THE FORBIDDEN LOVE OF AN OFFICER

JANE LARK

Boldwood

First published in 2014 as *The Lost Love of a Soldier*. This edition published in Great Britain in 2025 by Boldwood Books Ltd.

Copyright © Jane Lark, 2014

Cover Design by Head Design Ltd.

Cover Images: Head Design Ltd and Shutterstock

A CIP catalogue record for this book is available from the British Library.

Paperback ISBN 978-1-80557-984-7

Large Print ISBN 978-1-80557-975-5

Hardback ISBN 978-1-80557-985-4

Ebook ISBN 978-1-80557-986-1

Kindle ISBN 978-1-80557-987-8

Audio CD ISBN 978-1-80557-978-6

MP3 CD ISBN 978-1-80557-979-3

Digital audio download ISBN 978-1-80557-980-9

This book is printed on certified sustainable paper. Boldwood Books is dedicated to putting sustainability at the heart of our business. For more information please visit https://www.boldwoodbooks.com/about-us/sustainability/

Boldwood Books Ltd, 23 Bowerdean Street, London, SW6 3TN

www.boldwoodbooks.com

I dedicate this story to all those who serve in the military, and the families who support them. Much has changed in the two hundred plus years since men fought at the Battle of Waterloo, but I doubt the emotions people experience have changed at all.

HISTORICAL NOTE

While my characters are fictional, nearly all the scenes in this book are based on the facts leading up to the Battle of Waterloo; even down to the wallpaper in the carriage house where they held the last ball in Brussels before the battle commenced...

1

'Lady Eleanor...' A hesitant knock struck the door as Ellen's maid whispered through it, as if she feared someone hearing her, even though she used the servants' entrance to Ellen's bedchamber.

Ellen's father, the Duke of Pembroke, would be nowhere near the servants' stairway.

'Pippa?'

The handle turned and the door opened.

'My lady, a letter.' Pippa held it out as she came in. 'It is from the Captain.'

'From Paul?' Ellen swept across the room, her heart clenching as she moved. Paul was the reason the whole house had slipped into tiptoeing and whispering. He'd caused her father's recent rage, and now everyone was terrified of causing offence and becoming the next focus for her father's anger.

If it was rude to snatch it from Pippa's hand, then love had made Ellen rude.

Her fingers shook as she broke open the blank seal and unfolded the paper.

My love.

Holding the letter in one hand, the fingertips of her other touched his words.

My love... He'd only said those words for the first time a week ago, and yet she'd hoped to hear them for weeks, perhaps for months. *Paul.* An image of him dressed in his uniform crept into her head, his scarlet coat with its bright brass buttons hugging the contours of his chest. She loved the way he smiled so easily, and the way it glowed in his blue eyes. But he was a man of strength and vibrancy; life and emotion burned in his eyes too, and power cut into his features.

He was a breathing statue of Adonis; his beauty more like art than reality.

Her gaze dropped back to his words.

I'm sorry. Your father has said no, and by now I am sure you know it. I tried, Ellen, but he would not hear me out. He said I am not good enough for you. He would not even consider me. He will not have his daughter become the wife of a mere Captain, no matter that I am the son of an Earl. He wishes you to be a Duchess. He will never consider a sixth son who must earn his living. He actually had the audacity to tell me even if I had been my brother and the heir, he would not agree to our match.

But I refuse to give you up, and I must leave for America soon. My love. I want you with me. Will you come with me without his acceptance? Will you run away with me? We can leave at night and head for Gretna; elope. You know how much I feel for you. You know I cannot bear to let you go. Remember, my love burns brighter than the sun for you. You are my life, Ellen. Come. Send word via your maid if you will.

My heart shall ache until I can look into your topaz eyes again.

All my love, forever and ever yours,

Paul

Tears dripped onto the paper, blurring the words. She loved him too. They'd met in June. He'd attended a house party with his father, the Earl of Craster, and his brothers. His family had come to talk politics, but Paul had only come to entertain himself.

Ellen looked up from his letter, wiping away her tears. 'I will write back, Pippa. You will take the letter for me?' The maid hovered near the door, watching.

When Paul had come here, even though Ellen was not officially out and allowed to socialise in high society, her father had agreed to her joining the party.

She'd been sixteen then.

She'd eaten with the men during the day and entertained them in the evening, playing the pianoforte and singing while they stood or sat in groups and talked. But in those weeks Paul had singled her out. He had sat next to her for several meals, and turned the music sheets for her when she'd played; his thigh would brush against hers as they'd shared a narrow stool.

She'd known her father's intention had been for her to draw the interest of the Duke of Argyle, but she did not want to marry an old man. Paul had talked to her and made her laugh, whispering as she played, while the other men talked politics and struck bargains about the room.

They had communicated through the servants since the beginning of August.

Paul had befriended a groom while he had stayed here and

the man took letters back and forth, passing them through Pippa.

Ellen's conscience whispered as she turned to open her writing desk, which stood on a small table before the window.

The very first time she'd seen Paul, before they'd even been introduced, something had pulled her gaze to him.

Perhaps it was his scarlet coat which made him stand out among her father's political friends, or his dark blond hair, which swept sideways across his brow, as though his fingers had combed through it. Or the blue eyes which had looked back at her. Or the dimple which dented his cheek when he had smiled before looking away.

When they were introduced, her stomach had somersaulted, and when he had kissed the back of her fingers, her knees had weakened. It was as if she'd known him a lifetime as he'd held her gaze.

She had told her sister, Penny, she wished to marry the soldier, not the old Duke.

She should not have written to Paul though, not without permission... Thrusting her feelings of guilt aside, she put his letter down to start her own, sitting before a blank sheet of paper.

Paul,

My father has shut me in my room. I am to stay here until I agree to marry the Duke of Argyle. You would not believe how cruel he was about you. I know he is a Duke, but I have three sisters who may marry whoever he wishes. I choose to marry a Captain. Yes, I will elope with you. Only tell me when! Send word as quickly as you can. I do not wish to stay here another hour even.

I cannot wait to see you. Come and fetch me.

Love, love and more love.
Yours and yours always,
Ellen

Ellen blotted her words, then sealed the letter, dropping a little melted wax onto the folded paper. Then she blew on it to cool it, and waved it in the air. She finished by kissing the still warm wax, before she gave the letter to Pippa.

'Be careful, do not let anyone see you pass it to Eric.'

'I shan't, my lady. Did you wish me to bring you something to eat? I can fetch something from Cook.'

'No, do not take the risk, Pippa. If my father's steward or the housekeeper discovered it, you would lose your post and I will never forgive myself. I can manage. It is just a little hunger.' *It shall not be for long...*

'Then is there anything else, my lady?'

'Nothing, Pippa. Go.'

The maid bobbed a curtsy, then left, the servants' door closing behind her.

Ellen walked over to a chair by the fire and looked into the flames. Her fingers curled into fists as she held on to her excitement.

It was Christmas in a week, mid-winter.

She picked up the handkerchief she was embroidering for her youngest sister, Sylvia, and sat down, then took out the needle intending to sew again, but her hand dropped as anxiety twisted and spun in her stomach. She had felt muddled for weeks – quivery inside. She'd been confused ever since Paul had left in the summer.

Before he left he had slipped a note into a book he was reading aloud to her. It said simply, *may I write to you?* She had nodded, her heart blooming with relief that his leaving did not mean the end of their friendship.

Paul's first letter had come with her father's mail. He had opened it and read it before returning the letter to Paul, telling him not to write to her. There had been nothing condemning in it, no words of love, only facts and stories, but still she had endured a severe interview, and her father had not even known she had given Paul permission to write.

Paul's second letter, telling her about his first, had come via Eric, a groom, and Pippa. It had still been merely talk, but he'd said he'd taken lodgings nearby for a week or two so he might establish a way to communicate with her. Her heart beat rapidly even at the memory of that first letter. She had thought, surely if a man would go to such lengths, then his feelings were more than mere friendship.

A week later she had ridden out with Penny and Eric, and met Paul briefly. When Penny had met Paul, he had smiled his charming smile and bowed in his regimental way. Penny had been enchanted, and Ellen had liked him even more for being nice to her sister.

She and Penny had walked through the woods with him, at the edge of her father's land, near his tall, red-bricked folly, and they had all laughed. Laughter was a rare thing in her family. Only when she was with her sisters, somewhere private, did they ever find moments to laugh.

Paul had gone to London after that, but he had continued writing. Mailing his letters to the village inn, addressed to Eric, who had handed them to Pippa. For weeks the tone of the letters had been conversational, but in November it had changed. He had spoken of the summer, and said pretty things about the colour of her eyes and hair, and the fullness of her lips.

A week ago he had written to say he had hired a room at a local inn and asked her to meet him there. She had ridden out with Eric, and not even told Penny, fearing involving Penny if her father found out.

She had known what she wished Paul to say. Over the months since the summer, she had fallen in love with him.

Numerous hours had been wasted ever since she met him, lying on Penny's bed, or her own, whispering about Paul. Rebecca and Sylvia were too young to be confidants, yet she loved all her sisters, but now, if she went with Paul, she must leave them behind. Loss shot through her heart like an arrow passing through it.

A tear escaped. She wiped it away.

When they met a week ago, Paul had taken her hands and said he loved her, that there was no other woman he wanted, or would want. He had been ordered to go to America and wanted her to marry him and go with him. He had asked for her agreement to speak to her father. She had given it, her heart swelling and bursting with joy.

If she had stopped to think, she would have known her father would never accept a marriage offer from a Captain of the 52nd Regiment of Foot.

She did not want to marry anyone else, though, and if she wished to marry Paul, she had to leave. That was her father's fault.

Paul was one and twenty, but she was ten and seven – old enough to know her own heart but not to marry without the consent of her father, unless they went to Scotland.

* * *

'Captain, there is a letter waiting for you at the desk,' a maid said.

Captain Paul Harding crossed the bare boards of the inn's entrance hall to collect it, his gaze running over the wooden racks. 'My letter?' The clerk turned to pick it out from a pile.

'Thank you.' Paul turned away and headed to the taproom, his boots brushing over the beer-scented sawdust spread across the floor. Looking at the maid who served there, he said, 'May I have an ale?' The girl nodded and moved to pour it. After accepting the full tankard, he occupied an empty table in the corner of the room, ignoring the general conversation of the local labouring men.

His heart clenched at the sight of the familiar flow of letters forming his name.

Ellen had written them. Lady Eleanor Pembroke.

He had fallen hard for this girl in the summer when he had never fallen for a woman before. But Ellen was uncommonly beautiful. Her hair was raven black, and her skin like porcelain, while her eyes, which shone bright as she spoke, were the palest, most striking blue he had ever seen. She had captured his attention in the summer, like a siren.

Perhaps he'd been at war too long and now he just wished for peace and beauty to surround him, to shut out the bitter memories and images of blood and corpses strewn across fields. Who knew? But he had not wanted to leave Ellen behind in August, and now he had to go back to war he did not wish to leave her in England. He craved this girl, as he craved water after hours of fighting, dry-mouthed, thirsty and heart-sore.

She was young. But if he waited someone else would snap her up by the time he returned. To keep such a beauty, he had to take her with him. The girl could keep him sane, when all about him lay brutality and madness.

He had spent the last three years watching the few men whose wives had travelled with them, following the drum. It was not a pleasure-filled life, but at night they had each other, before and after a battle.

His choice had been the comfort of a camp whore or the camaraderie of jaded war-beleaguered men.

Not that he did not like his men; they had survived too much together. But there were times a man wanted a woman, and there were times only one woman would do.

He wanted solace, someone to take to bed and escape war with – someone who would help him shut out the visions of the death he'd left behind.

Of course more fool his heart – picking the daughter of a Duke.

He'd held little expectation Pembroke would welcome his proposal, but Paul had known he had to try to do things properly.

God. His father would go mad when he heard of this. It would set Pembroke against him for years, when his father sought a political alliance. But self-sacrifice be damned. He had given his life to society. Now he had discovered something he wanted more than others' good opinion. He wanted Ellen.

He had little to do with his father though anyway, since he had gone to war. His father had paid for his commission, and then his duty had been done; he had ensured his sixth son had an independent living.

At first Paul had kept in contact with his mother, but war was not a thing to write of, so he had grown distant from his family now. In the summer, when he had joined his father at Pembroke's, he had little conversation to share. He was not interested in politics, and they would not have been interested in his tales of survival and death.

He cracked open the seal on her letter and read it quickly, drinking his ale as he did. She'd said, *yes*. Not that he'd doubted she would, he'd known since the summer the girl was attached to him. But before he'd felt guilty. Now he did not. Argyle? God, her father was a bastard. Paul would be rescuing her from a life of hell.

Her father, and his, could go hang. This girl was meant for him, and he was right for her. He needed her too much.

He couldn't remember the point attraction had become love. At some point between catching her staring at him across the room the first day he'd arrived at Pembroke Place and hearing her sing as he sat beside her turning the pages of her music, while her thigh brushed against his through a thin layer of muslin, her cotton petticoats and his pantaloons.

Any day soon this girl would be his, and she may have to learn how to endure the hardship of an army camp, but regardless he would make sure she never regretted eloping. Determination to make her happy gripped in his gut, and determination to love the girl so she'd never feel she lacked a thing.

Setting his empty tankard sharply back on the beer-stained table he rose, left the taproom and returned to the clerk's desk, where they sold tickets for mail coaches and hired out horses and carriages. 'I need a fast carriage, have you any yellow bounders to hire?'

'I can find out for you, Captain. Are you dining? If so I will see what is free while you eat.'

'Yes, I will dine.' Paul turned away and returned to the taproom. Not that he was hungry. His stomach had been tied up in knots for more than a week. Ever since he'd received his orders to sail and decided to come back and get Ellen, he had hardly been able to eat a bloody thing.

She had taken over his thoughts since August, hovering in

his dreams at night and walking with him in daydreams in the sunlit hours. She had enchanted him, and he had found her unfledged and ready for flight.

Thank God he had joined his father and brothers on that visit to Pembroke Place. He could so easily have stayed away and gone to London.

But his father and hers were going to be mad as hell.

He asked for another tankard of ale and ordered the pork dish. He'd eaten enough bloody rabbit for a whole century during the Peninsular War. He would not touch the rabbit pie. It reminded him too much of the biting pain when hunger gripped inside you and you still had to march or fight. Yet he barely touched the meal, his hunger now was for a certain pale-blue-eyed, black-haired beauty.

Finding Ellen had been like finding treasure on the battle-torn fields in his head. His sanity clung to her, something beautiful to remind him that everything was not ugly. She was someone to fight for. Someone to survive for...

The clerk arrived. 'The day after tomorrow. Would that suit, sir?'

'Yes.' The sooner the better. Tomorrow would be torment. Now he'd made up his mind, and Ellen had agreed, he simply wished to leave. But he had no choice but to wait for a carriage. 'That will suit.'

'Thank you, Captain.' The man bowed.

* * *

Ellen's stomach growled with hunger for the umpteenth time as she lay on her bed. She'd been confined to her room for four days, but this would be the last day... She was leaving. The thought clutched tightly in her heart. No one knew. In ten hours Paul would come to meet her.

She had not even told Pippa, she was too terrified her father would hear it from someone if she said the words aloud.

Every detail of their plan to escape, in Paul's words, was safely tucked inside her bodice near her heart, pressing against her breast.

'Eleanor.'

Heavens.

'Eleanor!' The sound seeped through her bedchamber door; a deep heavy pitch that made her instantly wish to comply. Obedience had carved its mark into her soul – and yet she was about to disobey. Where on earth would her courage come from?

'Father?' The key turned in the lock on the outside and Ellen scurried off the bed.

When the door opened, she stood by the bedpost, her hands clasped before her waist, her back rigid and chin-high, but her eyes downturned. It felt as though she were one of Paul's soldiers on parade when she faced her father. She did not feel like his flesh and blood.

'Your Grace.' She lowered in a deep curtsy, sinking as far as she was able, in the hope he would think her penitent and be kinder. She did not look up to meet his gaze in case it roused his anger. But she need not even look at her father to know when he was displeased; displeasure hung in the air around him without him saying a word. Yet he never showed his anger physically, apart from barking orders and offering condemning dismissals.

Those cutting words and his exclusion were enough punishment though. He never looked at her as if he cared, never smiled...

What I am planning will horrify him...

Her father's fingers encouraged her to rise, with a beckoning gesture.

'Papa.' She lifted her gaze to his.

Paul's words, promising faithfulness, love and protection, pressed against her bosom as she took a deeper breath. A blush crept across her skin. She feared even the blush might give her away.

Compared to her father, Paul was water to stone, something moving and living.

Vibrancy and approachability – warmth – emanated from Paul.

Her father hid beneath coldness and disdain. If there was any warmth in his soul she had never seen it. He most often communicated in a series of bitter glares rather than words.

Yet Paul had experienced awful things. Death. Illness. He had cause to be bitter. He had watched friends die and killed others for the sake of freedom in Europe. He never spoke of those things, though, even when she asked. He always spoke of good things. But she supposed his months in England were months to forget the Peninsular War.

'Well? Have you thought about your behaviour, Eleanor?'

Paul's letter was warm against her blushing skin. Yes, she had thought, and she had made a choice – to leave. 'Yes, Papa.'

Until this summer she had thought her father was unaware of his daughters, they grew up in the hands of servants, with a daily visit from her mother. Then, last year, she had reached a marriageable age and he had seen her – but only as a bargaining tool. He wished her to marry to secure a political alliance.

'And are you sorry?'

Ellen's gaze dropped to his shoes. She felt no regret. 'Yes, Papa.'

'You will take Argyle?'

Ellen took a breath, longing for courage. She did not feel able to lie to that extent.

'Eleanor?'

Looking up, she faced his stern condemning glare. His expression was as unreadable as marble. 'I cannot, Papa. I do not wish to marry His Grace.' Her father had a way of making other people seem small and insignificant – incapable. 'Papa?' *Do you love me? Will you miss me?*

'You do not have a choice, Eleanor. You will do your duty.'

His gaze held her at a distance, blunt and cold.

Hers reached out, begging for a sign of his affection. 'I cannot, Papa. He is so old, and—'

'You are being wilful and defiant, Eleanor. You will do as I say and that is an end to it.'

Repudiating words pressed to escape, catching up in a ball in her throat as she longed to argue and plead, to make him accept Paul, but her father did not like emotion. As children they had been taken away from his presence whenever they cried, or shouted, or laughed. But today, today she could not quite hold herself back. 'Papa, please... What would be so wrong with Paul? I love him and he loves me...'

He gave no obvious sign his anger had escalated, yet she knew. It was in the stiffness of his body, in the cut of his silver eyes as they glared at her. He was like her in appearance – or rather she was like him. She had his eyes and his jet-black hair and pale skin. But she was nothing like him in nature, and she did not wish to be. What possessed a man to be so cold? He would be handsome if he smiled but he never smiled.

'Do not be ridiculous, Eleanor. Love... What is it?' *Something you do not feel, Papa.* 'You are talking nonsense. There is nothing in it. You are the daughter of a duke. You have a duty and responsibility, and that is what you must think of in a marriage. It seems you are unrepentant then, and you've learned no lesson at all. You will spend the next full day on your knees. Study the Bible, ask for forgiveness and pray for guidance. You will learn, Eleanor. Your mother has been too lenient, letting you dream of such fanciful things. I will return to speak to you tomorrow, until then you will stay in your room.'

I will be gone tomorrow. She could continue to argue, she could beg and try to cajole, but her father would never change his mind. He had never done a single thing out of kindness.

Eleanor lowered in another curtsy. 'As you say, Papa.'

'As I say indeed, Eleanor. It will be so. You will marry Argyle. I shall write to him today.' *You may write, Papa, but I shall never marry him.*

'Kneel at your bed, child.' She turned and did so, she had never disobeyed him and even now her heartbeat thundered at the thought of doing so in a few hours. Where would she find the courage? From Paul. Her father would be so angry.

As Ellen lifted her skirt and knelt, her father turned to the door and called to a footman. 'Fetch the Bible from the chapel, my daughter needs time to search her soul.'

No, she did not. She had found what her soul needed. She had found Paul.

* * *

A quiet knock struck her bedchamber door. 'Ellen?'

'Penny?' Ellen stood. It was dusk, her family had probably just eaten dinner, and their father would be sitting alone at the table drinking his port.

The handle of her door turned but it would not open. Papa had the key.

'Mama said I must not speak to you, Papa has forbidden it, so of course *she* will not come, yet I had to know you are well. Are you hungry? Do you wish me to send you something to eat? Has he beaten you?'

Ellen rose from her kneeling position, even though she had been told not to move yet, she could not shout across the room in case someone heard and told tales on them. Then Penny would be in trouble too.

Ellen pressed her fingers against the door, leaning to whisper through it. 'I know, and I know Mama cannot defend me, she must obey Papa. I do not want him to be angry with her or you. You should go, Penny.'

'Why is he angry?'

'Paul made a marriage offer. Papa refused it. He is angry because I encouraged Paul. Do not become caught up in this or Papa will confine you to your room too.'

'Captain Harding? Oh, Ellen. I like him.'

Resting her forehead against the wood, Ellen smiled. 'As do I, but Papa does not. He wishes me to accept the Duke of Argyle.'

'You cannot marry that old man. He is awful, Ellen... I shall come through the servants' way and speak with you.'

'No. Papa would be furious. Do not take the risk. I can manage, I am merely a little cold and hungry,' *and I will be gone soon.*

'But you will not agree to marry that old man. I saw him in the summer and—'

'Of course not.' An urge to share the truth and speak of her elopement shot through Ellen's heart, another arrow of love passing through it, but it would be wrong to involve Penny. Penny was fifteen, she would not be able to hide her knowledge if their father questioned her, and Ellen would not have Penny hurt.

'I miss you. Rebecca and Sylvia do nothing but play silly games. Life is so dull without you.'

Penny's words tugged as if a cord were tethered to the arrow through Ellen's heart, and Penny pulled it.

But Ellen could not stay. She wanted to be with Paul.

Her hands trembled as her palms pressed against the wood and she leaned closer, feeling the presence of her sister on the other side in every fibre of her body...

This life, this house, was all Ellen had known. She had never travelled beyond the local towns.

Paul had travelled the world. He had told her what life as an army officer's wife would be. Hard. She was not to expect luxury. But she would be loved and cared for and adored by him. She longed for it. Her heart ached for it. But voices in her head whispered, *be afraid...*

'You will manage without me, Penny.'

'I know I shall. It will only be for a few days. Papa cannot keep you locked away forever.'

'Yes, only for a few days.' *Years.* A desire to tell Penny the truth fought to break the words from Ellen's lips. But if her father discovered Penny had been told he'd hurt her. 'You'd better go. I'd never forgive myself if you were caught.'

'As soon as Papa allows you to come out, find me and tell me everything. Promise?'

'Promise.'

'Goodbye.'

'Goodbye.' Tears flooded Ellen's eyes as she heard her sister go.

Leaving Penny behind without explanation would cause Penny pain, but it tore at Ellen's heart too.

* * *

The room had become bitterly cold. Her father had forbidden anyone to tend the fire. It had burned out hours ago. Ellen's knees ached from kneeling, yet still she had not risen, even though no one watched her. Her father's will had been forced upon her for so many years it was her instinct to obey. She would break that tether at midnight.

She read through the Ten Commandments for the thousandth time. '*Thou shalt honour thy father and mother.*'

Was she about to sin, then, because she was going to run away and betray them? Her mother would be heartbroken – *she* knew how to love. She was even loyal to Ellen's father, respecting their marriage vows despite his coldness towards them all.

Ellen could not do the same. She could not stay here. She wanted a life with Paul – even if it was sinful and selfish.

It had been dark for hours, and every time the clock in the hall struck, she had counted the chimes. It was past ten.

Pippa had brought her some bread and cheese at eight, wrapped in a cloth, but Ellen had sent her away with a need to obey her father, at least in that. It was a penance for the moment she would break free and shatter any feelings he had.

Excitement and anxiety warred with guilt and sorrow; sadness weighing down her soul. She did not want to leave her sisters and her mother.

But the sadness was outbalanced by the happiness and expectation that she felt. She was going to Paul. Running towards love. Yet what else would she run to? All she knew was his love bore more weight than her mother's or her sisters'. It owned her heart and made it pulse – not simply made it feel tender.

The clock began to strike again, the sound echoing. One, two...

Ellen knew how many times it would chime.

Leaving the Bible open, she rose, even now unable to fully disobey and close it.

Her feet were numb and her knees stiff, the price she had to pay for what she was about to do.

Everyone in the house retired early to avoid wasting candles. They rose with the sun and retired with it. They would all be in bed.

The chilly air made her shiver, or perhaps it was the overwhelming blend of excitement and fear. She still could not believe she was doing this. She took a leather sewing bag from a cupboard and began emptying it of embroidery threads and ribbons. The clock outside chimed nine... ten... eleven...

Ellen's eyes adjusted to the shadows cast by the moonlight pouring through the open curtains. She looked about the room.

One hour.

She picked out undergarments and three of her muslin dresses. Then she fetched her hairbrush and the mirror her mother had bought her when she'd reached six and ten. That had been over a year ago, but she could remember the day as if it were yesterday. She had been here in her room, and Pippa had been brushing her hair out before bed with her usual one hundred strokes. Her mother had come in to say goodnight and she had carried a beautiful wooden box containing the set.

When she had given it to Ellen, she had said it was to mark Ellen becoming a woman. She'd kissed Ellen's cheek and wished her happiness.

That is what she was running to – happiness. But she could not fit the beautiful box in her bag, so she left it and just packed the brush and mirror.

She sifted through her gloves and picked four pairs, and she picked a dozen ribbons to change the look of her dresses, and some lace to drape at the necks of her evening gowns.

She had no ball gowns. She had never been to a ball, although she had watched one through a door that had been left ajar when her father had held one here.

There were many things she had to leave behind, bonnets, shoes, dresses, her lovely room with its pretty paper painted with birds – her sisters – her mother.

Pain caught in her bosom, sharp and tight, like the press of a little knife slipping into her flesh. How would she live without them, and yet how would she live without Paul? And if she chose to stay, what if Papa would not bend and he forced her to take the Duke of Argyle? No, she was doing the right thing.

She stopped and looked about the room. She could take nothing else. But she wished she had thought to cut a lock of her mother's and Penny's hair at some point, to remind her of them. It was too late now.

She wiped away a tear before closing the bag and securing the buckle. Then she took her riding habit from where it lay in a drawer and began to change. The thick velvet made it too hard to fit in the bag and it would keep her warm as they travelled.

It was a fabric her mother had urged her to buy, a burgundy red, as deep a colour as port. She was lucky that it fastened at the front so she could dress in it without Pippa's help.

When it was on, she looked in her long mirror which stood against the wall in the corner of her room, and saw a woman. Not a child any more. A woman about to desert her family.

Sighing rather than face the guilt which crept in, overlaying her excitement, she turned away to collect her bonnet, cloak and a pair of kid leather gloves. She would have taken her muff, but she feared carrying too much. Lastly she put on her half boots, and laced them neatly.

Then she looked into the mirror again, at the Duke's daughter. She would not be that now. She would be an officer's wife. She would no longer live in luxury but in simplicity. It was what she chose. It was what she wanted.

Her gaze spun about the room, looking at everything one last time. 'Goodbye, Mama,' she whispered into the darkness. 'Goodbye, Penny.' Her voice caught as tears burned her eyes. 'Goodbye, Sylvia and Rebecca. I will pray for you all, I will pray for your happiness and good fortune.' She paused for a moment as though she half expected them, or the house, to reply. No sound came. She picked up her bag and went to the servants' door, then out into the narrow hall. It was little more than a person wide and pitch-black. She hurried down the spiralling steps which would take her to the service area and the stables; the fingertips of her free hand skimming across the cold plaster on the wall to guide her way, while her heart pounded out a rhythm that made her light-headed.

2

As he heard the rustle of frozen leaves on the ground, Paul whispered, 'Ellen...' into the night. His breath rose in a mist into the cold winter air. He was on the Duke of Pembroke's land. He had not dared encourage her to take a horse, so he had come close enough that she might walk from the house and find him.

He waited at the end of an avenue of yews, out of sight of the house, in a place she could easily see him. His horse whickered, sensing something, or someone. 'Ellen?' he whispered again.

Still no answer.

He listened, wondering if she had been caught as she left the house. He hoped not. If she had been caught her father would allow her no freedom and short of leading a military assault on Pembroke's home, he would not be able to get her out.

The horse shook its head, rattling its bit, and snorted steamy breath into the cold air. The chill of the winter night seeped through his clothes. There would be a hard frost. He hoped she had dressed in something warm.

He would have to buy more clothes for her before they sailed. She would need garments to keep her warm in the sea breezes she'd face on their journey to America.

There was another sound.

'Paul...'

'Ellen.'

How did this woman manage to make his heart beat so erratically whenever he saw her? He could run into battle and not be so affected.

A band of silver light reached through the scudding clouds and caught her face. She looked even more beautiful in the dark. Ethereal.

He let go of the horse's bridle and instinctively moved forward. He had never held her. In the summer there had been no moments alone, she had been strictly chaperoned and when she had come to meet him she had brought the groom and her sister. Even when they met a fortnight ago, she had still brought the groom. This was their first time alone. 'Ellen.' He embraced her, his arms wrapping about her shoulders. In answer her arm came about his waist. It was the most precious feeling of his life. He would always remember this day. She was slender and there was a feeling that she was delicate.

She slipped free, but he caught her nape and pulled her mouth to his, gently pressing his lips against hers. It was her first kiss, he knew; he could tell by the way her body stiffened when he had pulled her close. He let her go, an unfamiliar tenderness catching in his chest.

'Come.' He took the leather bag she carried. 'Will you ride before me, or would you rather sit behind my saddle and hold my waist?'

'Would it be easier if I ride behind you?' Her voice ran with uncertainty. She was giving up everything to come with him.

'Do what feels comfortable for you, Ellen.'

She nodded, avoiding his eyes. 'I would prefer to ride pillion.'

'Then you shall.' He softened his voice, hoping to ease her discomfort.

Turning to the horse, he slipped one foot in the stirrup, then pulled himself up. 'Did you have any difficulty leaving the house?'

'No, the servants' hall was quiet, and the grooms had all retired.'

He rested her bag across his thighs, then held a hand out to her. 'Set your foot on mine and take my hand. I will pull you up.' He watched her lift the skirt of her dark habit, and then the weight of her small foot pressed on his, as her gloved fingers held his. She was light, but the grip of her hand and the pressure of her foot made that something clasp tight in his chest, and the emotion stayed clenched as her fingers embraced his waist over his greatcoat.

He shifted in the saddle, his groin tightening too. A few more days. Just days. He had been waiting months. As he turned the horse, Ellen's cheek pressed against his shoulder.

'Did you tell anyone you were leaving? Your sister? Or your maid?'

'No. I did not want them to have to face Papa knowing the truth. He would know they had lied, and then who knows what he might do.' Paul urged the mare into a trot as Ellen continued. 'He made me spend the day on my knees reading the Commandments because I refused to marry the Duke of Argyle.'

'Today?' He wished to look back at her but he could not turn in the saddle with her behind him. Her father had been diabolical to Paul, sneering as though Paul were nothing when he had done the decent thing and spoken to him to offer for her. He could imagine the way Pembroke treated his girls. He had to get Ellen to Gretna before her father caught them, so she never had to come back and face his retribution.

He stirred the mare into a canter as Ellen's arms wrapped about his waist, firmly hanging on to him.

'Yes, today,' she said, to his ear. 'He came to my room this morning, to ask if I was repentant.'

If she was repentant? She'd done nothing wrong, as far as her father was aware. He'd not told her father they'd been communicating since the summer. He'd expected to be refused, and he'd not wished their pathway of communication closed. All she had been guilty of, as far as her father knew, was that her presence and her company in the summer had attracted a man her father deemed unworthy. She bore no guilt for being beautiful and charming.

God, how had Pembroke brought up this untouched, unscarred girl? 'Did you tell him you repented?'

She laughed; a low soft sound he hadn't heard before. 'No.'

He smiled. It had taken him so long to make his offer because he had wanted to feel sure she had the strength to follow the drum. She had it. She had a core of iron. She would survive. He would make sure she did; though he didn't doubt his way of life was going to come as a shock to her. He had tried to warn her in letters, preparing her, but he could tell from her responses it was all whimsical rather than real. It would soon become real.

He stopped the horse suddenly, and strained to look over his shoulder, as it restlessly side-stepped. 'You're sure of this, Ellen? I mean, if you are not, I can take you back.'

In answer, her fingers pressed into his midriff, holding firm, stirring pain in his chest and his groin. 'I am sure.'

I am sure too.

'Then let us hurry.' He kicked his heels and set the horse off at a canter, his mind on the treacherous tracks they were likely to encounter on their journey north. This was a race now.

The ground was hardened by frost, and slippery. The horse's breath, and theirs, rose into the cold air in plumes.

They had a few hours' lead, but—

'Papa said I was to have nothing to eat either. I told Pippa not to bring me any food.'

Then perhaps, if no one was to speak to her, their head start would be longer. It could be twelve hours to a day before they realised she was missing. Even so it was the wrong time of year for haste. He hoped the cold weather and frost would hold. Better that than rain and mud bound routes when carts, horses and men became bogged down. His head had begun planning their flight like a bloody military campaign.

'The coach is waiting for us at the inn. It will be ready. I've hired a yellow bounder.'

'A coach and four?'

He smiled at the tone of excitement in her voice. 'Yes. You sound as if you fancy driving them?'

She laughed again, that low heart-wrenching beautiful sound. 'No, I would not have a clue, I have never even ridden in a fast carriage. It sounds exhilarating.'

Exhilarating? This girl was so wonderfully innocent. But that was another thing that had drawn him to her, her naivety, it was such a contrast to his own knowledge of the world; she knew nothing of the horrors he'd lived through, though he was only a little older than her. She was here to wash his soul clean of war and brutality.

They came to a gate, but he did not dismount, he merely

leaned down to open it, and then they were in the woods, where the frost had not yet settled.

Here darkness reigned. It left him reliant on the horse's sight as they kept low to avoid tree branches; then he had to slow and keep the horse at a trot.

When they reached the clearing at the bottom of the ridge on which her father's tall folly stood, he took a moment to regain his bearings and then set off through the trees again.

Due to the darkness, it took half an hour to reach the inn. When she dismounted, his mind counted the minutes passing, aware of her empty bedchamber and the people asleep back at Pembroke's palatial mansion. At some hour tomorrow they would discover her gone. His heart beat in a steady firm rhythm as he held her hand and she slid from the horse.

While she waited on the ground, her arms nervously clasping across her chest, he dropped her bag onto the cobbled yard then slipped his feet from the stirrups, swung his leg over the saddle, and dismounted.

The ice had not yet settled in the enclosed courtyard, but the street beyond was white with frost. He patted the mare's cheek as it snorted, and whispered a thank you, then looked at the small, yellow-painted carriage, and the horses which waited, impatiently shaking out their manes and snorting misty breath into the night air.

A groom took the bridle of the hired mare he'd ridden to fetch Ellen and another collected Ellen's bag to place it in the boot of their carriage.

'Come.' He held out his hand to Ellen and she took it, in complete trust. He was a lucky man.

The inn's grooms hurried ahead to open the door.

It was strange, holding a woman's hand. When he had walked with a woman before, she had only ever lain her hand on his arm. This was more intimate. She belonged to him. He was responsible for her now, even if it was not yet official.

Paul handed her into the carriage. She climbed the single step then slipped inside. Once her hand left his, he reached into his pocket for a small bag of coins. He looked at the groom beside him and then to the other two who stood in the yard. 'For your silence.' He passed it to one to share out among the rest. He could ill afford it and it would be no guarantee, yet he did not want Pembroke warned. He had not said who she was, but she had the distinctive Pembroke colouring and beauty, with her dark hair and very pale blue eyes. She would not be forgotten.

'Thank you, Captain.' The man pulled his forelock and the others bowed their heads as Paul glanced at the postilion rider and the man on the carriage's box. The small carriage would be steered by the rider on the front right of the four horses, the second man was so they could change over and keep going through the night, so one could sleep while the other rode the lead horse.

With a nod Paul climbed up into the carriage. The moment he closed the carriage door, the carriage lurched forward. Even before they left the silent village, shrouded in its blanket of night, the postilion rider had upped the pace into a gallop, not at all heedful of the frosty track as the carriage bounced over the hardened muddy ruts. 'We must make haste,' he had told the drivers three dozen times before he had left to fetch Ellen. It seemed they had heard his words.

'We are going to be mightily bruised by the time we reach Gretna,' Paul said.

There was that wonderful laugh again which stirred something incredibly masculine in his soul – an instinct to gather her up and protect her. He lifted his arm. She slotted beneath it, pressing close to his side. And there was that ache in his chest and his groin again. *Ellen.* He could see her face clearly in the lamplight which glowed within the carriage. Beautiful. Perfect. Flawless.

His arm around her, and her warmth clutched against him, he began explaining. 'It should take us about three days, I think; maybe less if we are lucky with the roads and the weather. Then after Gretna we shall travel to Portsmouth. From there we will sail with my regiment. I'll purchase the things you'll need as a soldier's wife in Portsmouth. You shan't be able to carry much, there is a need to travel light, but we can spare you more than a single bag of clothing.'

He couldn't see her smile, but it was in the press of her hand against his greatcoat over his chest and the stir of her cheek against his shoulder.

He would love this woman for the rest of his life. He knew it. 'Come now. Let us take off our outdoor things and use the blankets, then you may sleep a little, if the road is not too rutted.' He moved, letting her rise, and she set her feet on the hot bricks the inn had put on the floor and took off her bonnet, cloak and gloves. He took off his gloves too and gripped her hand as she moved back beside him, spreading the blanket over them.

It was even more intimate than before, holding her naked hand, skin against skin – their first physical contact without the boundary of clothing. 'Ellen, you need not fear me. I shall not press you. We will be travelling day and night. I shall not ask you to do anything with me until we are man and wife. If you change your mind...' He would not want to let her go, but if she wished to return to her father then he would take her back.

'I will not change my mind. I wish to marry you.' The answer rang with vehemence as she sat up and glanced at him, her eyes bright and determined. Yes, she had a core of iron. She would survive. 'I love you.'

Those words... He smiled. They had shared them for the first time a fortnight ago. It had been the first time he had spoken them, and the first time he had heard a woman say them to him. But the feeling was true, it was in his blood and bones. 'I love you, also, Ellen. And I shall make you happy. I swear it.'

* * *

When Ellen woke, her head rested in Paul's lap, and the weight of his hand lay on her shoulder. She sat up, blushing. 'Sorry.'

He was awake. He had been looking out the window but now he looked at her and smiled – that kind, warm smile she had become used to in the summer. 'It is of no matter, Ellen. You were tired.'

She smiled too. 'Yes. Did you sleep?'

'A little.'

'Where are we?'

'Close to High Wycombe.'

It had been foolish to ask. She had no idea where High Wycombe was, or how far that meant they had travelled.

His smile opened and his eyes glowed. 'We are the other side of London, eight or nine hours away from your father's estate.' It was as though he had read her mind, or perhaps her expression.

Her stomach growled, and she pressed her hand over it, blushing again.

A humorous sound came from his throat. 'Are you hungry?'

'Yes.' She nodded, her smile quivering. She had felt a close-ness between her and Paul, which had begun in the summer and gathered through their letters, but now awkwardness hung between them because she knew very little of him in the flesh, only his written words.

'We will stop at the next inn. But we cannot stop for long. We need to make sure we keep ahead if your father follows.'

A knot tied in her stomach as Paul leaned forward to open a slim hatch and shout up to the man on the box. 'We wish to stop at the next coaching inn!'

If her father followed, she would be in trouble. He would never forgive her for this. But she was not sure he would follow; there were her sisters. He had never shown any sign he cared for her. Perhaps he would decide to wait until Penny came of age, and let Penny take Ellen's place.

Guilt rushed in. What if Penny had to endure the fate Ellen had run from, and marry the Duke of Argyle? It would be Ellen's fault. But she could not regret this – because she was not running from – she was running *to*. She could never choose to give Paul up.

Paul sat back in the seat, and his fingers lifted and tucked a lock of her hair that had fallen from the pins behind her ear.

She smiled, sitting back, and tried to re-pin her hair without a mirror.

His fingers touched beneath her chin. 'You need not pin it, you look beautiful if a little tussled by a bumpy carriage ride.' She laughed, but she still re-pinned it, and touched it to feel if it was in place.

The carriage jolted over a deep rut as it turned off the road, sending her off balance and toppling her backwards. In an instant he had caught her upper arm in a firm grip, holding her steady. She smiled, warmth and emotion running through her blood. He would take care of her now. Moisture clouded her vision.

'Are you well?' His expression said he thought she was injured in some way.

She smiled, swallowing back the emotion in her throat. 'Yes.' She leaned forward and hugged him, aware her breasts brushed against his chest through their layers of clothing. This was only the second time she had held him, held any man. He kissed her temple a moment before she pulled away and her heartbeat thumped.

The carriage slowed, and through the window Ellen saw a row of thatched cottages, then they were turning into a courtyard.

'Come, let us get you some refreshment.' Before the carriage had even stopped, Paul opened the door, and when it did he knocked down the step and lifted a hand to help her out.

When they returned to the carriage less than half an hour later, refreshed and more awake, Ellen let Paul hand her in as he'd handed her out. She did not feel guilty about making him stop because the drivers had changed the horses while they had eaten.

The carriage lurched as they pulled off into a canter.

The ground was still frozen which meant the lanes were passable, but the frozen ruts cast by previous carriages in the mud-strewn tracks made the journey bumpy.

The day was freezing, but new hot bricks had been placed inside at the inn, and Paul drew the blankets around them.

'Come here, let me hold you, then you will not be so thrown about by the rough track.'

She smiled, sliding to sit against him. Her thigh pressed against his and his arm lifted so she might slot beneath it. He was warm and solid. Dependable.

She rested her head against his shoulder but his palm touched her cheek and his head turned and he kissed her, gently at first as she tilted her neck to better receive it. But then he kissed her more ardently as he parted his lips and brushed the seam of hers with the tip of his tongue, in a silent command that implied, *open your mouth*. She did, and then... *Heavens*. His tongue slipped into her mouth searching and exploring. *Paul*.

Her hands instinctively clung at his shoulders as her tongue circled about his. She could not breathe. He had lit a flame which melted her heart as though it were wax, and it dripped into her blood.

He kissed her for a long while, his hands either side of her waist, a gentle, secure pressure.

Then a hand came up to the back of her head, steadying her as for a moment his tongue pressed deeper into her mouth before he broke the kiss.

Her stomach somersaulted as she looked into his eyes; their blue was the same colour as the winter sky outside the carriage. His lips tilted in a half-smile, a dimple denting his cheek.

Heat flared under her skin as she blushed. She had not known kissing could be like that. What would come next? Images spun through her head as she imagined their wedding night.

3

They had spent a day and another night in the carriage. Paul ached from too many hours of confinement, so they had stopped again to break their fast and for him to stretch a little. Now they had eaten, he had left Ellen to refresh herself and walked about the yard of the Bull's Head in Leamington Spa. He did not dare take a proper walk and venture out onto the high street in case Ellen followed. An officer and a dark-haired beauty might be remembered. So he kept to the confined space at the inn, walking a circular route a dozen times.

Anxiety raced through his blood. His senses were as heightened as they would be before a battle. But he had no idea where the enemy was. The Duke of Pembroke could still be in Kent, or he could be a few hours behind them, riding at a gallop, eating up the ground, pursuing them as they lingered here. Paul hated stopping and yet they had to eat, and... Well, they could not simply stay constantly in the carriage.

Bored with walking in a circle, he stopped at the stable and moved to a stall where a horse whickered from within; one of the horses they had just relinquished from their traces, to be returned to the Black Horse at Bicester, the inn they had stopped at before nightfall.

'You have a connection with horses, and you ride well.' Ellen stood beside him. 'I remember from the summer.' Her fingers touched his arm as his reached out and patted the mare's neck then stroked its cheek.

'Why did you not join a mounted regiment?' she asked. 'I would have thought you would be in the cavalry instead of a regiment of foot soldiers.'

'Because I could not have borne to watch a horse that I brought to battle die. I made my choice to fight. My horse would not have had the same luxury.' He patted the animal once more, denying the images of battles crowding into his head. He did not want to remember. He turned to her and immediately all the memories of war and brutality faded.

She did not speak; perhaps he had said something too morbid.

Her eyes held questions. He did not wish her to know the answers – with her he wanted to forget those memories. Yet he was taking her to a battleground, albeit not to fight.

Perhaps it was wrong of him...

But he could not regret it. In their hours in the carriage, the attachment she had planted in his heart in the summer had emerged like a shoot from a seed, germinating and growing to full flower. Ellen Pembroke was the woman his soul chose; he could not leave her behind. Love clutched about his heart, a vine wrapping around it. 'I love you.' The words slipped from his mouth without thought.

She was young, she knew nothing about brutality. He did not wish her to, but she would learn.

He was young too, but the experiences of war, and now having her to protect, made him feel much older than he was.

She smiled. 'And I you, Paul.'

'Come, we had better be on our way. There is no knowing how much ground your father has gained on us, if he is following.' His fingers closed gently about her elbow, and turned them both.

When they were back in the carriage he kissed her, desire and need roaring in his blood. He could not wait until they were out of this damned carriage and in a bed. But he did not press her for anything more. She was innocent, and they were unwed, he could wait. For now he just revelled in her kisses and her tender, beautiful responses as shallow sighs slipped across her lips and her tongue tentatively entwined with his, while the weight of her arms rested on his shoulders.

This girl was a treasure. He was going to protect her and love her all his life. He would not allow the brutality of war to touch her.

* * *

Ellen woke. Shouts echoed outside the carriage. The vehicle hit a rut, tipping and throwing her into the corner. She gripped the strap above her head, fearing the carriage might roll, but it righted itself. Outside another shout rang out, then gunfire. She jolted forward as the carriage suddenly rocked to the side again then slowed.

Paul had been asleep too, but now, wide awake, he moved and turned the damper, to put out the lantern. The light died instantly.

She watched, still half asleep. 'Paul?'

'Stay quiet, stay in the carriage and stay down.' The sharp order cut her as he pulled the curtain back from the window and looked out when the carriage came to an abrupt halt.

'I said get down,' Paul whispered harshly, bending down himself, but he was not trying to hide, he pulled something out from beneath the seat. A pistol and a sword. She caught a glimpse of the metal in the moonlight.

Ellen slid off the seat and landed on the now-cold bricks on the carriage floor. She started to shiver. 'What is it?'

'Highwaymen. Do not say a word. Act as though there is no one in here. I am going out.' He pulled the curtain closed again.

'Paul...' She grabbed his arm, to stop him, but he shrugged her off as he opened the carriage door. The door banged shut behind him. She clicked the lock into place.

Her heart thundered. She was having a nightmare. She would wake in a moment. But the cold air and the hard bricks beneath her bottom felt real.

Outside Paul shouted, his voice low in timbre and threatening. Her heartbeat rang in her ears, loud and deafening. A gun went off. Then another.

She could not stay in here. 'Paul!' Scrabbling off the floor, she reached for the door handle and clicked it open. She heard more shouting and almost fell out onto the frosted earth. Her feet landed on the ground as her hand still held the handle, wrenching her arm as she slipped but stayed upright.

Paul was a silhouette cast by the moonlight and the frost-covered earth. He faced away from her, a sword held in one hand, the tip pointing towards the ground. Something dark dripped from it. His other hand still held the pistol. A wisp of smoke rose from the barrel and the cold air carried the bitter smell of gunpowder. He dropped to one knee as she watched. She was unable to speak; shock had solidified every muscle in her body. There was a figure on the ground. A man.

Paul rested his hand which bore the gun on the man's chest, while his sword slipped from his fingers and fell on the grass.

He reached to the man's throat and pressed it for a moment, then searched through the man's coat.

'What are we going to do with him, Captain?' one of the drivers shouted, climbing down from the box.

The statement brought Ellen back to her senses. This was no dream. 'God help me,' she whispered.

Paul rose sharply and turned to face her. 'Get back in the carriage, Ellen. You do not want to see this.'

But she had seen it.

Her hand let go of the door handle and she walked forward.

'Ellen, go back,' Paul barked at her. But she could not stop herself.

'Who is he?'

The man on the ground had not moved.

'A highwayman, chancing his luck. Go back inside, Ellen. Please. Let me sort this.'

The man was still motionless. A macabre desire to see pulled her towards him.

'Ellen,' Paul snapped as she got closer, in another warning. But her body refused to be warned. She kept walking, and it only took a few more steps. The man lay there, as white as the frost-stained grass beneath him. Except the grass beside his head was not white but dark, marred by something fluid that glistened in the moonlight... and half his forehead had been blown open.

Ellen turned away and cast up what little she had eaten when they had stopped for supper. Paul's hand touched her back. 'Ellen, I told you not to look.'

She was sick again.

He pressed his handkerchief into her palm as she fought to catch her breath.

'Ellen.' Paul's voice was quiet, as though he was afraid of her reaction.

After a few minutes, she straightened, the world about her turning to dust. 'You killed him.'

'I had to—'

'Could you not have merely wounded him?'

'It was self-defence, madam. The Captain had no choice. The highwayman had his pistol aimed at the Captain's head. If he'd not sliced the man's leg open to get him off that horse—'

'Would that not have been enough?' Ellen's words echoed back on the night air.

Paul raised a hand, his fingers reaching for her. 'Ellen, come.' She backed away. 'That man would have raped and murdered you without a thought. I had no choice.'

'I'm glad, you did it, Captain. The bastard hit me.'

'Hit you?' Paul faced the man who must have been riding the lead horse.

The man walked towards them, clutching his upper arm.

He looked as pale as the dead man.

'Bullet's gone clean through my arm, Captain. He wanted to stop the horses.'

'Sit on the backboard, before you fall down,' Paul said. Then he glanced at her. 'Ellen, tear a strip off your petticoats.'

She bent to do it. Any moment she would wake up in her bed at home, and this whole journey would be a dream.

Her hands shook too much, she could not tear the cotton.

'Wait.' Paul walked back for his sword. She straightened as he wiped it clean in the grass.

Her gaze caught on the dead man. Paul seemed so unemotional.

He rose and turned to her. Ignoring her observation, he squatted, gripped the hem and sliced into it with the sword's edge. After he had done it, he dropped the sword and tore a strip with his hands. She stood still. Frozen.

When he straightened, he said, 'Ellen, can you tie this about the man's arm? Here...' He clasped one of her hands and pulled her towards the postilion rider who sat at the back of the carriage. 'Do not worry about taking his coat off, just tie it over the top, just above the wound, as tightly as you can to stop the bleeding. Do you understand?'

She nodded and began as the man watched her in silence, in pain, looking faint as blood dripped from his limp hand onto the ground.

Paul walked away. She heard him talking to the driver and realised they were moving the highway man's body. Her trembling fingers struggled to tie the cotton, but she managed.

Cold seeping deep into her flesh, she shivered, her teeth chattering.

'Ellen, get in the carriage.' Paul's words were an order. Not knowing what else to do, she did. It was just as cold within, and dark, and lonely.

After a moment he opened the door. 'I am going to ride on the box to the nearest inn. We will sort everything out there.' There was a dark stain on his grey pantaloons. Blood.

She nodded. She had left everything she knew behind her. This was a world of unknowns. She had never imagined anything like this might happen.

The carriage lurched into motion. She heard Paul talking on the box above her, but not his words.

Images of the man lying on the grass and Paul standing over him cluttered Ellen's mind. Her senses waited for something to happen as the carriage rolled slowly on towards the next inn, their pace restricted to protect the wounded man who must be sitting beside Paul.

Every sound reverberated through her body. She could still smell the gunpowder as if it were in the carriage. She shivered, her arms folding over her chest as she swallowed, trying to clear her dry throat. Then she gritted her teeth to stop them chattering.

The next inn was in the middle of nowhere at the edge of the road. The golden light of an oil lantern bleached out the moonlight when they turned into the courtyard, but the carriage was still dark inside, since Paul had put out the lamp.

Ellen looked through the window, her fingers shaking as she put on her cloak and bonnet.

Yawning men appeared from the stalls, grooms ready to change their horses.

She saw Paul jump down from the box and say something, and a man's eyes opened wide, staring at Paul. Then the man ran into the inn.

Paul turned to the carriage, opened the door and knocked down the step, not meeting her gaze until he offered his hand to her. The hand that had recently killed a man. But then it must have killed many men during the Peninsular War. Her fingers shook as she took it.

'Ellen,' he whispered, 'I have told them you are my wife. I have asked for a private parlour for you to wait in while I sort this mess out. Do you wish me to order a warm drink for you? Chocolate? You look in shock.'

She nodded. She was shocked.

His fingers holding hers, he led her across the courtyard, and she tried not to think of the dead man whose body lay sprawled over the back of the carriage, on top of Paul's trunk.

But she did think of the injured man as she heard him climb down behind her. There was a word spoken, 'Surgeon'.

Paul had killed the man to protect them.

This was the ugly world he knew, she had only known the sanctuary of her father's property.

A lone rider left the courtyard, she presumed to fetch a surgeon.

'Ellen, wait here,' he commanded when she was seated in the parlour. But he did not then walk away; he squatted down and rubbed her gloved hands as he held them together, as if warming them. Then he said more gently, 'I will be back in a while, as soon as I can.'

She nodded.

He had not returned when her warm chocolate arrived. She sat in silence, sipping it – drowning. How would she cope on the edge of a battlefield? Paul was more than the man she knew, the man who overflowed with vibrancy, who smiled and laughed easily – he had killed a man with no thought, or remorse.

She had taken neither her bonnet nor her cloak off, and the fire in the hearth blazed, but she was cold.

Paul arrived an hour later – an hour which she'd endured in the form of a statue, sitting in the chair staring at the cup of chocolate in her hands.

He shut the door behind him; the action sent her nerves reeling. She was unused to being in a room alone with a man, and yet they had spent days confined in the carriage. But now she knew she had spent those days with a man who could kill so brutally and close his heart off to it.

An expression of pain flickered across his face as she looked up. He had seen her flinch.

He no longer wore his blood-stained clothes and he had put on his greatcoat.

'Have I made you dislike me?' The words held anguish. He looked younger. His age. 'I am sorry.'

She stood, setting her cup down.

How could she balance the man she loved against the soldier who could kill? There was a lethal warrior residing inside the gentle man she had met in a drawing room.

He was not gentle.

But she did not dislike him. Her heart loved him. She had known he was a soldier, she had not understood what that meant. Now she was terrified of the choice she had made.

She went to him, sobbing, and her arms embraced his midriff; doing what she had longed to do for an hour – hold him and cry – and pretend that what had happened had not happened.

His hand slid her bonnet back so it hung from her neck, then he kissed her cheek and her forehead as his hands held her waist. 'I have spoken to the magistrate. The villain was known here. There will be no prosecution against me, and the driver who is injured is being replaced. The injured man will stay here until he is well enough to travel back. I have given him money for his lodgings.'

Ellen nodded against his chest, not knowing what else to do.

His palm lay on her hair, a gentle weight of reassurance.

How could he touch her with such gentleness yet do what he had just done?

'You have had a taste of death tonight, Ellen. Has it made you wish to turn back? I will take you back if it has changed your mind.'

Had it?

She would not remain with her family if she returned. Her father would force her into marrying Argyle.

But Paul had killed a man...

Yet that man was a thief, he had chosen a fate to kill or be killed. He had shot the carriage driver.

She pulled away from him, although her hands held Paul's greatcoat either side of his waist in fists. 'Was killing him the only way?' Maybe she showed her naivety by asking. But she was a little afraid of him tonight.

His eyes studied her in the flickering orange light of the tallow candles which burned in the room. 'Not the only way, no. I could have brought him down from his horse and shot him in the shoulder or the arm. But it is my instinct, Ellen. In battle, a soldier cannot risk simply wounding a man. Otherwise, as you fight on, a dozen men could be aiming a pistol at your back and... you were in the carriage... and I did not know if there were more men in the woods.'

She could not judge the colour of his eyes in the candle-light, but she could see regret and pain. He had killed, but he did not wish to kill. He was not a murderer. Sorrow caught in his gaze, as if ghosts walked about him.

She pressed herself against him, holding him. This time it was not to receive comfort but to give it.

'Ellen?' His hand ran over her hair. 'Do you want me to take you back?'

'No.' She did not want to go back, but she did not know how to go forward.

* * *

Ellen's answer was warmth seeping through the clothing covering his chest, into his heart. It would have hurt to let her go. But he would have done it, if she had wished it. Thank God, she did not. He'd promised himself barely hours ago to protect her from the brutality of this world, and he'd not even reached Gretna before he'd failed. 'You are strong, Ellen. You will face unpleasant things if you follow the drum with me. But you will survive, and I will make you happy.'

She sobbed and more tears dampened his collar in answer. He held her tighter for a moment. But then he set her away. If her father was behind them, they had lost hours... 'We need to leave. Are you ready?'

Her gaze met his, flooded with the uncertainty he had dispelled before this incident. She was brave and strong, and she loved him, he knew it, but he could see she was also a little afraid of him now.

A sigh left his throat. He could do nothing. He had been trained to kill, and he had killed to protect her. He was a soldier; it was his instinct to fight and protect.

He pushed his thoughts aside, along with the memories of dead, dying and wounded men. They had to reach the border before her father reached them. *If* he had followed.

Within a quarter hour they were in the carriage with freshly heated bricks, his weapons tucked away once more, and blankets piled over them as the temperature had dropped still further. The next stop would be Penrith. They were nearly there... nearly.

Ellen pressed against him, seeking comfort, her arms about his midriff, but her body felt stiff and her fingers trembled a little, implying her shock had not really ebbed.

Neither had his.

She fell asleep, her head resting against his chest. He laid his arm over her shoulders and took comfort in her beauty as he tried to hold her steady while the carriage bounced over the frozen ruts in the road.

He could not sleep. The call of battle still raged in his blood. There had never been any real danger, he was by a mile more experienced in a fight than the highwayman, but a murderous desire had swept over him; the same which captured him on a battlefield.

Kill or be killed.

Ellen was right; he was skilled enough to have maimed the man and no more. But the thought of her in danger... *God*, he could not bear it. He had not stopped for one moment to consider doing anything less than kill.

Visions of battlefields, of corpses, and men's eyes clouding with death before they fell played through his head, but his heart only felt Ellen and nothing of the bitter world he fought in.

He had fought for her, to keep her safe, to return to the beauty he had found and forget death.

What was his intent for the future then?

To keep her safe, he would have to march into enemy lines and slay every man.

A throaty sound of self-deprecation erupted from his chest. *Bloody hell.* It was what he wished to do, but he would end up dead from such stupid ideas, and that would hardly protect her, and what was the point of her companionship and comfort if he was dead?

He looked through the window, his gaze scanning the passing treeline. He had left the lantern smothered, and the curtain open, so he might look out for any risk of attack, merely to ease his battle-ready nerves. But now what he saw was snow. *Ahh. Damn.* Why tonight? Why could it not have waited one more day?

As the carriage rolled on, he watched the large white flakes fall and settle. It was the sort of snow which could form deep drifts. But maybe it was a blessing. If it fell thick, it would hold her father back too. *If* he had followed.

The snow formed a swirling cloud of white and Paul's heartbeat pulsed, his blood racing as hard as the carriage horses' pace. This was not now only a race against her father, but a race against the weather. How soon before the roads become impassable?

He watched the white flurries for what must have been two hours, as they swept against the pane of glass in the carriage door. Then the snow subsided and instead he watched the blue glow which shone back off the white blanket covering everything. The carriage slid a number of times but fortunately the frozen ruts in the road, beneath the white layer, gave the horses and carriage wheels grip.

He remembered all the travelling he had done in the years of the Peninsular War, marching hundreds of miles. He had not been tucked inside a warm carriage. He had been outside, trudging through the cold and urging his men to ignore their numb feet, when his were also numb and his fingers burning with cold too.

How would Ellen survive days like that? True, she would be with the baggage train and have the luxury of a respite in the carts. But there were times when the carts got stuck and the women had to get out and walk through knee-deep mud, snow or thickets, and then in the summer there were days of blistering heat...

He had been a fool to bring her with him. Cruel. Selfish. But yet again he shoved the thought aside as he did with the haunting memories of war. She was happy to be with him. He would not take her back. She was his now, his comfort, and he would be hers. She would be the thing that brought his mind back from war to peace.

Maybe it was good that she'd faced the encounter with the highwayman, maybe it meant, when she faced the reality of war and wished she'd not left England, he could say, 'But you did know...'

Had he become such a selfish bloody bastard, then?

Yes, where Ellen was concerned. A thousand times, yes. He loved her.

It was not until the sunshine finally began glinting on the snow, reflecting gold light as it rose above the horizon, that Paul finally rested his shoulder against the corner of the carriage, lifted one foot up onto the opposite seat and fell asleep.

4

Ellen woke to find the carriage flooded with natural light. It appeared to be late morning. When she sat upright she saw a carpet of snow outside. Everything was white. The world looked pure again, denying the memories of a man lying still on the ground beside a dark pool of blood as Paul stood over him with a sword and a pistol in his hands.

She shivered at the memory but her stomach growled, despite her revulsion. She'd eaten nothing since it had happened, and she'd been sick last night.

She looked at Paul. He slept, leaning against the corner of the carriage, one elbow resting on a sill beside him, so his curled fist could support his chin. His other hand lay slack on his thigh. One booted foot rested on the opposite seat, with his leg bent, the other still rested on the carriage floor. His thigh had become a pillow for her head.

Every muscle and sinew in his body was honed. He was a soldier. Even in sleep he looked ready to fight. Now she had seen the aftermath of his killing, she knew what that meant.

Her heart had chosen this man. Yes, he knew how to be

violent, but he knew how to be gentle too. She could not deny him now.

In his sleep, he looked younger. Yet he was young, merely one and twenty, just a little older than her, and he had endured so much...

He needed a sanctuary and he'd chosen her. She would willingly play that role, even if at the present moment, the idea of his capability to kill frightened her.

The carriage jolted and instantly his eyes opened. He sat up, his hand going to his hip, as though to grasp a sword or pistol. But then he saw her, and smiled. His hand lifted instead and raked through his hair, hiding the instinct to be ready to fight.

As the image of the dead highwayman hovered, she wondered how many pictures of dead men on battlefields played through his head.

She could perhaps understand a little more of the soldier now she knew what that meant.

She smiled.

'How are you?' he asked. 'You slept well. You have been asleep nearly all night.'

'Were you awake then?'

'Yes. I did not like to sleep while it was dark, in case, well...' He did not end the sentence but she understood. He had been nervous of more highwaymen. But he could not be worried for himself as he was able to defend himself – he had worried over her.

He looked down, lifted his fob watch from his inside pocket and flicked open the catch. 'It is nearly noon.'

She was not surprised; the hunger in her stomach and the sunlight implied it. But he looked surprised that he had slept.

She wondered how much last night had disturbed him. He'd seemed cold and unemotional then, but now...

'We'd better stop soon.' He leaned over the carriage to open the hatch in order to speak to the man on the box. 'Where are we?'

'Two miles from Penrith by the last marker, Captain.'

'Stop at the next coaching inn, will you?'

'Aye, Captain.'

Paul sat back again and then stretched, lifting his arms and arching his back. It showed off the lean, muscular definition of his torso and his thighs, which his uniform hugged so perfectly.

A warm sensation fluttered low in her stomach. They were nearly at Gretna. Soon she would know what it would be like to share a bed with him. She smiled, excitement and anxiety skittering through her nerves; warring love and fear. It tangled up like a muddled ball of embroidery threads within her.

'I cannot wait to stretch my legs a little,' he murmured as he dropped back against the swabs. Then he looked at her. 'I admit I am sick of this carriage.'

Her smile parted her lips. 'I am also.'

'Shall we take a break once we are wed, before we travel to Portsmouth? We may find lodgings for a night. It will be our wedding night.'

His blue eyes shone.

She nodded, the flutter stirring low in her stomach again – desire and disquiet. 'It will be Christmas Eve too,' she said. 'There may be poor service at the inns. We should feel guilty dragging our drivers away from their families during advent?' He looked at her oddly. 'Paul...'

'My apologies. I had completely forgotten it was nearly Christmas Day. My mind has been focused on gathering my men and then coming to fetch you ever since we received the order to sail. I have also not celebrated this time of year for many years. My family will not expect me to be there, but yours... You will miss your sisters...'

She nodded, her vision clouding with tears. The twelve days following Christmas were for feasting and celebration, and on the twelfth night, at Pembroke Place, they held a servants' ball, when someone would be crowned the Lord of Misrule and order all the entertainments. Ellen and her sisters were allowed to watch for a little while.

He pulled her into a firm embrace. 'I should not have mentioned them. I am sorry.'

'You need not apologise. It is nice to know you think of what will affect me. I do miss them. I will miss Penny most. I wish I had been able to explain to her. But I do not regret leaving with you. I will be happy with you even though I will miss them.'

His palm rested on her hair. 'You can write to your sister when we are married.'

'Yes. What of your family?'

He laughed, a low deep pitch. 'My family are long forgotten.'

'But you came with them in the summer...'

'Because I had returned to England and sought my old self, the privileged sixth son of the Earl of Craster, but I am not that now. I am first a soldier. Christmas with my family would be like living in the past. My family is the army, and my men.'

'You are no longer close to them?'

'As close as it is possible to be when I lead a very different life to them. They will not miss me, and I will not miss them.' His fingers lifted her chin, and he looked into her eyes. 'You will be my family now, and I will be yours. We will be each other's comfort and companion. That is what I wish for us.'

His words sent shivers running across her skin. 'That is all I want too – to make you happy and to be happy with you.'

'As I wish more than anything to make you happy, so we have hope, Ellen.' His head lowered and he kissed her.

The ache in her stomach swept out to her limbs – yet along with the pleasure of his warmth and gentleness came concern; his gentle hands could kill a man...

When they pulled into an inn a little while later, having driven into the town of Penrith, Paul moved immediately, letting her go so she could sit up. He climbed out of the carriage in a moment, lowered the step and then lifted his hand to help her.

She took it and smiled as he smiled at her. 'Let us go in search of refreshment.'

The cobbles of the courtyard were slippery from the snow, so they walked tentatively. He kept a hold of her hand. It was protective – the way he had been with her ever since they'd been together.

She had never seen her father be even slightly attentive to her mother. She had only seen him give orders and her mother obey and defer to his wishes. This side of Paul, the man she had first met in the summer, was precious gold in her eyes. If only there was not also the part of him that frightened her a little – the image of the highwayman lying dead in his blood lingered in her mind.

Paul ordered cured ham, cheese and freshly baked bread to break their fast, and then asked how many miles they were away from the Scottish border and how long it would take them to get there. The innkeeper implied they could make it by nightfall, if the snow neither melted nor started falling again.

By nightfall. In hours they might be wed.

They ate hurriedly, not wishing to delay, then Paul suggested they walk away from the inn, a little way up the road, so he could stretch his legs before having to endure the cramped carriage again.

She offered his arm and she held it, but his long-legged stride made it difficult for her to keep up, especially as the layer of snow caught on the hem of her skirt, making her velvet habit heavier as it soaked up the moisture. But she liked the gentle give of the crisp snow beneath her half boots, and she began sliding her feet through it to keep up.

She slipped, and her fingers tightened about the firm muscle of his forearm.

The solidity, his security, caught at her heart.

But his strength enabled him to kill men.

Her gaze turned to the picturesque village green on the far side of the road. Its fresh white coat looked pure and beautiful.

'Shall we walk through it?' Paul asked. 'I think it is too late now to make any difference if anyone were to remember us.'

Ellen nodded, her fingers clinging to his arm more firmly, denying her thoughts of the warrior within him.

'Come then.' He led her over.

On the village green, his arm dropped from her grip as he bent, then he quickly grasped a handful of snow and tossed it at her, a wide smile cutting his face and laughter glimmering in his eyes.

Ellen squealed, turning away as it hit the side of her bonnet. 'Oh, you brigand!' She laughed.

He laughed too, stooping to gather another handful of snow.

Ellen bent and filled her hands, crushing the snow in her fingers to make it denser, then threw the snowball at him.

He threw his. It hit her breast. The snow stuck to her cloak.

The cold, the exercise and the laughter tumbled through her senses in an exhilarating rush.

He still laughed as he brushed snow from his shoulder and she ran a few steps away then turned and threw another handful at him. It nearly missed him, only brushing his ear as he ducked. She bent and filled two hands, as a missile of cold snow hit her back.

She laughed again, smiling so widely it made her cheeks begin to ache, and lifted both her hands, and the pile of snow she held. Still laughing, she ran at him. He did not try to avoid her ambush as she neared and thrust the snow at his face, he only shut his eyes and his lips.

She laughed even more as he brushed the snow away, and some clung to his eyelashes and brows. A look of retribution slipped across his face, although his blue eyes glinted with laughter and a smile hovered at the corners of his mouth.

His smile parting his lips, he gripped her shoulders and tumbled her backwards so she fell onto the snow. He fell with her, on top of her, though he did not crush her.

All the air left her lungs as her gaze caught his. Laughter no longer lingered in his eyes, but something else shone in them, something deep, warm and heartfelt. Her laughter died too, a moment before his lips pressed to hers. It was unlike any kiss they had shared in the carriage. They lay on a green before the inn, with several cottages about them. He just pressed his lips over hers for a moment. But the pressure of his body, the knowledge that last night he had killed a man and knowing that in a few hours they would be married, fought a battle to dominate her emotions. Her heartbeat drummed.

He rolled away, knelt, then stood. He offered her his hand. She accepted it and he pulled her onto her feet, then dusted the snowflakes from her cloak.

It had been good to laugh. She had needed laughter, and perhaps he had known. Perhaps he had needed laughter too.

Her beautiful, elemental, warrior was not invincible. He did feel pain over the loss of life, which meant he must be weighed down by memories. She would protect him too, love him and comfort him, and she would make him happy.

'We had better be on our way,' he prompted, his voice implying the threat which still hung over them, of being caught by her father. 'Things will be good between us, Ellen. I promise. I know last night was abhorrent to you. Death is a terrible thing, no matter that a man is your enemy and trying to kill you. I hope you will not have to face it often, and I will do everything I can to protect you. I love you.'

'I know. I love you too.'

She could face living on the edge of a battlefield, as long as he endured fighting on one, and when he came back she would help him fight the ghosts.

'You will withstand, Ellen, and we will be happy. I swear it.'

* * *

It had turned to dusk as the carriage dashed the last few miles towards Gretna. Paul mentally willed the horses to gallop faster. The carriage rolled far too slowly. There had been no more snow, *thank God*, and no thaw to make the roads turn to a quagmire of muddy slush, but even so the weather slowed their pace. The tracks they travelled over were hard yet slippery, so they could not race at full tilt.

Hurry. Hurry. He still had no idea if her father followed. But they had lost time last night and it would be the worst thing to be caught just before Gretna.

Come on. Faster.

He wanted to jump out and pull the horses. *Come on!*

Ellen sat beside him, and his hand held hers, probably too

tightly. He relaxed his grip. He knew she was anxious too. They both sat forward on the seat, looking from opposite windows, listening for the noise of a carriage or riders in pursuit.

Hurry up. Come on.

Ellen glanced at him. He smiled, trying to reassure her, though he doubted he succeeded, because he was not sure they would make the Scottish border.

Once they were across, they just needed to find another person to witness them pledging themselves to each other, and in Scotland that meant they were married. Where they made their vow and before whom did not matter, it was a legal bond. Anyone could bear witness to a wedding under Scottish law. As long as the bride was older than five and ten. So if he and Ellen stood before a Scotsman and said they wished to marry, then the deed was done. They had no need for parental consent or a priest.

They had left Carlisle behind hours ago. They could not be far from Gretna, which was the first village in Scotland, the place where all runaways searched for a witness.

Come on.

Night had begun to creep across the sky, and he was not sure they would find a witness if they crossed after dark. Would anyone rise from their bed at night to perform the favour, and confirm the ceremony? For enough money, maybe; but he would be spending the precious funds he needed to clothe Ellen. Heaven knew he had spent enough years penniless during the Peninsular War. He had only received his accrued arrears of wages a few weeks back, along with a small inheritance from a deceased aunt. Still, he was not rich.

The sky turned darker and became a bleak half-light. He saw the slightly darker line of the sea against the sky on the horizon. As the carriage rolled on he saw the inlet of a river mouth; the estuary which marked the Scottish border.

He looked at Ellen, the tension inside him spinning in a sudden eddy, disorientation tumbling over him for a moment. Ellen leaned across him and looked through the window on his side.

The driver slid the hatch open. 'We've crossed the border, Captain.'

Thank God. 'Hurry then. Stop at the first place you think we will find a witness.'

The carriage hurried on, travelling past the estuary, where a few small boats rested on the sand, left stranded by the low tide.

Paul let go of Ellen's hand and drew the window down, to look ahead. They passed over the bridge beneath which the river ran out to sea. He saw nothing as the chill night air rushed into the carriage.

He heard Ellen slide down the opposite window. A harsh cold draft swirled through the carriage penetrating his clothing.

Come on, he urged the horses. He leaned out of the window and looked back along the track. There were no carriages, or horses, pursuing them.

'I see something!' Ellen called. 'A little forge beside the road.'

He looked ahead and saw nothing on his side. Looking up at the box, he yelled, 'Driver. We will stop at the forge!'

Slipping back into the carriage, he turned to Ellen.

She smiled broadly, her fingers holding the sill of the open window as the breeze swept a few loose strands of hair off her face. She had taken off her bonnet. It rested on the carriage seat between them.

She glanced at him. The colour of her eyes engaging with the last bluish light of the day. She was magnificent; he'd never seen a woman as beautiful as she. Every man in his regiment would envy him, and when he went into battle, he would have this beauty to come back to, to refresh his battered soul.

He held her hand again as they travelled the last few yards in silence, in the freezing cold carriage.

A few moments more and they would be safe. Married.

The carriage slowed and pulled up, sliding a little, and Paul braced his hand on the side, holding himself steady.

The forge was a squat, whitewashed building, only little bigger than a stable, with a thatched roof.

'Stay here,' he said as he let go of her hand.

He opened the door, climbed out and shut the door behind him, leaving Ellen inside until the arrangements were made. As he walked about the carriage, the blacksmith came out, wiping his hands on a rag. The man's face and hands were stained with dark smut, and he wore a tarnished leather apron.

'Ye looking to get y'urself hitched?' The question was bluntly put, implying this man had done the deed a thousand times.

'Yes. Will you bear witness?'

'For a price... What will ye give me?'

What Paul offered first the man rejected. Paul's uniform marked him as an officer, and Paul would guess the man assumed he had enough to pay more. But unwilling to throw money away, Paul haggled until they reached a price he was prepared to agree.

'Bring your woman,' the blacksmith said as they shook hands, 'and let's get it done.'

After handing over the payment, Paul turned to the carriage. Ellen watched from the open window. His heart jolted and a tight sensation clasped his chest – elation. He smiled. Her smile rose like sunshine in answer, cutting through the dusk.

She was not only externally beautiful, her beauty shone from inside her too. She was like a brook of bubbling joy that spilled over into a refreshing pool he wished to bathe in. It was like slipping away from the army camp on the edge of war to swim naked in a cool river, to feel clean when you had been dirty for days.

The horses stamped at the ground and shook out their manes, rattling their harness and tack, restless from their hard ride. They whinnied into the cold air as Paul moved to help Ellen from the carriage.

The spare rider, already on the ground, had lowered the step, and now he opened the door for her.

'Wait.' Paul stopped the man with a hand on his shoulder to move him aside, then he lifted that hand to Ellen. 'Will you marry me?'

Her smile shone in her eyes. If she had been unsure when they had left, she was not any more.

'Oh, yes.'

'Come then. Let me make you my wife.'

She laughed, holding his hand, then looking down to watch her step.

The snow crunched underfoot as he walked her to the forge, holding her hand as he might if they were parading about a ballroom. Of course they had never done that; she was not officially out. He had snatched her from the nest, as it were.

'Stand here,' the blacksmith called from within. The man had not washed his hands, or his face, and it meant he was absorbed in the shadows inside the forge. He stepped into the orange glow emanating from the fire. 'There.' He directed them to stand on the opposite side of an anvil.

Paul held Ellen's hand more firmly, his fingers weaving between hers, uniting them before the words were even said.

'Have you a ring then?'

Yes, he had; where were his wits? Letting go of her hand, he took off his gloves, as she removed hers. He took the ring from the inside pocket of his coat. It was a simple band of gold, nothing special.

A plump woman came into the smithy through a door at the back, and as he and Ellen turned, she smiled. 'Another couple come to exchange vows then.' Two young children followed her. A girl who was probably eight or nine, and a boy of about five.

'Aye,' the blacksmith answered in a gruff voice. The children hovered near their mother, watching as she came closer.

'Margaret can bear ye witness too,' the blacksmith said, calling Paul's attention back. 'Say y'ur piece and I'll pronounce ye man and wife.' The cold dispassionate words turned Paul's stomach. He needed this to feel a little more than something rash and hurried. He wanted it to be a moment Ellen would look back on with fondness. He wished to make a memory they could treasure their entire lives.

He faced her, searching for the right words. Words that would profess all he felt, but he had never been a poet. 'I love you, Ellen.' Her eyes searched his, shining orange in the low light of the smithy, and her lips pressed together, slightly curved. A few strands of her hair had fallen about her face, the ebony curls caressing her jaw and neck. His chest filled with a warm sensation. Her beauty could steal his breath away.

'I promise to protect you. I swear I shall cherish you every day of my life. You may trust me, you may rely on me. I am yours. I wish to give myself to you – my life to you. Will you be my wife? Will you marry me?'

Her lips parted in a smile.

'Yes,' she answered. But she did not hold her fingers out for him to put the ring on. 'I love you, Paul. I wish to be your comfort and your sanctuary. I pledge my life to you. I will be your wife. Will you be my husband? Will you marry me?'

A smile touched his lips. 'Yes. I will. Give me your hand.'

He held her hand steady and slid the ring on her finger. It stuck a little on her knuckle, but then slid over. A pain, like a sharp blade, pierced his heart as her hand dropped.

Forgetting the other occupants of the smithy, he pressed a kiss on her lips.

A loud ringing clang, a hammer hitting the iron anvil, broke them apart as Ellen jumped.

'I pronounce ye man and wife, forged together now ye are.' They both looked at the blacksmith, and his lips lifted in a smile of acknowledgement. The deed was done. Her father could not prevent it now. They were married.

'Congratulations,' the blacksmith's wife said.

'Thank you,' Ellen answered, looking at the woman before glancing back at Paul, and giving him a self-conscious smile, her cheeks turning pink. He loved her like this, a bit tousled and unkempt, and looking young and slightly lacking confidence. To see her perfect beauty a little awry made her appear more human, more touchable.

'I shall fetch ye a piece of parchment to show we witnessed y'ur vows,' the woman said, before turning and hurrying back inside the living space of the forge; it must be no more than one or two rooms.

Ellen's hand reached for Paul's. Her eyes said she truly thought he could master the world if he wished, her trust appeared absolute. He prayed her faith would be honoured. *Please, let all be well.*

'Here ye are, Donald, here's the marriage paper. I 'ave signed it.'

The blacksmith took the document from the woman's hand and held it out to Paul. 'Ye sign it first. Then I'll put me mark.'

The woman had brought a quill and ink as well as the paper. Paul signed the document on a rough wooden table. The woman's name had been carefully written in a very precise script; it was probably the sum of her education. Paul handed the quill to Ellen who signed it too. Then the blacksmith signed it with a smutty hand, marking the paper with a scrawled, unrecognisable name. It did not matter; it was evidence enough to prove they were married within English law.

Paul lifted the paper and blew on the ink, as outside they heard horses. He handed the document to Ellen.

The blacksmith looked at him, a dark eyebrow lifting. 'An angry papa? Or another couple come?'

Paul's heartbeat stilled for a moment, then pounded. *Damn.* He had hoped to save Ellen from a scene with her father. He turned and followed the blacksmith outside. Ellen followed them.

An unmarked carriage raced along the road towards them. Not her father. If it had been her father, the Pembroke coat of arms would be emblazoned on the door. Yet it looked like a privately owned vehicle; fresh polish glowed in the moonlight that breached the layer of light clouds and reflected back from the snow.

The postilion rider, who sat astride the right-hand lead horse, pulled on the reins as the carriage drew closer, slowing the horses and therefore slowing the carriage. Paul took a breath and held it for a moment, an uncomfortable feeling running up his spine.

Ellen joined him on the road outside the forge, her gloves were now pulled on and her bonnet tied, ready to progress their journey.

Her hand embraced his elbow. 'They are my father's men.' Her other hand contained the confirmation of their marriage.

Paul watched the carriage slide on the snow-covered ground as it slowed. He straightened, feeling the lack of his sword and pistol. Both were in the carriage. Not that Pembroke would fight. Paul was married to Ellen and any thought of annulment would be foolish, it could not be undone; she had been on the road alone with him for days. She was ruined regardless.

Whoever was within waited for one of the men to climb down from the box.

Accustomed to charging into battle, Paul's arm slipped from Ellen's grip as he walked forward. He reached the carriage at the moment the man opened the door. Another stepped out. Not Ellen's father. Though this man had blue eyes very like Ellen's.

'It is Mr Wareham, my father's steward,' Ellen whispered.

Paul glanced into the carriage and saw no one else within. Her father had sent someone for her, not come himself.

The man stared at Paul. 'Captain Harding, I presume.'

'Mr Wareham,' Ellen said.

'Lady Eleanor.' The man's gaze passed to Ellen, his expression stiff. 'I have come to prevent this nonsense—'

'You are too late to stop us,' Paul answered.

The man continued looking at Ellen. 'Am I, Lady Eleanor?'

She nodded, holding out the document on which the ink was still drying. 'The evidence is here.'

'My journey is wasted then.'

Paul did not answer, neither did Ellen, and for a moment the man just stood there looking at them as if he expected something else.

Then he said, 'Very well...' and reached into his inside pocket. 'I have this for you. I was to give it to you when I found you, if you were already wed.' He held out a folded letter, the red wax seal on the top had been stamped with the Duke of Pembroke's mark. Ellen took it.

'I will leave you then.'

'Wait,' Ellen said. 'Will you take letters for me, Mr Wareham, if I write them quickly?'

The man had already moved away, but he turned back, agreeing with a nod. 'If you wish me to.'

'I will only be a moment.' Ellen looked at the blacksmith. 'May I purchase some paper?'

The blacksmith nodded, looking at Paul to agree the price.

Mr Wareham returned to her father's carriage as they entered the small smithy.

It did not take her long to write three separate letters and fold them, as Paul watched. The first she wrote to her father, asking for his forgiveness. The second she addressed to her mother, asking for understanding. The third was to her sister, Penny, expressing regret at leaving her behind.

He remembered writing letters home when he had joined the regiment. They had been full of light and hope as hers were. He had given up writing because who at home wished to hear of his desperate need to keep his men fed, and alive, and how many men had been killed in battle, or how far they had marched that day? He hoped Ellen's joy in life and the hope in her words would not die when she learned his life.

But he refused the thoughts of consequence or future now. This was their wedding day, their wedding night, and tomorrow was Christmas, the first day of the twelve days of feasting; a time to count blessings.

'Here, Mr Wareham.' Ellen rushed back out into the road, bearing her letters. Paul could see her willing her family to support her marriage as she handed the letters to the man in the carriage. Her father would never approve. Paul had seen her father's face when the man had turned down his offer, as though it were a piss-pot that he had offered.

The Duke's man took the folded pieces of paper without a word.

Ellen looked at Paul, biting her lower lip.

He went to her. 'Ellen.' He took both her hands. 'Do you regret this?'

'No.' The denial came immediately.

He smiled, ignoring the Duke's carriage pulling away behind her. 'Shall we go to Carlisle and find an inn?'

'Yes.'

He turned towards their carriage. 'Do you think he even tried to catch us in time to stop our marriage? He did not seem overly concerned.'

'He is committed to my father. He has worked for him for several years.'

'Time is not the thing that makes a man loyal. Trust and respect make a man loyal. I do not think he cared one way or another that we were married.'

5

Ellen's heartbeat pounded. A part of it was heavy with sadness because they had married without her family present. But it had been beautiful and Paul's vows had made her heart overflow with joy, pushing her guilt and fear aside.

She loved him. She did not regret her choice.

Paul had left the lamp unlit again, so she opened her father's letter, rested her shoulder against the side of the carriage and held the paper near the window. The clouds had had begun to clear and the moonlight was brighter than ever on the snow, so she could see.

There were just two lines of his precise, formal script.

Eleanor

You have made your decision and by doing so, made me look a fool. Do not expect a welcome back. You are no longer permitted here.

The Duke of Pembroke

His words hurt. He had not even signed it 'your father'.

They had been brought up by her mother to call him Papa; he had not once used the childish name himself. Father, he would concede, but he never said it with any emotion.

'What does it say?'

Ellen looked at Paul. 'That he wishes nothing more to do with me. I think it would have been the same even if Mr Wareham had arrived before we wed.'

'Then why send him?'

'Perhaps just to look as though he tried to stop me; for appearances' sake...' She shrugged. She had never understood her father. She would have to be much wiser to fathom his depths.

Paul smiled. 'Put him from your mind. You have no need to worry over him now.'

She was not worrying over him but she was concerned about her sisters and her mother.

Paul lifted her hand to his lips. The warmth of his breath seeped through her glove. Then he turned her hand and kissed her wrist above it. Sensation skimmed up her arm. 'Do not fret about your sisters either. They have time to mature, and I am certain your eldest, Penny, is tough enough to fight her own battles. She did not seem demurring when I met her.'

Ellen smiled, although moisture filled her eyes. Then she laughed, just a sudden sharp sound. 'No, she is not demure, she will stand against him if he tries to force her hand, and she will use my disobedience as her example.'

'And the others will learn from her...'

'Yes.'

Paul had such an aura of confidence; it filled the air around him.

'Very well then. No more sulking.'

Her smile lifted. 'No.'

'And no more tears,' he added, wiping one away from the corner of her eye with his thumb.

Her next laugh was a little choked, and then foolishly she burst into tears. But she was happy too; they were part happy tears. He pulled her close and held her, as the carriage rolled on.

Another hour or more passed before they reached Carlisle and the snowy frost bound mud roads turned to cobble. The noise about the carriage changed as it rolled through the streets, and the strike of the horses' hooves, tack and carriage wheels bounced back from brick houses.

When they turned into an inn, Paul pulled away from her and gave her a smile. It burned with compassion. 'I know you've left a lot behind, Ellen, but now is the time to begin our new life.'

'I know.' She was his wife and she was about to become his wife in full. A pleasant ache clasped low in her stomach. She took a breath and her breasts pressed against her bodice.

The carriage halted and all outside was noise. Within, her nerves rioted in anticipation of her wedding night.

'Come.' He opened the carriage door, then climbed out and lifted his hand, as he had done so many times during their journey to the border.

She stepped out, her head spinning with emotions.

'Do you wish to eat in a parlour or in the room we hire for the night?'

'In the room.' She was not hungry. Her stomach had tied in knots.

'Well, then, we had better claim one.'

They walked across the courtyard that had been cleared of snow. The ostler was already helping to free the horses from the traces.

Paul asked for a room for Captain and Mrs Harding and ordered a meal of gammon pie for them both.

Mrs Harding... That was her name now. Her lips lifted a little as the novelty flowed through her.

A maid showed them to a room at the front of the inn. She walked across and closed the window's shutters, blocking out the view of the dark street. The room contained a huge four-poster bed, carved in the Tudor style with garish-looking men and women, and oddly shaped animals and birds. Beyond the bed, two chairs stood before a small hearth. The candelabrum on the mantle spread flickering gold light, and a fire burned in the grate, doing its best to fend off the cold winter air.

'Your dinner will be with you shortly, Captain.' The maid bobbed a curtsy.

As soon as the door shut, Paul turned and held Ellen by the waist, then swept her off her feet and spun her in a circle. 'My bride. My wife.' He grinned broadly.

Her happiness burst into a smile.

'I am in love,' he said. Then he put her back on her feet and kissed her firmly, pressing his lips against hers then opening his mouth. It became a kiss like those they had shared in the carriage. Her hands rested on his shoulders as it continued and he pushed her back against the bedroom wall.

All the air left her lungs and a spiralling sensation twisted through her middle, tumbling down as her fingers slipped into his short hair. He plundered her mouth and she fought to keep up, yet she could sense his restraint as his hands held her hips in a stiff embrace. Her body longed to be pressed against his.

A knock struck the door.

He broke away with a sideways smile and a dimple cut into his cheek as his hair fell over his brow. He swept his hair back as he turned to the door and called, 'Come in.'

A blush heated Ellen's cheeks as men clothed in the inn's livery entered, carrying Paul's trunk and her bag from the carriage. A few moments later another man arrived with a small trestle table that he set up in their room. Then their dinner came.

Ellen stripped off her gloves and dropped them onto Paul's trunk, along with her bonnet. This was Christmas Eve; her sisters would be at home in their beds missing her.

'Sit down and eat,' Paul said with a smile, pulling out a chair for her.

Ellen glanced at the bed as she sat down. *Soon, they would lie together in that bed...*

Paul sat in the chair opposite, then cut the pie. He put a piece on her plate.

'Thank you.'

'No need to thank me.' He smiled. 'Has anyone ever spoken to you about what will happen in our bed?'

The heat of a blush crept over her skin. 'No.'

'Then I will be mindful, Ellen, but you have no need to fear it.'

'I know. You have been kind...' Her words dried, not knowing how to express the things she longed for and feared at the same time.

'A physical relationship between a man and a woman can be a beautiful thing. I think it will be beautiful between us.'

Her face grew warmer still; she must be as red as a ripe strawberry.

'But I have said enough, have I not? Eat and then you will find out how beautiful it is.'

Now she could eat nothing, each mouthful was tasteless as she forced herself to chew and swallow.

He ate heartily, discussing America. After tomorrow they

would travel to Portsmouth to meet his regiment and then catch a ship to Cork, in Ireland. Then from Ireland they would sail hundreds of miles across the Atlantic.

When he slid his empty plate away from him, Ellen ceased pushing the last of her food about her plate and put her knife and fork down side by side.

'You did not eat much. Are you anxious?'

She was not hungry because she was so nervous and she could not smile.

He smiled. 'I will have the inn's staff clear the table. I will be back in a moment.'

When he had gone, anxiety hit her harder.

She stood up and turned to the window. She unfolded one of the shutters and looked out. Clouds had hidden the moon, it was so dark all she saw was her image reflected in the glass, with the light from the candelabrum.

She did not look like herself; the duke's daughter who must always be perfect. The woman who faced her was Mrs Harding. Some strands of her hair hung to her shoulders, having fallen from the pins, and her habit was creased from days of travel. This woman would follow the drum and live on the edge of battlefields. She was the woman who would give solace to a soldier.

The bedchamber door opened behind her. She turned as Paul entered. He was followed by two of the inn's attendants. He directed the men to clear the table. One carried their plates and leftovers away, the other folded the table and took that too.

Paul closed the door behind them. Ellen's stomach somer-saulted as her hands clasped together before her waist.

His smile said, *don't worry, trust me, you will be safe with me.*

She knew that was true, but it did not prevent a rush of concern through her nerves.

He walked towards her, intent shining in his eyes, leaned past her and closed the shutter. Then he faced her, and the awe she saw in his eyes reflected the love she felt for him. He kissed her, his palm embracing the back of her head.

It was a brief kiss. 'I am utterly in love with you,' he said over her lips.

She smiled. 'I also – I mean, I am in love with you also.'

His smile tilted sideways, then he looked down and his fingers began tugging the buttons securing the front of her habit loose.

Her heart pulsed so hard it pounded in her ears.

'Relax,' he whispered, as he looked up to her face, but continued freeing buttons.

She could not. Her heart beat far too quickly.

Beneath her habit she wore only her chemise. She had not been able put on the short corset alone.

The last button slipped free, then his hand reached beneath her habit and his fingers cupped her breast over the cotton. He looked into her eyes as his fingers held and then released her breast and his thumb brushed across her nipple.

A sharp little pain caught like a pin pricking through her nipple. But that pain felt pleasant.

His hands slid the habit from her shoulders and down her arms. It fell to the floor. The cold air touched her bare arms.

She shivered.

'Are you cold?'

'A little.'

'We will get into bed soon, and then you will be warm.'

She nodded as her stomach did another somersault.

He kissed her bare shoulder and smiled as his hands cupped her buttocks over her cotton chemise and pulled her body flush against his. Then he kissed her again. A kiss like the one they had shared when they had first come into the room, his tongue pressing into her mouth.

When he pulled back all the air had left from her lungs.

'Ellen...' he whispered. It was a question but she didn't know what he asked. 'Take my coat off for me,' he encouraged then.

She bit her lip, realising she was too naïve. Of course he would expect her to take part.

Her fingers worked on the glinting brass buttons of his military coat, but her hands shook too much to free them.

A sound of amusement left his throat as he took over the task.

Then he stripped his shirt off too...

She could not meet his gaze as he took it off. An aura of strength and masculinity radiated from him and it travelled through her flesh to her bones leaving her limbs as wobbly as aspic.

Heavens. He was beautiful. She touched his stomach and chest, where ripples of muscles defined his body, his skin was warm.

When she looked up, he smiled, with humour in his eyes. She smiled too.

'Will you help me with my boots?'

She nodded as he turned to sit in one of the chairs. He began tugging at the heel of one boot. She helped him.

After his second boot fell to the floor he stood again, and still smiling, his hands gripped her chemise by her hips and fisted, clasping the fabric. Her stomach flipped another turn when he lifted it. But she raised her arms so he could strip it off over her head. It left her naked.

'You are beautiful.' His fingertips ran across the lower curve of her breast and her nipple. 'You have the look of a goddess.'

She rose to her toes and kissed him. She needed that contact to ground her and hold her nerves steady.

His tongue pressed into her mouth as his hand closed about her breast and kneaded the soft flesh.

I love you. The words roared through her mind. She was not afraid of him.

When he broke the kiss, gentleness, and love, shone in his eyes. This battered, hardened, and young, warrior, who had the marks of war in scars on his skin, who she had seen kill a man – had a heart of gold.

'Take off your stockings on the bed,' he said, 'then climb beneath the covers, so you do not become too cold. I will stoke the fire.'

As she sat, he walked to the hearth. She untied the ribbons holding up her stockings as he tipped coal from a scuttle onto the embers. The first stocking dropped onto the floorboards as he reached for a poker, then the second as he stirred up the embers so flames flickered into life.

She lifted the covers and lay between the sheets.

Her father would have called for a maid to tend the fire, and been angry that a servant had not already thought of it. He would never tend a fire himself. But then Paul had been his own master and servant for years.

The sheets were cold, and the dense feather-filled quilt which lay on top pressed the cold sheet against her naked skin. She shivered as her nipples peaked and pulled the covers up to her chin.

Paul smiled as he came to the bed. He unbuttoned his falls, holding her gaze, then bent as he slid both his pantaloons and his underwear down. The air caught in her lungs and her heart thundered again; the movement of the muscles in his buttocks and thighs as he bent was something to behold... then he pushed all his clothing off his feet and stood before her as naked as the day he was born.

She could not breathe.

He lifted the covers and she moved back to make room for him. He had not snuffed the candles but left them burning.

Immediately, his lips pressed against hers and his warm hand ran over her cold skin, from her hip to her breast, then he kneaded her flesh once more.

Blissful sensations twisted in her stomach as she rolled to face him and reached her arms about his neck.

His kiss travelled from her lips across her chin, down her neck to her shoulder. Her back arched as if she knew what he was about to do, but she did not, not until the moment his lips kissed her breast once quickly, then closed over her nipple. The pressure as he sucked was warm and gentle as his hand slid lower, brushing across her hip, making her shiver, but this time not because it was cold. His fingertips reached her inner thigh.

'Paul?'

He continued sucking her breast as his fingertips brushed over the private place between her legs. The place she knew a man and woman would join. That was all she knew about what would happen tonight.

His fingertips sent tingles across her skin and an ache skipping upwards through her body.

She was warmer now. Her fingers combed through his hair.

He looked up. 'Do you trust me, Ellen?'

She nodded, staring into his blue eyes and noticing the length of his brown eyelashes. 'Yes.'

His fingers slid inside her body.

'Oh.' Her hands gripped his shoulders.

'I will not hurt you.'

She nodded; she knew that. She bit her lip as his fingers

slipped gently and intimately in and out of her body, invading then retreating.

His lips returned to hers, his tongue pressing into her mouth, distracting her mind. *Paul.* She did love him. She did.

His mouth left hers and returned to her breast, as his fingers continued their caress. He was cherishing her; absorbed in her, she could feel it. Warmth spread throughout her body, reaching in ripples as far out as her fingers and toes. Her legs bent and her knees parted wider for him, as his invasion grew in speed and depth.

She was damp where he touched her, and the dampness increased as the warmth did too.

His head lifted. 'Ellen, will you touch me too...' His fingers slipped free of her then he clasped her hand and moved it to the part of him which would join them. He curled her fingers around him and moved her hand up and down.

Shyness prevailed over every other sense. His fingers slipped back inside her as she tried to do as he had asked. It was awkward and strange...

'Lie on your back, Ellen.'

She rolled backwards, letting go of him and opening her legs wider as he came over her, so he could settle between her thighs.

'It may hurt for a moment.'

She nodded as that part of him touched her, and then as she looked into his eyes, he thrust in, and yes, it did hurt, a bursting sensation pierced her, and then there was an uncomfortable pressure.

She felt a little sick. But it was done now; they were man and wife.

He withdrew then pressed in again.

She gripped his arms, realising it would not just be a single invasion. His jaw had been taut before but now a smile played with the edge of his lips as he withdrew again, and pressed in. Her hands lay on his shoulders.

'You are the most beautiful woman I have ever seen.'

She smiled, her shyness receding, and her senses absorbing the odd new feelings.

'I will look after you, I swear it.'

She nodded, watching his face as he worked, casting spells in her body.

She could not take her gaze from his and he did not look away from her. She loved him so much. 'This is wonderful,' she told him.

He smiled more, and moved more quickly, pressing in and pulling out, again, and again. Her fingernails dug into his shoulders as her knees bent higher so her toes could curl into the sheet, against the wool-filled mattress beneath it.

Her body was a flood of lovely sensations; they were tight in her lungs, catching at her breath and trembling through her stomach. She had no breath left when he thrust harder and deeper... Once... Twice... On the third movement, his body went as stiff as stone and his eyes shut as he sucked in a harsh breath before releasing it in a sigh which brushed over her cheek. The part of him that was inside her pulsed.

He did not move for a while, and while he lay still, the pleasurable feelings he had engendered tingled through her nerves then ebbed away.

He opened his eyes and smiled, then withdrew and rolled onto his back beside her. 'Come.' He lifted his arm. 'We will sleep now.'

She pillowed her head on his chest. She felt as though she had been shown a precious secret other people had been keeping.

He fell asleep. She listened to his breathing, watching the flickering orange candlelight dance about the room.

She was Mrs Harding.

* * *

Ellen woke in a silent room as daylight peeked through the cracks in the shutters. She was curled up against Paul, who had turned on to his side in the night. It was Christmas Day. Her sisters would be waking. They would have come to her room if she had been at home. She presumed Sylvia and Rebecca would go to Penny instead. They would attend Mass and eat an informal luncheon with her mother, then dine formally in the afternoon with her father and there would be guests invited from local families.

Paul rolled to face her. 'Good morning.'

'Hello. Good tidings.' She whispered her seasonal greeting.

His fingers stroked her hair back from her face as a smile curved his lips. 'Merry Christmas.' He kissed her for a while, then the weight of his hips rolled her backwards, and he was between her legs once more and pressing into her. She lost her breath.

He did delicious things, moving within her, the soft hair on his chest brushing against her breasts as he did so.

Both her hands embraced his nape as she held his gaze. He was so steady and strong. Her fingers slid down his back, exploring.

When his end came this time he growled, his eyes shutting again as he ground against her for a moment, then stilled.

He sighed when he rolled off her.

'We will stay here today,' he said. 'I will order breakfast. I am hungry, and then I will ask for a bath and we can bathe together.'

That sounded naughty. She was certain no married couples she knew bathed together. Certainly not her parents. She laughed at that thought.

She missed her sisters and her mother, but she was with Paul and she was his wife.

They spent the rest of the day doing as he said; relaxing. They ate breakfast in their room; she back in her habit for propriety's sake as he sat in his pantaloons and shirt. Then the inn's attendants brought up a copper bath, and pails and pails of steaming water along with some lavender water to scent it. It was a tight squeeze for them both to fit in it. But Paul sat behind her with his legs bent and parted, and she draped her shins over the edge of the tub. They lay in the water for an age as he ran the soap across her skin and brushed the water over her breasts.

They made love again when they got out and stayed in bed until he was hungry once more and wanted supper. Then they returned to bed and languished there without sleeping for hours.

She was happy.

6

'It is a shame you have to endure another long journey so soon, Ellen.'

Tiredness shadowed her eyes. He had kept her awake half the night. He smiled. She did too. She did not look unhappy about it.

The inn's grooms were readying their carriage behind her.

'It does not matter. I knew it would be so,' she answered.

He nodded and tapped her under the chin. Stalwart, that was his wife.

The snow had melted yesterday, the tracks would now be slush and mud, and it would be a much slower journey to Portsmouth. Travelling was a game of endurance she was going to have to become used to.

It took five days. Five days of dull inactivity within a carriage. Five days in which he was unable to fully appreciate the beauty of his wife. Although, on two occasions, as they had travelled through the night, he had persuaded her to sit astride him and lift her petticoats. She had blushed both times he had

asked, so he had tamped the lamp to save her embarrassment.
Yet he knew such moments would often be hurried and stolen
when they joined the regiment – she would have to adjust and
become used to others being in earshot.

The carriage pulled into the courtyard of an inn near the
docks in Portsmouth. The time for carefree living was at
an end.

Once the wheels had come to a halt, he opened the door,
climbed down and handed her out. 'I'll settle you into a room,
then leave you here and find the lieutenant colonel. I need to
tell him I'm here and find my men. I'll come back afterwards.'
Lifting his fob watch from his pocket, he flicked it open to check
the time. It was two after midday. 'I should return for dinner.
But if I have not, order a meal and eat in our room.'

She nodded, but he could see she was nervous. She caught
her lower lip between her teeth, as if holding back the words,
don't go. He did not want to leave. Yet this was his life, many
times she would be left alone.

She smiled; it trembled a little. 'I know you must go, it is
your duty.' Her answer implied she had read his mind, and he
thanked God she was brave enough to override the words her
heart wished to say.

At least she understood. 'Come then.'

He settled her into a room, which looked out onto the busy
street, although to the far right you could glimpse the sea, then
said, 'Goodbye,' after kissing her lips.

He wanted to stay, but her words were true – he had a duty.
That came first, and pleasure afterwards.

It took a half hour to walk through the docks and up the hill
to the barracks. The other officers were there, with the lieutenant colonel. Paul was told who had arrived and who was still
to come, the date they would sail and the name of the ship he

and his men were to use. Then he went to visit his men who shared a room in the barracks.

They greeted him, after saluting, with smiles and laughter, and he was smacked on the shoulder a dozen times when he told them he had married a few days before. The 52nd was different. They had a rule that officers drilled with their men, and it developed a camaraderie and friendship which did not exist in other troops. As Ellen had said, he could have ridden in the cavalry, but the closeness of these men had carried him through the last years. They had endured horrors together, lost comrades and survived to fight again.

He could not walk out and leave them when he had told them of the plans for their sailing, so he sat down and shared a drink with them, then played a hand of cards, but all the time his blood itched to be back at the inn with Ellen.

When he finally found an excuse to leave, it was dark. He looked at his watch. Seven. She would be bored and lonely. He quickened his pace.

In fact, she was asleep. She lay on top of the large bed in their room, fully clothed.

She'd taken the pins out of her ebony hair and it spread across the quilt, her pale skin in stark contrast. He had not seen her hair loose since Christmas Day. She was such a precious sight. He let her beauty ease his soul; the memories of war, the sounds of cannon fire and rifles that had invaded his thoughts when he had sat among his men slipped away.

'Ellen.'

She sat up and blinked.

She stole his breath when he saw her for the first time each day. She was a balm to soothe his battle-sore soul. 'I have ordered dinner.' The innkeeper had told Paul she had not eaten.

He sat on the edge of the bed. 'Is sleeping all that you have done?'

She nodded. 'I was tired.'

He lifted her hand and kissed her fingers. 'We are to sail in four days. Tomorrow, I will take you to meet the other officers and my men.' She looked nervous. 'They will like you, Ellen.'

She nodded. A knock struck the door, announcing the arrival of their dinner.

* * *

When Paul ushered her into his lieutenant colonel's quarters, cold fear tightened in Ellen's stomach. It had been one thing to travel with Paul, it was completely another to become a part of his life. She had stepped into a world far beyond her father's sheltered realm. This was a world she did not know, one in which Paul was the warrior who still frightened her a little.

Paul's body stiffened as he entered. It felt as though his thoughts detached from her. Here, he was the soldier who had killed the highwayman, not the man who had turned music pages for her in her father's drawing room – the man who could make her smile and laugh.

All the men she was introduced to were just as intimidating, dressed in their smart red and gold regimental coats, looking tall and confident. But all of them smiled and bowed over her hand, wishing her well, and giving both her and Paul words of congratulations. Only his commanding officer, the lieutenant colonel, made her continue to feel uncomfortable, because he never stopped watching her from the moment she and Paul had entered until the moment they left. But the conversation progressed and all the men were polite and jovial. Particularly a man Paul said was his closest friend, Captain George Montgomery. He followed them out of the office and onto the parade ground.

'I am pleased for you, Paul. You've picked a pretty little piece...' His smile was for Paul, but passed onto Ellen. 'We will have a ray of sunshine to look forward to in our baggage train, ma'am.' He gave Ellen another swift bow.

'She will be *my* ray of sunshine though,' Paul answered, the jest half joke and half warning. His friend winked in Ellen's direction.

A blush burned her skin.

'Quite the diamond,' Captain Montgomery commented, looking back at Paul. 'And all yours, yes, I know. No wonder you do not wish to leave your wife behind.'

'Come.' Paul's hand gently embraced her arm. 'Let me introduce you to my men. Good day, George.' Glancing back at his friend, he nodded in parting, the pressure of his fingers encouraging Ellen to move away.

'Good day, Paul.' His friend's smile passed from Paul to her again. 'Ma'am.'

She smiled. He was a rogue; she could see the twinkle in his eye, and as they walked away Paul confirmed it. 'George is a charmer, but you are to pay no mind to it, he is harmless in reality. Simply a slave to a pretty face—'

'A sublime face!'

The shout came from behind them, and they both looked back. Captain Montgomery grinned, lifting a hand in a gesture that said goodbye. Paul scowled when she looked at him, but then his gaze grew depth and warmth. 'It is true, though – you have a sublime face,' he said, with humour in his voice.

A smile she could not have held back parted her lips. She could live in Paul's world when there was a soft look in his eyes to carry her through. He let go of her arm, and instead she held his, as he pointed to a two-storey, red-brick building on the far side of the parade ground. 'My men are quartered there. Tomorrow I shall have to be here at eight o'clock to run them through their paces. I imagine they will have been lax during leave. It is time we returned to routine.'

She could not even begin to imagine the routine of her new life.

When they entered the room full of soldiers, it was very different from meeting the officers. There were shouts and whoops, and a mass of masculine energy surrounded her. She pressed close to Paul, holding the sleeve of his scarlet coat tighter as his other arm lifted, calling for quiet.

'Show my wife some courtesy!'

The men then paraded past her, and Paul gave their names as they bowed.

She did not lift her hand to any of them but feeling wide-eyed and unnerved, nodded at their comments and congratulations. Her mind spun with names at the end of it, and she could not match one to any man in the room.

'Will you stay and take a drink with us?' Paul's sergeant asked Paul.

Paul looked at her, a question in his eyes. *Are you comfortable?*

She was to live among these men, in closer quarters than she had lived with her sisters. She refused to be feeble. She nodded.

The sergeant flicked his hand at one of the soldiers who moved to begin pouring from a jug, and others then moved too, refilling pewter beakers. She was given one full of frothing small beer, as was Paul, and then the sergeant encouraged them to take a seat on a long bench beside a long wooden table.

The sergeant stood to make a toast, holding up his dented tankard.

'To the Captain and his wife.'

'To the Captain and his wife!' the room chorused at a deafening pitch.

Ellen looked along the table. At least fifty faces stared back, smiling. She was probably as red as it was possible to be, but still she lifted her beaker. 'Thank you.'

'Aye, thank you, for your good wishes,' Paul added, and then they both drank.

Ellen looked at him as he set down his empty tankard. She set down hers, still half full.

He appeared different among his men; energy, mastery and pride oozed from his stance. He was definitely the warrior here, and he looked older.

He turned to her, as if he sensed her staring, caught her hand and lifted it onto his thigh.

Love welled up inside her. Yes, he was a soldier, but his strength was protective, and with her, his touch was always gentle.

When they left the barracks, they walked along the seafront, returned to the inn and ate their dinner in a private parlour.

'When I drill the men tomorrow, you may come with me if you wish? Not to stand on the parade ground, you understand, but you may watch from the barrack room I will have been allocated. You will be among the men all the time as we travel, it is best you get to know this life.'

She smiled. 'I will come.' She wanted to learn and to fit in. At the moment, it was all alien.

A smile tilted his lips, forming the dimple that stirred her heart with tenderness. Warmth and depth filled his eyes. 'Shall we retire?'

That same warmth turned her stomach over as he took her hand and kissed her knuckles. She rose and followed him upstairs.

* * *

When Ellen woke in the morning, Paul stood before the wash bowl in the corner of the room. He held a razor in his hand, as he looked at his image in a small mirror, shaving.

He wore no shirt and his feet were bare, he was only dressed in his grey pantaloons with his braces hanging loose.

She watched the muscles moving in his back, shoulders and upper arms, as they etched shifting lines beneath his skin. Her husband's physique was as superb as the ancient marble statues lining the halls in her father's Palladian mansion.

Ellen stretched. He must have caught her movement in the mirror and met her through his reflection, smiling. 'Good morning, my love.'

My love. Those words made her stomach tumble over and the sight of his smile made her giddy with joy.

'Once I am clothed, I will order breakfast. We will eat in the parlour, so I shall send a maid up to help you dress.'

Ellen nodded. She remained in bed, and watched him finish shaving and dress. As he secured the buttons of his scarlet coat, smiling at her observation, pride flared in her heart as well as love. He was a man to be proud of.

He came to the bed and brushed a kiss on her cheek. 'I will go downstairs then and send up a maid.'

As soon as he had gone, Ellen rose. She washed and prepared herself, her heart beating swiftly. She would start her life as a soldier's wife today.

After breakfast they walked up the hill to the barracks. As

they walked through the gate, the guards saluted Paul. He saluted them in reply.

He led her to a small room in the red-brick building. Light broke into the dingy room through a narrow window in the outer wall, illuminating the single cot-like bed.

When Paul left, she leaned her elbows on the windowsill and looked down onto the parade ground.

In a few minutes she saw him down there, walking to the centre. His men came from the far corner and gathered in lines. He did not merely stand and order them to walk this way and that, but marched with them, shouting for them to form a square, then lines, three men deep. They walked about, but he frequently ordered them from one structure to another. Then he called for them to lift, arm, kneel and aim their rifles a dozen times, before checking that they all held their rifles as they should.

It was an impressive spectacle, but again she had the feeling she did not really know the man she watched.

At the end of the activity, he spoke with each man and checked their equipment before letting them leave. Of course, here it merely looked a theatrical show, but it was preparation for battle, not entertainment.

When he came to the room to fetch her, he was still in the guise of a military man, so although she wished to hug him, she did not. She did not think he would welcome it. But outside the barracks, he offered his arm and said he would walk her back to the inn and eat luncheon with her before returning alone to speak with the officers.

She wondered if this would be her new life, watching his through occasional windows, while he fulfilled his duty and excluded her with stiff, silent coldness? In order to do his duty, he must close off his emotions – she understood – but she did not love the soldier, she loved the man.

When he left after luncheon, he did not leave her with nothing to do, though, he ordered her to make a list of everything she would need to take to America, and bid her to write an advertisement for a woman to act as her maid, and general help. He said they would employ a woman when the regiment reached Cork.

7

Ellen stood on the ship's deck clutching the rail at its edge, watching England disappear. It had been two days since she had first watched the regiment parade. Four days since they had arrived in Portsmouth.

It was midday. Paul had taken her aboard, then spent the last hour instructing his men and ensuring they were all aboard and their kit stowed away before the ship sailed on the high tide.

She had met the other four wives who were travelling with the regiment, all married to men of a lower rank than Paul. They were on deck too, keeping out of the way as the men worked below decks to organise the space the regiment had to share.

Only an hour ago, Ellen had learned she and Paul were to sleep in the open galley with his men. There would be no privacy. But they would reach Cork in two or three days. Yet when they sailed to America, there would be weeks with no privacy.

A longing for home caught in Ellen's breast. Her fingers

closed about the wooden rail, holding it tightly. She thought of
Penny at home, possibly sitting before a warm fire working on
her embroidery at this hour of day, or perhaps she was prac-
tising the pianoforte, or the harp.

Something touched her waist, a hand, and then a tall, strong
presence settled behind her. Her husband. 'You look sorrowful,
Ellen.'

She looked up and back. She breathed out a breath she had
not even known she had held in. *I am a little sorrowful* – but only
because she could not yet picture the future. She was happy
now, but there were so many unknowns, and she missed her
sisters. She did not admit her insecurity; that would be disrespectful... 'I am well. It is simply odd to leave England when a
month ago the farthest I had travelled was barely ten miles
from home.'

His fingers tucked a lock of hair, which kept catching the
breeze and blowing across her face, behind her ear. 'This must
be difficult for you.'

Ellen held his gaze. 'I am not afraid.'

'I think you are, if you take the trouble to say you are not.'
His fingers brushed over her cheek and tapped beneath her
chin. 'Remember, I have seen enough recruits preparing for
battle to know the signs, Ellen.'

She swallowed, then licked her lips to stop them feeling dry
and saw his gaze lower to watch the movement of her tongue. 'I
am a little afraid,' she admitted. 'But only of what I do not know
– what life will be like.' In recent days, he had become more the
soldier she did not know well, and less the man she had met in
her father's drawing room.

'Ask the other women. They shall tell you. Make friends. I
know at times it will not be easy but I shall do my best to make
you happy.'

'I know I will be happy, I have you. I am not afraid of that.'

'Then I am content. I must go and speak to the lieutenant colonel. You will forgive—'

'You do not need to ask forgiveness for fulfilling your duty, Paul.'

His palm cradled her cheek and he smiled, before walking away.

The beat of her heart thumped steadily. The other women had not really spoken to her, she presumed because they thought she was too wellborn compared to them. Paul had not told anyone she was anything other than his wife, yet her voice, posture and clothing made her stand apart from the other women. She was not and never would be a common soldier's wife. She was an officer's wife, from a titled family. She would never quite fit in. But she longed to, she missed the company of her sisters, their whispered conversations and laughter. But Paul's men did not seem to judge him by his birth, perhaps she could at least make friends with the women.

She looked back at the thin line of green and grey along the horizon, England.

If her father knew she wanted to be accepted among commoners, he would scold her.

* * *

The women dined with the men, clustered at the end of a long, scored, dark oak trestle table, giving Ellen an opportunity to speak with the other women as Paul sat among the men, further along.

Now was her chance to be accepted.

'How do you travel with the men in general? I presume we

must walk behind them...' she asked of the woman beside her, before taking a sip of the watery broth in her bowl.

The woman glanced at her with uncertainty; all the women had been sitting stiffly since she had joined them. On deck earlier, they had talked easily with each other.

Ellen longed to say, *you need not be afraid of me*, but that would sound patronising when she was much younger than most of them. 'I have no idea how I shall be living now...' Ellen added, her uncertainty and fear slipping into her voice.

'Simply, ma'am,' a woman said, 'we mostly ride on the baggage carts if the men are on the march, but sometimes we must walk if the terrain is too difficult for the horses, or the carts. When we travel by boat, then we must make do with whatever accommodation we can obtain.' The woman lifted her spoon and ate another mouthful of the weak broth.

Ellen looked across the table at another woman. 'And where do you sleep, and live, when the men are camped?'

'Wherever we may, ma'am. We share our men's tents, and they are put up and taken down often if the men are on the march. It is only if they are defending a place or preparing for battle that we camp in one place—'

'But the Captain will be billeted,' one of the other women interrupted, looking at her friend, not at Ellen.

'Yes,' her friend agreed. 'The officers, if we are to remain in any one place for long, will find an inn or a farmhouse to take them in, or anywhere they may be sheltered. They are only in their tents if the regiment is marching and there is nowhere close by.'

'If the men are in barracks though,' another woman added, 'our husbands must find us accommodation nearby.'

Ellen looked along the table at Paul. He talked animatedly with the men, then laughed before he took a sip from a tankard.

Ellen swallowed another spoonful of the foul broth, then asked, 'What have you seen of war?' She looked from one woman to another, asking them all.

The women glanced at each other, expressing a silent unease. Then one of the women leaned forward and answered in a whisper, 'Many horrible things, ma'am. Many things a woman should never see. But that is war, and I would rather be with my Michael here than in England alone, not knowing if he is alive or dead, or will ever return to me.'

'And I could not bear to let Tommy go to America and not see him for months or even years, ma'am,' another woman chimed in, smiling nervously at Ellen.

She looked the closest to Ellen in age, perhaps a couple of years older. Nancy. Her name flew into Ellen's head, plucked from all those she had been told in the last few days. She had been introduced as Mistress Bowman but had asked Ellen to call her by her given name.

'And what do you all do to fill your days?' The question came out on a breath of longing, as the life Ellen had left behind tumbled through her thoughts... a life very different to the one she would have where she sat now.

The women smiled, apparently amused by the question. 'Why, we wash the men's clothing and cook for them,' the first woman who spoke answered. 'There is little time for anything else, ma'am.'

The question proved Ellen's naivety. Their needles would work on clothing not embroidery, and they had possibly never seen a pianoforte, and certainly never sat in the warmth of the sun engrossed in a book – they probably could not read. A warm blush rising in her skin, Ellen asked what the men did when they were not fighting or marching.

When it came time to sleep, the trestle tables and benches were collapsed and secured along the sides of the galley.

The low-ceilinged room, which forced Paul to bend over constantly, then became a dormitory for a hundred or more men, all rolling out pallets. Ellen watched as Paul laid out theirs. The thin mattress was only wide enough for one.

'Do you wish to undress, or sleep in your clothes?' he whispered as he slipped the buttons on the coat of his uniform free.

Biting her lip, Ellen shook her head. 'I will sleep in my dress, but I will remove the pins from my hair and plait it.' She had shared a room with her sisters when she was younger, but sharing a bed in a narrow space with over a hundred men... She would suffer two nights in her dress.

She sat on the mattress as she withdrew the pins from her hair, and lay them into a handkerchief. The women's conversation haunted her, they had spoken mostly of a harsh way of life. What if it was always to be like this? Must she endure such sleeping quarters all the way to America?

The crowded low-ceilinged space was too enclosed. Most of the lanterns hanging from the low beams had been extinguished, but a few still burned, one near the ladder leading to the upper deck and a couple beside some of the men's pallets. They creaked as they swung with the rock of the ship.

All about her the men were in varying states of dress and undress as they retired, though none were naked; she tried to look only at the ship's wooden planking.

She turned her eyes to Paul. He lay down, clothed in his shirt and underwear, and lifted the wool blanket for her to join him on the mattress. Nervousness warring with embarrassment, she lay down with her back against his chest, and rested her head on his muscular arm. His other arm surrounded her, and his palm settled over her stomach.

'The women said that when the regiment camp, you are billeted,' she whispered. 'Do you share that accommodation too?'

'Sometimes,' he whispered back. 'But that is only during war, when we are fighting. In America we will most often be in barracks, and then I will hire lodgings to share with you and not live among the men. America will be different to the Peninsular War. The situation is not the same.'

'And the woman you said you will hire for me...'

'Will have her own room. She will be your maid of all work, Ellen. You shall not live exactly as the wives of the soldiers live.'

She was out of her depth without servants; she longed for a woman to help her navigate her new life. She did not think herself proud but she had been sheltered. This was so different from the rooms in her father's Palladian mansion. She would beg Paul to secure them a cabin for the longer journey.

She did not sleep, merely lay there, her thoughts absorbed by the odd rock and sway of the ship, and the sound of so many men breathing heavily in the shadow-filled space.

When she woke, Paul was rising, moving from behind her, and about them others stirred. She felt as though she had just a moment's sleep.

'I am sorry, you must get up,' he said quietly as she pulled on his scarlet coat. 'You will learn to shut your eyes and sleep no matter where you are in the end, because if you do not, you will never rest.'

Ellen nodded and sat up, rubbing her eyes. Then she stretched. He had said this life would be hard. She had not imagined it like this...

'Go with one of the women to freshen up while we set up the benches.' He looked away. 'Mistress Porter, would you help my wife?'

This was all so strange.

* * *

The ship swayed constantly – it was no different than the trepidation rocking inside Ellen. She was doing her best to fit in among the women, but everything was so alien it was not easy.

Paul had spent a couple of hours with her on deck, as she stood at the rail, just watching the acres of ocean reaching to the horizon, but beyond those hours she had mostly stood alone. She had no idea what to say to the other women who worked in the galley below, repairing their men's clothing.

When it was time to retire, she slipped beneath the blanket quickly, leaving him to undress.

When he lay with her, as last night, he wore only his underwear and a shirt. As he lay against her back, holding her, she could feel the muscular definition of his body. The breathing of the men about them calmed as people drifted into sleep and the movement in the room stilled as the last few lamps were extinguished. Without the lamplight, the galley sunk into a depth of pitch-black.

She had not heard Paul's breathing change. He was awake.

He pressed a kiss on her neck.

Her stomach turned a somersault.

His fingers that rested against her stomach gently pressed, silently urging her to move back and press tighter against his body.

The column of his arousal was solid within his underwear and it pressed against her bottom through the layers of her gown and her petticoats.

'Lay on your back,' he whispered into her ear, 'and I will move on top of you.'

She did as he asked, rolling to her back, and he lay over her.

'Here...?' The word was spoken quietly on a shocked breath.

'Here or never, Ellen, there will be hundreds of nights like this when the men are about us; we will be quiet, they need not know.' His words were spoken in a very low whisper.

Ellen looked left and right, to check if anyone watched them, but it was too dark to see. No sound indicated they did.

'Help me raise the skirt of your dress, and your petticoats.'

Her heart pounded as her hands pulled at the garments, as his did so too, working the hems up over her knees and thighs to her waist. It was so dark, she could not even see his face.

Two of his fingers slipped between her legs, stroking across her for a moment, then sliding inside her, the movement slow and gentle, drawing her thoughts away from the room and anyone but him. Then, one hand and one side at a time, as he held his weight above her on one elbow then the other, he pushed his underwear lower. His hand gripped her thigh, his fingertips sinking into her flesh, as he moved her leg aside.

She opened her legs, making room for him.

She bit her lip when he entered her, and she carried on biting it as he moved within her, in a slow steady motion, as her legs wrapped about his hips. Her heart thumped. It was as though the air had disappeared from the galley.

He pressed a kiss on her temple as he continued moving, as though he sensed her insecurity, but he did not speak, probably to avoid increasing the risk of waking his men.

They were covered by the blanket and it was dark, none of the men would see anything if they did watch. But they might know what was happening.

The spell he could create began to weave its charm, whispering through her blood and spinning into her limbs.

Her hands grasped his hips, her fingertips pressing into the muscle moving beneath his skin.

'Paul...' She could not prevent his name escaping.

'Hush, Ellen,' he whispered.

As he moved quicker, she closed her eyes and bit her lip again, absorbing every heavenly sensation.

Her fingers touched the dimple in his cheek. It implied he had gritted his teeth.

The sensations inside her swelled, and then there was one deep last push and his seed spilled into her. She opened her mouth, her breath releasing – while his body shuddered. Then his weight came down onto her and she held him as he lay still for a moment.

He brushed a kiss on her cheek before lifting off her and laying on his side. She did her best to right her clothes, then lay with her back to him.

'I love you,' he whispered into her hair.

Tears slipped from Ellen's eyes.

'Are you well?' He could not have seen her tears, though perhaps he had sensed them.

'Yes, I am well.' She was. She was happier than she had ever been; no matter the oddness of his world she could still feel the intensity of his love for her.

'Sleep now.'

She understood there were two sides to Paul; here he must mostly be the soldier, but even so, there would be moments when the other half of him could be expressed – the man who loved and needed her.

She fell asleep in his embrace, and she slept well.

8

Ellen sat with a quill poised in her fingers, and an empty page lay on the oak table before her. After four weeks in Cork, the weather had not been good enough to sail. She had written to her mother and to Penny to tell them where she was. She had told her mother she was well, but impatient to complete their journey. To Penny she had written a dozen amusing little stories of her adventures, describing Paul's men and their atrocious ability to maintain polite language in her hearing – and about the women, who were kind and supportive yet kept their distance.

She had a woman to help her now, as a maid, cook, washerwoman and everything else, though currently, while they lived in the inn, her only duties were as a companion and ladies' maid.

Ellen stared at the blank page. She wanted to write to her father, but she had no idea what to say. The quill twirled in her fingers. No words came.

She looked through the window at the busy street. Paul was restless. He wanted to be on his way. The waiting was difficult.

Words came at last. She looked back at the paper and
dipped the quill in the ink then wiped the nib clear of drops,
before writing simply.

Dear Father,

I hope you will forgive me for marrying Paul. But I am
happy. We are happy. I have told Mama how we are waiting
to sail to America, but the winds will not calm enough to
allow it. I think we shall be here another couple of weeks, if
you wish to write to me before we leave, I have given you my
address.

Your daughter,

Eleanor

She looked at the words for a moment. In the past she
would have written, your obedient daughter, but today she was
his disobedient daughter and she could hardly write that. She
blotted the ink, then folded the letter, struck a flint and sealed it
by heating the edge of a small block of red wax over the flame
until a few drops fell on the folded page. She used Paul's seal,
pressing the small pendant he had loaned to her into the wax.

Once she had addressed the letter, she placed it with the
others, fetched her cloak, then went in search of her maid, to
ask the woman to accompany her to the posting inn. She could
ask the woman to take them, but Ellen wished to stretch her
legs, and Paul would not be back until dinner.

* * *

Ellen stood on the edge of the harbour wall watching the waves
crash against it. The sea was still too angry for the ships to sail.

Foam and spray spewed over the top of the wall as the waves hit it, and tiny droplets of salty water blew into her face.

This was her favourite thing to do, to come down to the harbour and watch the sea. She liked to come during the hours Paul drilled his men because at this early hour, the harbour was less busy as long as the tide was out.

Another four weeks had passed and more since she had written to her family, but there had been no reply. Each day she looked out across the sea thinking of her mother and her sisters, wondering how they were, and what they thought of her desertion. Were they angry with her? Was that why they had not written? Ships reached Cork from England every week but no letters came.

Ellen stood for a little while longer, just watching the tug of war the tide played with the waves, throwing them against the harbour wall, before pulling them back.

She felt like the sea. She was happy with Paul, and this life had become normal, yet when they left for America it would be abnormal again. The part of her which missed her mother and her sisters still tried to pull her back.

Ellen turned her back on the water and faced her maid. The woman stood a few steps back. 'Jennifer, I am sorry to leave you standing in the cold. We will go home.' It was odd to call an inn home. An inn was not a home – yet they had been here for weeks.

When would she have a home again; if they were to always travel where would ever be home?

Paul is my home – and so the inn was home – that was the answer. She did not need a place, just him.

To stave off boredom, she had begun sewing shirts and cravats for Paul. The task filled the hours she sat alone. At home she would have embroidered the hems of garments to fill her time, but embroidery had little purpose here.

Sewing was the occupation she decided to return to as she walked back through the cobbled streets, with Jennifer keeping pace beside her.

The streets were busier than they would normally be and everyone seemed to be huddled together in small groups and talking in hurried whispers. A group they passed splintered and began another conversation with others. Ellen could not hear.

'What are they talking about, Jennifer?'

'I do not know, ma'am.'

Something was happening, something ominous. The whole atmosphere of the day changed; it had rained last night; the cobbles were damp and glistening; their appearance held a metallic glow, and the grey stormy sky reflected back from the puddles. As Ellen walked the last hundred yards a sense of doom draped about her.

In the inn, instead of going to their room she sat in the parlour Paul had hired for their private use, with Jennifer, and they both picked up the sewing they had left there. Her fingers trembled, making it difficult to thread the needle. It was silly to feel anxious merely because people talked in the street. Yet Paul did not return for luncheon, nor dinner, and as the day turned to evening, her anxiety grew.

She looked towards the door of the parlour each time she heard footsteps on the flagstones beyond the door, her heart setting up a sharp rhythm... Each time the door did not open.

'Should I order your dinner, ma'am?' Jennifer asked.

'No, Jennifer, I will wait for Captain Harding.'

But half an hour later, Paul had still not come.

Ellen wondered if she should ask someone in the inn to

send a message to the barracks. But surely he would have sent word if something were wrong.

She put her sewing down on the arm of the chair to go. Then, finally, she heard familiar strong heavy footsteps in the hall.

Paul!

She stood as the door opened and rushed to embrace him. The scents of the sea and the outdoor air and cold seeped from the cloth of his greatcoat. He did not embrace her in return; his whole body was possessed by the stiff poise of a military officer. Something was wrong; she released him and stepped back a pace.

'Have you heard, Ellen?' He spoke sharply – his voice that of the military officer too.

'Heard what?'

'You have not.'

She shook her head.

'Napoleon is free.'

'Free...' But the war with France was over... Napoleon was imprisoned...

'He escaped the island of Elba at the end of February, and is gathering an army. We are no longer going to America. We have orders to sail to Ostend immediately.'

A lead weight fell in her stomach. She had seen the names of the dead in the newspaper her father read. Many men were killed fighting Napoleon's forces, and many more crippled soldiers were begging in the streets in England now.

He took her hands. 'You must pack tonight and make ready. We will sail back across the English Channel soon. I am sorry, I cannot stay to dine. I will eat with the officers. We need to plan. But I wanted to let you know what is happening, so you could prepare.'

Fear rushed through her – a sense she would lose him. But how silly. He'd survived years of the Peninsular War. She knew he was capable. Even so, she hugged him again, her arms reaching about his neck. 'I love you.'

'And I you, Ellen. I shall return as quickly as I can, but you must eat without me.' His arms came about her for a moment, but he held her stiffly, then set her away, smiling quickly before he left the room.

Ellen faced Jennifer, a warm blush touching her cheeks. Her intimacy had been inappropriate before a servant, yet it had still hurt that he had broken their embrace so quickly. But he had done it because he was a soldier today and he needed to focus on his work, not his wife. Now they would be sailing towards a war there would be many more moments like this.

In the weeks they had spent in Cork, waiting to sail the wild Atlantic, she had learned enough about a soldier's life, though, to know what she could do; when she lay in bed at night with him, she would cling hard to the man she had met first.

The pain of brewing tears hurt Ellen's throat and pressed at the back of her eyes, but she swallowed them away and breathed. 'Would you order dinner for me, Jennifer?'

After dining alone, and eating very little, Ellen retired to their chamber, asking Jennifer to help her undress. Once the maid had gone, she slipped between the cold sheets and waited for Paul, and the moment when the soldier became just the man to her.

9

Paul carefully closed the door to their chamber, trying not to wake Ellen, who lay sleeping in the bed.

She had left a candle burning for him.

Quietly he slipped off his greatcoat and laid it over the arm of a chair. His heart thumped hard. It had been doing so all day. The news still shocked him. Napoleon had escaped when they had thought that battle won. It should be over. He had spent enough years starving and exhausted, battling his own men to keep them fighting when at times they would have rather turned and run, as well as battling the French and their allies. Memories of the horrors of war had been spinning through his head all day, the sounds of imaginary cannons deafening him at times.

He did not want to go back, and yet he would not allow that damned tyrant to have his way. The whole regiment was angry and ready to fight again to put the man back in his jail. But it was galling that they had to, though. Napoleon had already been defeated.

Paul's fingers slipped the brass buttons of his military coat free.

He just wanted to be in bed with his wife, and feel her softness. She was his safe harbour, his sanctuary. His sanity. All he lived for now. Just as he had known she would be from the first moment he had seen her at her father's house.

When he set his coat aside, exhaustion hit him. He ran his fingers through his hair. It had been a long day, but there would be many more long days in the next months. Napoleon was gathering an army to return to Paris. The message had said hundreds of men.

Paul pulled his shirt over his head and let that fall on top of his military coat. Then he unbuttoned his falls, watching Ellen in the bed they had shared for weeks.

Her dark hair rested across her shoulder in a braid and her breaths lifted it a little, as her bosom rose, lifting the sheets too. She looked so young.

He slipped off his pantaloons, underwear and stockings all in one.

She did not only look young, she was young. Perhaps too young to face the conditions on the Continent. They'd been bled dry by the previous years of war. But he had been her age when he had first left England – he had survived and trained recruits younger than him. They had to walk into battles, kill men and risk being killed.

She would cope. She was strong. He said the words to reassure himself. But still there was a fear low in his stomach that he had never known before; a fear for her, not for himself. It accused him of being juvenile himself, and therefore incapable.

When he moved across the room, he was careful not to let the floorboards creak. He blew out the candle, casting the room into darkness, before climbing into bed beside her. The sheets were cold at the edge of the bed, but near Ellen they were warm, so he moved closer. She lay on her side. He shaped his body to hers and gently rested his arm about her. She did not wake.

When he woke in the morning, Ellen turned beneath his outstretched arm, and as he opened his eyes, he faced the very pale blue of hers.

Her gaze was warm and welcoming. 'Good morning,' she whispered.

'Good morning.'

'What hour did you return?'

'Past ten.'

Her fingers brushed across the stubble on his jaw. 'As I have said before, you need not feel guilty for doing your duty.'

He smiled, his hand embracing the curve of her waist, beneath the sheets. 'Things will become hard over the next few months.'

'I know.'

'And you will cope?' he asked.

'I will cope, because I am with you.'

Again, there was that clasp of fear, low in his stomach, the one he had never known until he met her. It did not trust his judgement, or his ability to keep her safe. But he was not the only man in the army and she would be in a camp away from the battle. There would be hundreds of men between her and danger – she would be safe.

For now, though, he needed to feel her security. The light in the room implied it was a little past dawn; there was time. 'Let me love you,' he said, already moving over her. Perhaps it was selfish to press straight into her when she opened her thighs, and yet it was what he needed.

The weight of her arms rested on his shoulders, crossing

behind his neck, her fingers brushing his back. The rock of his hips as he moved slowly rocked her body too, making her breasts stir.

He adored her. There was a blissful intensity when they did this. Because it was lovemaking, it was nothing like any encounters he had known with whores. This was his wife he honoured, and she was warm and wet for his invasion. Little sighs left her lips, as colour scored her cheekbones. Her eyes had been open, looking up into his, but now they closed, dark lashes settling on her pale skin, and she bit her lip to keep her silence.

This is what she had learned from the time they had made love on the ship – to always be silent. He did not encourage her to be more vocal. There would be many times they must be silent. It was better she had this skill.

The heat between her legs increased as he worked harder, pulling out and pressing in, captured by the primal call of her body. Three. Four more strokes. And then... *Oh*. He firmed the muscles in his arms to stop his whole body from falling onto her, as her gentle fingers ran over his hair.

She was so beautiful.

* * *

Paul eased out of the bed as carefully as he could, trying not to wake Ellen. As he moved, she rolled to her back and stretched her arms, her sleepy eyes opening and looking up at him, the pale blue slightly misty. Her skin was reddened in places from the heat of his embrace and the brush of his stubble.

When she lay in bed looking like this, with her hair only loosely braided and escaping about her face, he loved her more – the imperfect, approachable, Ellen.

He leaned down and pressed a kiss on her forehead, longing

to return to the bed but knowing he could not; he had things to do. 'Be ready in case we are to sail today, I shall send word as soon as I know.'

She nodded.

As he washed and dressed, she sat upright in bed, watching him, her arms lying over the covers. He kept occasionally smiling at her in the mirror. They would be well. They would be happy. And he would keep her safe. He would accept no other conclusion. But even as he assured himself, his mind threw images of dead and dying men at him.

When he looked at her, and walked back to the bedside, she looked at him with the awe he had seen in her eyes in the summer. The look spoke to his heart as it had done then, stealing away all the memories of war. He bent and kissed her forehead. 'Goodbye, Ellen. I doubt I shall return for luncheon, not unless we are to sail. But I shall send word.'

She nodded again then said, 'Good day.'

As he turned away, there was the sensation low in his stomach. Fear; for her. He hated the feeling. She was a quiet woman, she often withdrew into her thoughts rather than join a conversation, yet despite her shyness, his men adored her, because she would speak to them in the same way she spoke to the officers. Of course, the other officers were enamoured too – though most had expressed shock over her decision to follow the drum. He had not told them she had no choice.

Perhaps that was why he felt concern – because it had not been her choice. She had chosen only to be his wife, the outcome of that had been decided for her.

Casting that thought aside, he left the room. It was too late to worry over such things. Their course was set.

* * *

When a soldier arrived, almost bursting into the small parlour, dressed in the scarlet coat and blue-grey pantaloons of Paul's regiment, Ellen stood, setting aside her sewing without thought. Jennifer stood too.

'Madam.' He bowed deeply.

'Tell me your news. I presume my husband sent you?'

'Ma'am.' He bowed again. 'The captain did. He asked me to inform you that the regiment is to sail on the high tide at six this evening.'

It was today then. 'Very well. Did he say how our things are to be taken to the dock?'

'Some of the men will come with the captain after four and bring a cart to take your items, ma'am.'

Ellen nodded. That was it then. The end of the peace they had known here.

'And there are these, ma'am.' He held out two letters.

'Letters from my husband?'

'No, ma'am, they came with the regimental mail.'

She took them from his outstretched hand and turned one over. The coat of arms imprinted in the seal was one she'd known all her life... her father's. She recognised the writing on the other, Penny's.

Ellen's heart leapt, then pounded as she looked at the young soldier. 'Thank you.' Her voice came out much quieter than she had expected and a little shakily with the emotions gripping in her chest. She urged more strength into it. 'I am grateful. Please tell Captain Harding I shall be ready.'

The soldier bowed again, with a stiff posture, then walked from the room.

'Jennifer, would you fetch us some tea?'

As soon as Jennifer had gone, Ellen broke the seal on her father's letter. It was short.

I did not, and do not, welcome your letters. They have all been destroyed and you are not to contact your mother or your sisters. Do you understand? I do not wish to hear from a disobedient child, and I shall not have your ill behaviour reflect on the others.

You have made your choice, now live it, and be done.

The Duke of Pembroke

'The Duke of Pembroke...' The title escaped from her mouth. 'You are my father, Papa.'

She held the letter against her bosom for a moment, thinking of her mother, Penny, Rebecca and Sylvia as tears clouded her vision and slipped onto her cheeks. This was the moment a tide, like the sea, tried to pull her back home. Soon there would be even more miles between herself and them. Yet that home was gone forever for her.

She looked at the second letter. It was also marked with the Duke of Pembroke's seal. But the address was written by Penny's hand.

Ellen's heart pumped even harder as she broke the seal, a beat of excitement and anxiety drumming through her limbs, all the way to her fingertips, making the paper tremble.

Eleanor, my dearest sister,

I am sure you must feel guilty for leaving us, but do not. I am glad you have run off with Paul. Papa is furious; he has not let any of us mention your name, not even Mama. But I know she has cried, and I have tried to comfort her, but she must obey Father and so she will not let me say your name to her, though, I see her concern for you in her eyes all the time.

When I saw him scribbling a letter with a look of steel on his face, then I knew he must be writing to you, and so I wrote my own and hid it in the packet with his. He does not know I have written, and I am sure you will not be able to write back. This is just to tell you that I understand and miss you terribly, but I would not have it different for the world. I hope you are happy.

I saw an article in Papa's paper; there was a paragraph. 'Lady P, the daughter of the Duke of P, is known to have run off with the 6th son of the Earl of C, without the consent of either influential home. One does wonder over the abilities of these noble lords if they cannot even control their sons and daughters. The eloped couple are now believed to be abroad.'

Papa threw the paper at a footman. I have never seen him so obviously angry. You know what he is like for cold disdain, but this was definitely heated. I had to hide a giggle.

Oh, Ellen, I miss having you to talk to, so much, but you must not come back. You must stay away and enjoy your life. I wish you happiness. I can hardly imagine what it must be like to be an officer's wife. You shall have a life of adventure, while I pine away for you. But do not let that put you off, you must enjoy every moment.

All my love,
Your sister,
Penelope

Ellen collapsed into a chair, tears tracking pathways down her cheeks, as her heart bled for her home, her sisters and her mother.

*** *

Ellen heard Paul arrive with his men through the window, the noise of carts and shouts. A few minutes later his boot heels struck the wooden floorboards in the hall.

She stood as he entered the bedchamber.

'Are you ready, Ellen?'

'I am, yes.' Externally – but not internally.

'Come in!' He looked back and called to the open door.

She was dressed to leave. She wore a pelisse, which he had bought for her to wear when travelling, it had a military theme with frogging like a hussars' uniform, gold braid and brass buttons, and beneath it, her travelling habit was made from calico. It was thicker than the muslins she usually wore, so the chilly sea breezes would not penetrate the cloth. When he moved out of the way to let his men enter the room, he smiled towards her.

A torch lit within her heart, light and warmth, and she smiled too. His smile belonged to the man she had met at her parents' home; the smile that had captured her heart the first time she had seen him.

The soldiers lifted the trunks and carried them out. When they had left, Paul lifted his arm. 'Come then.'

Her fingers embraced his arm through the layers of his clothing as she walked out of the inn room beside him.

They left Jennifer to oversee the loading of their items and walked along the cobbled street to the dock. It was not far from their lodgings.

'My father wrote to me,' she said. 'That was one of the letters your man brought.'

'And...' Paul encouraged her to say what the letter had contained.

'He told me I may not write, not to him, nor Mama, nor any of my sisters.'

His arm dropped away from beneath her fingers as he turned sharply and embraced her. It was so uncommon for him to show her affection in public when he was in the guise of a soldier, it made her wish to cry. But Paul would not want a weeping wife when they boarded the ship. She wiped away her tears as he let her go.

'The other letter was from Penny. She wanted me to know that she is happy for me, and wishes me well...'

Paul held her hands. 'I know you miss your sisters. If he had accepted my offer—'

Ellen met his gaze. 'It is not your fault he refused you, and to acknowledge us. You are more than worthy.'

His eyes shone with heartfelt anger.

'The fault is my father's. His rigid judgement...' Ellen concluded.

Paul touched beneath her chin. 'Even so, I regret that this is the outcome of marrying me.'

'I do not regret. I am happy to be your wife, and if I had wanted to see you I would have had to travel alongside you anyway.'

'Then I am a very lucky man.'

'Well, that makes us equal, because I know I am lucky to be with you.' She smiled, denying the sadness inside her.

She could tell from the expression in his eyes he wished to kiss her, but that would be a step too far in the street when he was in the persona of a soldier.

'Come.' He raised his arm, offering it to her to hold on to.

She did hold on to him, in so many ways.

When they reached the dock, the other officers were present and casting various orders. Instantly she noticed his lieutenant colonel on the deck of the ship. She sensed his gaze on her, he always watched her. She did not look up as Paul acknowledged him. She was under no obligation to do so, and there was just something about the man which made her skin crawl, as though she had lain on an ants' nest.

Paul's arm fell from beneath her fingers then he walked quicker, moving a few paces ahead as he called a couple of the soldiers over. She heard him telling them his belongings would arrive soon...

When he returned to her, he leaned forward. 'I have managed to secure us a cabin as you were so uncomfortable with our conditions previously,' he said quietly.

Beyond Paul, his senior officer watched them. She focused on Paul. 'Thank you.'

'Shall I take you to it? Or would you rather wait on deck until we sail?'

'No. Take me there.'

'Very well then.' Instead of offering his arm, he took her hand, and she was well aware of her fingers shaking despite her brave words.

He led her up the gangplank and stopped before the lieutenant colonel for her to curtsy. She did so, briefly, without looking up to meet his gaze, she looked instead at his cravat.

'Good day, Madam Harding, I hope our weather is fair and the journey shall not be difficult for you.'

He said nothing wrong – nothing offensive – there was nothing factual to cause her discomfort, except that he stared. But that tingle of disgust which kept running up her spine whenever he was near shivered through her nerves.

'I will show Ellen to our cabin and then return and instruct the men.'

'Indeed.' With that she was dismissed.

Paul's hand tightened around hers, gently leading her across the deck. The cabin was tiny, probably only a yard wide, with one narrow cot and another above it, but at least it would be private.

'We will be at sea for three to four days, Ellen. I shall send Jennifer to you once she arrives.' Paul closed the door, leaving her alone. She sat on the lower bunk.

Everything felt so strange. She supposed this would be the way it was now – she would become used to one place and then it would be time to move to another.

She lay down on the bunk. If he wished for relations tonight it would be impossible as her bleed had begun. Her lower back ached a little as she rolled to her side.

10

Paul looked about the port for what seemed like the fiftieth time. It overwhelmed even him. They had docked an hour ago. The place was already teeming with soldiers, and among the men in uniform were dozens of people here for pleasure. It seemed as though half the fashionable world had descended on Ostend, as well as the military. He had intended to leave Ellen on the ship, but she had not wished to stay while he went ashore, so she was clinging to his hand as they navigated the crowd.

She had not been well during their journey; she had her bleed and her stomach had been painful and queasy. It was a problem which would arrive each month as they travelled, a thing a man would never need to think of – another thing to make him wonder if he had done right by her.

But this was no time to fret over her stamina. He needed to find somewhere for them to stay until he knew where the regiment was to go next – and there were many others here hunting for accommodation.

'This is madness,' Ellen said.

'It is.' The noise about them was deafening, with so many voices all shouting over one another seeking someone to carry luggage, and asking directions, while working men shouted orders over that, to load and unload ships.

'We will walk this way.' At least Paul knew his way around Ostend.

On a street away from the docks he managed to hire a hansom cab, but the streets were overflowing with carriages and people, just like the docks, and it took an age for the man to navigate through it. The world had truly gone mad.

It was only a few streets. They would have probably reached his destination quicker on foot. But to his relief, the boarding house he had used previously had a room available. It was nothing grand, yet it was adequate and they would not be in Ostend for long.

'Stay here in the room. I will go back and bring our trunks.' Ellen only nodded. She looked exhausted. 'Rest. I know you have not slept well during the journey.' He had slept in the wooden bunk above hers as she had been bleeding, but he had heard her moving restlessly each night.

She nodded agreement, then bent to unlace her half boots.

He knelt before her and took over the task. Once her boots were off, she unbuttoned the front of her pelisse and he slipped it from her shoulders. Then she lay down on the bed, not even looking at him, she was so tired. He watched her, unwilling to leave her, but he needed to go back and tell the men where to bring their possessions, and of course he had to fetch Jennifer and bring her here too.

'Do you have the headache still?' He leaned and brushed a lock of hair from her brow, gently stroking her temple. She nodded. 'I shall have a maid bring up some remedy.' She nodded again, her eyes closing.

There was a pain in his stomach once more; the one that kept challenging his ability to protect her. Ignoring it, he left.

It was two hours later when Paul returned. He entered the room to wake her before allowing his men to carry in the trunks. He had left Jennifer with the female proprietor, to be shown to a bed in the servants' quarters in the attic above.

When he let the men in to set the items down, Ellen sat in the only chair in the room, still looking pale and tired.

They were to move on in four days. Then Ellen would discover what it truly was to be the wife of an army officer; there would be no laying abed.

Once his men had gone, he shut the door. At least he could stay with Ellen until tomorrow now.

'Is this all too much for you?' he asked.

Her eyes focused on him. 'No, I am simply unwell. I shall be well again tomorrow now we are off the ship, and my bleed will cease in a day or two.'

Fortunately, she would have a month before she had to endure this again and hopefully within that month they would reach Brussels. The plan was for the Allied forces to gather and wait in and around Brussels, while their leaders argued over the politics of Europe at the Congress of Vienna. Napoleon had already been named an outlaw, though, so it was only a matter of time before war began.

'Let me help you undress,' he offered, 'then you may rest properly.'

She stood and let him begin releasing the buttons at her back. Once they were all undone, he helped her step out of her dress and put it aside, then unlaced her short corset. When it slid off, he kissed the skin above the line of her chemise at her shoulder. She shivered.

He knew she was in no condition to be bedded, but his body longed for it. 'Lay down,' he encouraged.

Thoughts of war, memories, and dreams had been haunting him since the day they had left Cork.

She lay beneath the sheet and the coarse blankets covering the bed, shut her eyes and fell asleep in moments.

It was only three in the afternoon. He could go out, but he did not like to, he preferred to stay here and watch over her. There would be so many times to come when he would not have that choice.

He sat in the chair she had vacated and ran his palm over his face. *Damn it. Why did that bastard Napoleon have to continue his war?* Paul was tired of the endless hunger and effort, and the need to close himself off to avoid the pain of constant death.

He looked out from the window at the street below. People flooded it, people who seemed to think following the army to Ostend was fun. There was a party atmosphere in the street. These people had come to cheer the soldiers on, while the soldiers, all tired of war, longed to sit back and let others fight.

Paul could not help being reminded of the amphitheatres he had seen on the Continent, those that hundreds of years ago would entertain crowds with men battling until death. It was macabre. These people had come to play audience to men killing and being killed. It did not hearten him. It turned his stomach.

11

By the time they reached Ghent, for the first time in his life Paul regretted joining the army. They had travelled from Ostend by barge to reduce the time it would take to reach Brussels but Ellen had not been allowed to travel with the regiment; she'd journeyed on another craft, and the isolation from her had been unbearable. He had worried over her, although by all accounts, her journey in the company of the battle tourists was as good as a pleasure cruise with excellent food and entertainment, as if this were no more than a festival parade.

There were so many tourists.

They did not understand war.

He did not wish them to.

He wished them a hundred miles away.

At least, having reached Ghent, he could be with Ellen again.

Paul sighed and his hands settled at his waist as he watched Ellen sorting out items to be laundered and passing them to Jennifer. They were to spend four days in Ghent. He was to meet with the other officers in an hour and speak with other regiments and find out how the 52nd fitted within the whole, and obtain their orders before progressing.

He knew Ellen was relieved to have a break from travelling, and he felt that he should say something to reassure her. But he could not apologise for what could not be different, and he did not think she expected him to. She had been stoic and resilient throughout their journey. He had no complaints. It was just that damned tense queasy feeling in his stomach that feared for her and wished to protect her – and it was from things he had no capability to prevent.

'I shall come with you when you buy supplies, Jennifer,' Ellen said.

She had changed. She had learned how important it was to plan ahead. She had travelled to Ghent with the other women and he could tell they had been educating her about the next weeks they would spend marching.

'Is there anything I may fetch you?' he said at last.

She turned and looked at him, smiling, though it was not the carefree stunning smile he had received at the time they had wed. It was careworn. He smiled back, feeling the same weight she probably felt in her chest. Tonight, he would retire early with her and love her. That would make them both feel better.

'There is nothing I can think of...'

'Well, then, if I can be of no assistance here, I shall return and meet with the officers.'

She nodded.

'Goodbye, Ellen.' He longed to move forward and kiss her, but Jennifer was still in the room. 'I will return soon.'

She nodded again.

* * *

Ellen's hand clasped the edge of the cart to stop herself swaying, so tightly her knuckles were white. She was sitting beside the driver and the lieutenant colonel's servant. Two of the other wives and Jennifer sat in the back on top of some of the regiment's supplies.

The cart rocked, jolted and creaked along the muddy track. They had to stop and climb down from it on three occasions today to lessen the weight so the horses could pull the cart out of the mud. She had secured the skirt of her dress by tying a knot at her waist so it would not spoil, but her petticoats were stained with mud and there would be nowhere to wash them. A year ago, she would not have worried, but now every item of clothing was precious; she could not simply buy more.

She had not imagined an army life would be as hard as this, yet it had not even really begun; the regiment were not fighting.

She gritted her teeth as the cart jolted heavily to the left, and she bumped her side. She had not complained to Paul. That would be unfair. He was marching towards a battle, wading through the mud, and striving to keep others moving. She had the luxury of a cart. But she was black and blue with bruises from being thrown about on it, and he knew that, and at night he would kiss all of her bruises in the privacy of their narrow canvas tent.

There were some special moments, though, for instance when they sat about the campfire among his men, the other wives and Jennifer. She would huddle close to Paul, his muscular thigh against her softer one, and, because it was dark and they were wrapped beneath a blanket so no one would see, he would put an arm about her waist.

The conversations around the campfire were unlike any she had known before. Her father would have called their language coarse, but camaraderie ran so easily among the men she did not mind it. Paul would laugh with them; a laugh which seemed to come from low in his stomach. His laughter had become a precious sound.

'Lieutenant Colonel.'

Ellen jumped a little as one of the women in the back of the cart spoke.

'Good day, Mistress Porter,' the lieutenant colonel acknowledged.

The man beside her, who was his servant, looked back. 'Sir.'

The lieutenant colonel was the only man on horseback, and he often road alongside the cart.

Each time he rode beside them, Ellen's skin prickled, as if a million beetles crawled over her. She wished he would stay away from her.

She felt his gaze as though his eyes had drilled a hole into her back.

He stared all the time and spent hours riding beside the cart as the men marched. She felt as though he only rode beside the cart to watch her.

Why does he watch me? That thought had slipped through her head a thousand times since they began this journey.

Paul had deliberately not told anyone in the regiment which family she came from. He thought she would be safer if no one knew her status. If anyone was captured during a battle, they might be tempted to bargain with the enemy for their freedom, offering her up as a captive for a ransom.

She wondered if the lieutenant colonel suspected; her father's black hair and pale eyes were distinctive and she and all her sisters had inherited his colouring. That still did not really explain it, though. Even if he knew, why did he stare constantly? He did not need to keep looking at her.

She had thought of saying something to Paul. He had no

idea how many hours the lieutenant colonel spent beside the cart watching her. Yet this was his superior officer.

If the lieutenant colonel spoke, it would be easier. It would at least break the unbearable atmosphere. But he did not speak, merely rode in silence, staring.

She had thought about speaking to the lieutenant colonel, to see if that stopped him staring, but she had no idea what to say – other than *go away*. So she only spoke with the women, and he did not participate in their conversation. That conversation was always stilted anyway, though, because of the gaping class divide between her and them.

As they rode on, she wondered if the others in the cart found his presence uncomfortable. If they did though, they would not share their thoughts with an officer's wife.

Ellen looked into the back of the cart. 'Nancy, is your wrist better?' Nancy sat on top of a chest there.

'It is a little, ma'am.'

'Well, Jennifer will help you with the meal and washing if you need her to, if it is still too painful for you to work.'

'Yes, ma'am,' Jennifer responded from her position on the opposite side of the cart.

'Thank you, ma'am,' Nancy answered. Nancy was only a couple of years older than Ellen, and she had fallen onto her wrist as they had walked earlier, twisting it, meaning she would have difficulty fulfilling her role in supporting her husband and the regiment. The soldiers' wives did not just help their own men, but others too.

Of course, as an officer's wife, and genteelly bred, it was not for Ellen to do the same, but she loaned them Jennifer and supported where she could.

She had not really formed friendships with these women, they were too mindful of her class, but they did talk with her.

Later, when the men set up camp and put up the tent she shared with Paul, Ellen helped Jennifer sort out their bedding, wondering again whether or not to say something to Paul about the lieutenant colonel.

When they had finished the task, Paul was nowhere in sight, and it was late, the sky was a rich deep blue waiting to turn to black as dusk hovered.

'The Captain will be among the officers, Jennifer. Shall we walk across to fetch him and stretch our legs a little?'

Jennifer nodded.

Ellen missed Pippa, her nurse since childhood. Pippa had become a part of her family, Jennifer was simply a maid. She did not converse with Ellen, although she spoke with the other wives. She walked with Ellen now because it was her responsibility. Having been brought up, waited on and cared for by servants, Ellen wondered if the maid's awkwardness was her fault. She had never had company or friends beyond her sisters, perhaps it was because she did not know how to speak and act among others.

Mistress Porter looked up as Ellen passed. Ellen lifted a hand. Mistress Porter smiled, stopping in her task of sorting through cooking provisions, straightened and bobbed a shallow curtsy. Smiling too, Ellen acknowledged the gesture with a little nod before walking on.

She could think of nothing to say to break the silence between herself and Jennifer. Sometimes she felt imprisoned by her past – she felt unable to fully fit within this life. *Would she ever fit?*

Sometimes her heart longed for all the luxuries she had left behind – her soft bed, quiet rooms, tea and easy conversation. She missed warm baths to bathe in, spare hours to embroider pretty images, her pianoforte to play music – music she could escape into; afternoons spent with her sisters talking of the fashion, and the books in her father's library.

The pace of her strides quickened as she hurried to see Paul, longing for his company – and the time of day that made up for all other times.

The officers stood gathered about a large table within the marquee that was set up as a living space for the lieutenant colonel.

Ellen was permitted entry, and left Jennifer to return to the area where Paul's men camped.

Only the lieutenant colonel and one other officer were married. The other wives had been left in England. Perhaps that was why the lieutenant colonel stared – because he disapproved of her presence? She was more of a burden to the regiment than an aid. The other women worked for the men. She did not. Lieutenant Colonel Hillier looked up and gave her a stiff smile. 'Mrs Harding.' He was the only one who had been able to see her at that point. The others leaned over the table before him, on which a large map was spread. They all straightened, looking back at her.

Paul turned. 'Ellen...'

She smiled, looking only at her husband. 'Sorry to interrupt.'

The lieutenant colonel answered, 'It is not an issue. We are almost done.'

She looked at the lieutenant colonel. She could judge nothing from his eyes. There was no warmth or depth in his expression.

Paul looked back too. 'Is there anything else you need from me, Lieutenant Colonel?'

'I think not, Captain Harding. You may go.'

'Thank you, sir.'

Paul saluted and then nodded to the other officers in parting. Ellen noticed a man standing across the room, wearing a
different uniform from the 52nd. It was spattered with mud. He
was clearly a messenger who'd been sent back to give the regiment direction.

Paul held her arm. 'Ready?'

She smiled. 'Yes.' As they stepped outside, she added, 'I am
sorry, should I not have come? Was I intruding? Were you
talking secrets?'

'If we had been talking secrets you would not have been
allowed in,' Paul whispered in her ear in a teasing voice, his
fingers still gently encircling her arm.

She looked up at him, engulfed by the joy of his proximity.
Whenever he was close, heat ran within her blood and chased
up her heartbeat. 'Are you hungry?' she asked him.

'Starving. I wonder what the men have found to eat.'

'When I left them,' she said, 'they were bargaining for a pig
from a farmer, with a note that promised recompense.'

'And as we know, Wellington is generous in that regard...'

She had seen the members of his regiment resort to begging
and hunting on a daily basis, because no pay had come down
the line. But the Duke of Wellington was insistent local people
were refunded for any loss the army caused as they progressed.
Money was always found for them so the soldiers did not incite
unnecessary bitterness and create more enemies of the British.
Meanwhile his soldiers marched on empty stomachs.

'Well, I am remaining hopeful there is pork for dinner,' she
said.

He smiled. 'Then I shall hope for your sake.'

No one was looking at them, so she stopped and hugged
him briefly, slipping her arms about the sinuous muscle of his

waist. His body had become leaner and firmer since he had been marching daily.

She let him go and walked on.

'Your petticoats are filthy,' he commented.

'We had to stop the cart and walk so the horses could pull it through the mud.'

He caught her arm, stopped her and turned her back. Then he cradled her chin with one palm, lifting her gaze so she looked directly into the turquoise blue of his eyes. 'Such a decline from the pretty parlour I found you in. Do you miss those comforts and playing your pianoforte to entertain visitors?'

How did he know she had just been doing so? She would not admit it to him; that would be disloyal, and she wished more than anything to be a dutiful wife so he need not worry over her. She merely rode in a cart all day and had to bear the lack of the friendship of others; he had to march for hours and prepare his men for war. And besides, she had his friendship, she was not completely lacking companionship.

She shook her head, lifting her chin from his touch. 'Not when I would have to trade them for your presence.'

He smiled. 'I would trade nothing to have it different. I wish you here.' Then he said more gently. 'I need you here...'

She wished to lift up on to her toes and kiss his lips but it would be wrong to do so here, and so instead she longed for privacy – for the time they would retire to their tent – their cocoon – the place where they could be private and express their love. The place where he always made her feel beautiful and happy. 'And I need you...'

* * *

As Paul made love to Ellen, thoughts of war plagued him. The messenger who had come yesterday had said that since Napoleon had reclaimed Paris on the 20th of March, he had recruited even more men and begun training them to be his new army.

Meanwhile, Great Britain's ambassadors sat with the representatives of other European countries, fighting their verbal battle in Vienna over who would own what land when this was done; their armies had not won the land yet.

The lieutenant colonel received new information daily from the spies the Allied army sent out. But the Duke of Wellington's decision was not to race towards Napoleon, but to hold back and wait. That way, they could prepare and be ready, and they could pick their ground.

Damn it, focus.

He had begun this with Ellen to forget these things, to escape thoughts of war, if only for a short while, but it was becoming harder to – even though he had Ellen's beauty to bathe in. Birdsong seeped through the canvas about them, increasing from odd chirps to a constant vibrant swelling sound. The morning chorus was the first true sign of spring. It was a time of rebirth. But for a soldier, time always held a measure of death.

Quiet, he commanded his thoughts. He did not want to think of war, only Ellen. Only the body he moved within, a body which received him willingly, with soft, warm, moist reassurance.

Her fingers brushed through his hair, as if she knew his thoughts were splintered and she sought to bring him back.

He focused on her eyes, losing himself in the pale blue, and his thrusts sharpened, as the sound of yawns invaded their haven and fires being stirred up for kettles to be heated, and slopping water against metal.

Ellen became breathless, but she bit her lip to stop any sound as his strokes grew more urgent, hard and firm, and, and... Release came in a rush, flooding into him and onto him all at once. Relief. Escape. Freedom. He shut his eyes and let it fill him for a moment, resting his forehead on hers. She kissed his cheek. He rolled on to his back, and she turned to her side, holding him. They had not undressed. It was too cold and so their clothing mostly covered them as well as the blankets.

She kissed his jaw with such tenderness it made his heart ache. He was tired now. He hoped exerting this energy would not affect his stamina today. He did not normally make love to her in the morning, but today the thought of what was to come and the haunting memories of battles had brought on an intense desire to seek the safe harbour of Ellen's body, and he had let himself indulge.

He held her close for a moment more, willing time to cease for just a little while, but the sounds outside their tent grew stronger, men speaking and washing, and the edge of kettles striking tin cups.

'We had better rise,' he whispered to Ellen.

She held him tighter, clearly wishing time to be held back too.

He ran his fingers through her hair, and sighed, then kissed the crown of her head. 'We have no choice, darling.' As he spoke he was already moving, sitting up to right his clothes. Ellen rolled to her back. He looked down at her. 'I shall send Jennifer to you.'

She nodded.

12

Captain George Montgomery bowed over Ellen's hand. 'Will you dance with me, Mrs Harding?'

Ellen glanced at Paul, who smiled to give his consent. 'Go along, have fun.'

Looking back at Paul's best friend, she agreed. 'Of course.'

His hold firm about her fingers, he stepped back a few paces, pulling her away from Paul. His hand lifted hers and his other arm came about her to provide the secure frame for a waltz. Her heart thundered. She had danced the waltz more than a dozen times. Paul had taught her in their rooms. It was the thing here, the rage. Everyone danced it, and at the lieutenant colonel's parties he insisted it was the only dance.

Her heartbeat thundered as they began to move. She was not comfortable being on show in a room full of people, nor with the intimacy the waltz created with a partner as it made her feel awkward. Yet the steps were swift and there was something enchanting about being spun through the dance, so she did have fun once she forgot who she was with and where she was.

She glanced at the other couples dancing and those looking on.

Brussels was as busy as Ostend, Bruges and Ghent, or perhaps even more so. There were people everywhere. When she had imagined her role as a camp follower, she had imagined she would be one of a small number, but there were thousands of people here to support the army.

The army was not based in Brussels, though. It had been dispersed over miles around the city. Paul had told her that outside the city, there were over a hundred thousand of the Duke of Wellington's army in makeshift camps, and even more than that in Blücher's Prussian army that were camped about the city too. All of these men sought food and lived on depleting local resources, while their rich audience of tourists lived lavishly in the heart of the city and danced waltzs.

Paul had said the way people lived here outdid even the rash extremes of the London life he had experienced during the season last summer. She had never known anything like it. But of course, she had only lived in her father's house, sheltered from all this.

There were balls and parties daily, picnics, and the theatre continued as if there were not two hundred and fifty thousand men camped in an arc about the city preparing for war.

During the day, these fashionable people walked about in the parks, laughing and thoroughly enjoying themselves. Women flirted with the soldiers in the city, and men thought themselves something important because they were here, absorbing the atmosphere. But they would not be the ones who fought.

They had been here weeks, though, and there was no news of when Napoleon might come or when the army would invade France. The 52nd, Paul's regiment, was camped five miles outside the city, in the direction of Nemur, and each day, while the hordes of novelty seekers sought entertainment, Paul rode out to his men, and Ellen waited in Brussels for his return.

He had told her his men and others had been exploring the local terrain, learning every hill and hollow so they would have the advantage if Napoleon brought the battle to them.

She felt surplus. There was nothing she could do to help him except love him, and be a companion for him when he returned, to take his mind from the preparation for war.

In the evenings, they generally avoided entertainment like this. But they did walk through the parks, along paths edged with early flowers, and a few times Paul had taken her to the theatre. They had seen the Duke of Wellington once, in a box at the theatre. Paul had pointed him out, and she had felt in awe of the nation's hero.

She had said a prayer that night – that the Duke of Wellington would be wise. Because Paul's life lay in his hands and the skill of his decisions.

'It is a rare treat to have you in my arms, Mrs Harding...'

Ellen merely smiled at Captain Montgomery. He was always flirtatious.

Paul had urged her to participate more in the city's social life, for her own sake. At the first party, the lieutenant colonel had offered his arm and walked her about the room, introducing her to everyone, as though she was something special to him. Afterwards, his guests had invited her to afternoon teas and picnics. She had not accepted. She did not think all this merriment right, and she knew Paul did not. Even though he had wanted her to attend to fill her time; she would not, because it would feel disloyal to him and his men.

'You would just be entertaining yourself while I work. I would not mind, Ellen,' Paul had said, but still the thought of spending

time among those cold-hearted, shallow people she did not really know, and certainly did not care for, did not appeal. She was not unhappy to sit and wait for him. Jennifer was with her each day and Paul had bought her books and sewing threads, and she walked outside, perhaps along the river. It was not an unbearable life. She had a roof over her head, a comfortable bed to sleep in and food in her stomach, even though they were now living upon credit as the army had not paid Paul's wages... and every evening Paul came home to her.

But then there were nights like this, when the lieutenant colonel hosted a lavish dinner party in the house he had rented, a very pretty and rather large town house, and the officers and his guests would be expected to dance almost until dawn.

'I never realised until I came to Brussels that ostriches came in every colour of the rainbow. Have you ever seen a blue or pink one in a zoological garden?'

Ellen focused on Captain Montgomery and bit her lip to stop herself from laughing, though she knew he must see the humour in her eyes. She understood why Paul liked him, because he was always light-hearted, and always making jokes. 'You are naughty...' But even as she spoke, her gaze passed over his shoulder glancing at a dozen ostrich feathers waving like the regimental flag on its staff, from the highly coifed hair of so many over-dressed women. They did look a little silly.

She smiled at him, and then for the rest of the dance they talked, mostly about others in the room – the pleasure-seeking people she thought fools.

But then perhaps her view was coloured by Paul's, who continually called them fools.

When the dance was at an end, Captain Montgomery bowed swiftly, lifting her hand and kissing the back of it. 'Paul is a very lucky man,' he said, before giving her a swift smile. He had said the same at the end of every dance they had shared in Brussels. Paul knew he said it too, because he was forever telling Paul how lucky he was to have her.

She smiled broadly, even as the heat of a blush warmed her cheeks.

'Come, seeing as you have a husband, and he is my friend, I am duty-bound to return you to him. I had better do so.'

'Paul,' she acknowledged as they neared him. He stepped forward and took her hand. Paul's smile passed from her to his friend.

'I have just said to your wife, again, you are a lucky devil. I cannot believe you have the pleasure of looking into those fine eyes for hours at a time. I am so very envious of you.'

'Well, you may remain envious, because this lady is mine.' The two of them laughed.

'Are you warm now, Ellen?' Paul asked her. 'Shall we fetch you a glass of punch?'

'Yes, please.'

Both men walked beside her to the refreshment table. As she walked, with her hand on Paul's forearm, looking from Paul to his friend as they talked, her gaze was pulled to look further away. The lieutenant colonel was seated at a card table in a room beside the one in which they danced, watching her.

She smiled, it was how she had learned to manage his interest. He smiled in return, then looked away.

She had become more accustomed to his measured stares, but perhaps that was because she did not have to endure them overmuch. Since they had reached Brussels she rarely saw him. It was only when the officers were invited to his parties, or to dine here that she encountered him. She looked at Paul, listening to him speak with his friend. He had not noticed her exchange with the lieutenant colonel.

Paul had told her the lieutenant colonel had submerged himself in the hedonistic life here. He socialised and was constantly playing cards, gambling, as he was now, until the early hours. He encouraged his officers to participate. Paul had excused himself, giving Ellen as his reason.

She and Paul were happy here, living their quite way of life, spending all their time together when he was not working. If only there were not a war looming like a dark, swirling storm cloud.

13

On the 10th of June, word reached Brussels that the Congress of Vienna had signed a final agreement over the state of Europe. It gave Napoleon no rights to France. But prior to this Napoleon had signed a new constitution for the Empire he had claimed, and paraded through Paris to celebrate, cheered by thousands of supporters who had come out on to the streets to see him.

In response, the parks and streets of Brussels were full of people eager to discuss the news with excitement and expectation, all gossiping in high-pitched, hurried voices, wondering what would happen next.

Ellen hated their speculation. She did not go out in the day, but she and Paul walked in a park at six o'clock, enjoying the evening light and the last of the sun's warmth. It had rained a lot recently, so the clear night was a novelty. Paul said the fields and tracks they were scouting were muddy, and terrain would not be at its best if there was a battle now. But it was likely it would be soon, because the French army were renowned for moving quickly.

Ellen held his arm, but as they passed another huddle of obnoxious tourists, she slid her fingers down to grip his hand.

At least half a dozen voices in the group were agreeing that the battle would be soon.

Her heart had been pounding for hours as she tried not to think about it.

Paul held her hand firmly as they walked on past. 'You know, Ellen, if I could assure you of my safety, I would say it...'

She wanted to stop and cover her ears. She had known this conversation would come but she did not want to hear it. Yet it would be cowardice not to listen, when he was brave enough to risk his life.

'There can be no guarantees in war, Ellen.'

She knew.

'I have written to my father, and asked him to help you, financially. If anything happens to me you must write to him. You understand?'

She nodded, unable to speak past the lump of tears gathering in her throat. She bit her lip to hold them back, biting down hard as her fingers curled more tightly about his hand.

'If things do not go well, I have asked George to see that you are safe. He will organise a route to get you home, and if anything were to happen to George then any of the officers would help you, you may appeal to any of them.'

Again, she nodded, as her stomach became hollow. She could not and would not imagine him gone. She could not live without him. He was her whole life. She sometimes thought of her old home, but those memories were beyond reality now, it was with dreamlike affection.

'And you must write to your father and encourage him to forgive you and show compassion...'

She did not think her father capable of compassion, but again she nodded.

'I have written a will. George has it. It was properly witnessed. I do not have much. We have too many debts. But the few things I have you can sell to help pay your way home.'

He spoke as though it would happen, as though this was a plan, not a contingency. She stopped walking, turned and held his hand in both of hers, as she looked him in the eye. 'You will not die. I shall not let you. I cannot allow it... I am too much in love with you. I cannot lose you. You will survive.'

His hand slipped free of hers as his eyes glowed aquamarine with moisture. *Was it tears...*

He enfolded her in his arms, pulling her tight against his chest, ignoring everyone else in the park. 'I love you, more than mere words can ever express,' he whispered in her ear. 'But I cannot control fate, Ellen. Believe me, I shall fight as hard as I can, both to beat back the enemy so they can never reach you, and to stay alive. But we must be sensible and plan in case...' He did not say the last words.

She was betraying him by letting emotion get the best of her. She needed to be brave for him. Not send him into battle with tears that might distract his thoughts, but with love. She leaned back and braced his face, a palm resting against his shaven cheeks. 'You must not fear for me. You must focus on yourself. I will manage here.'

* * *

Ellen's eyes were bright with unshed tears, they sparkled in the evening sun which flooded down on the busy park. This woman had so much beauty inside her, and so much love for him. It glimmered there.

After she had spoken, she bit her lower lip, and he could see how hard by the white line beneath the press of her teeth.

She was being brave for him. He could ask no more.

She was such a delicate-looking woman, and yet she was not delicate at all. Inside, she was strong, and he knew she would survive. 'If the whole army fails, Ellen, you must leave as soon as you hear the news. Do you understand? I will leave you what money I have, and you are to buy a passage on any coach or cart you can find. Do you hear me?'

'Yes.' Her soft lips trembled as they parted to answer him, and a single tear slipped from her eye.

'I will have to leave you in Brussels soon, in the next few days, I think, and you may stay here. But if you hear that ill fate has befallen us, then you must go.'

She nodded.

He held her to his chest again, with a fierce love, as the pain he had become used to clasped in his stomach. He hated that he could not protect her, that he could not offer her any certainty of his return. He hated having to leave her every day. But in a few days, it might be to never return. He was not afraid for himself, but for her. *What would happen if he died? He had done his best to help her, but if they lost the battle George would not return either...*

He held her for a long time, ignoring the stares of others in the park. Perhaps they should have had this conversation in private, but when he had heard the men talking, he had known what was passing through Ellen's mind and he had not been able to hold his words back any longer. The information he needed to tell her, about what to do if he died, had been passing through his head for hours, days, weeks, during their whole journey here.

When he released her, he pressed a brief kiss to her temple, then said briskly, 'Let us think and talk of other things...' It was better having said what needed to be said that they did not dwell on it. What was the point? He would live or he would not.

* * *

Ellen had prayed last night, over and over, while Paul slept, whispering the words out loud in case God could not hear them if they were spoken in her mind. She pleaded and begged God to keep him alive and bring him back.

When she went out for a walk with Jennifer just after midday, an exodus had begun; carriages and carts were being loaded with furniture and baggage. People were fleeing the city before the fighting began – people who, before the danger approached, had laughed and danced as though they had no fear.

Not everyone was leaving though; there were still many hardy revellers in the parks.

Yet seeing people rushing to leave increased the fear Ellen was struggling to hold back. She had been sick this morning, fortunately it was after Paul had gone. She knew he worried about her too and she did not want him to worry more. But the fear slept inside her, gently breathing, and then something would stir it and it would wake, running into her blood, gripping about her heart, and capturing the air in her lungs. But she continued walking beside Jennifer as if nothing was wrong, refusing to acknowledge any chance Paul might not return. He would. She would not accept another outcome.

When they returned to their rooms, Ellen picked up her sewing with an aim to focus her mind away from fear. It felt as though sand ran through an hourglass, each grain marking the footsteps of the approaching French army.

14

Ellen looked up as Paul entered their little parlour. Jennifer stood and bobbed a curtsy. His hand lifted, holding up two gilt-edged slips of paper. 'We are invited to the Richmond ball.'

They had laughed about the lavish event and the battle to obtain invitations a week ago. Those who had remained in the city had not stopped their parties; if anything they entertained themselves even more determinedly and the Duchess of Richmond's was the ball everyone wanted to attend.

The Duke of Richmond had rented a house in the Rue des Cendres and the ball was to be there.

Ellen set down her sewing. 'How? Why? I thought you did not want to go – and stand among the gawping falls.' She mimicked his voice.

'I did not. I do not. But the lieutenant colonel desires our presence. He insists all his officers attend. At least the Duke and Duchess are holding it for the right reasons, the most annoying tourists will not be invited.' Paul had told Ellen previously that Lady Richmond was entertaining solely to hearten the soldiers and keep their minds off war for a few hours. The Duke of

Richmond commanded the troops who were to remain in the city and defend Brussels, should Napoleon reach this far.

The ball was to be held in four days, on the 15th of June.

'So Captain Montgomery will be there too?'

'And the others. We are to make it appear as though nothing is afoot beyond us enjoying ourselves. Apparently, even the Duke of Wellington wishes it so.' He dropped the invitations on a side table. 'You may leave us, Jennifer,' he said with a smile.

The maid dropped a swift curtsy in both their directions, then left the room, closing the door behind her.

'And for now, Ellen, I want to enjoy myself...' Paul said as he walked across the room to her. He leaned down and captured her chin between his finger and thumb, 'by feeling the flesh of my wife against my flesh.'

'Do you not want dinner first?' Ellen smiled as his eyes shone with love and longing for her.

He shook his head, smiling too. 'I suppose you would rather I was civilised though and let you dine first.'

She held the sides of his scarlet coat. 'I can wait.' She would let him do anything he wished for as many days as she had him still – she hoped that would be forever. The tears which had been threatening to fall all day finally flooded her eyes. She blinked them away, pushed him back and rose from the chair. 'I will go and find Jennifer, and ask her to buy supper and bring it here, then we can eat afterwards without rising from the bed.'

Jennifer had gone up to her attic room. Ellen tapped on the door. 'Jennifer...'

The door opened. 'Yes, ma'am.'

'Will you bring us something hot from a local inn for dinner, a pie, perhaps? Oh, and purchase wine too, and of course, something for your own meal.'

'Yes, ma'am.'

'Thank you. When you return, please bring it to our bedchamber.'

When she entered the bedchamber, Paul was seated on the bed undressing. Ellen shut the door, leaned back against it, watching him sitting in his pantaloons, bare-chested, as he worked to pull off his boots.

He looked up at her. 'All I have thought of all day is you, and being back in bed.'

She smiled. It was good to know he thought of her, and now she could help him escape. She watched the muscles move beneath the skin of his torso. The hard contours were more defined since he had lost weight from working so hard, but it only made him more beautiful. Yet he looked so young today. He was young. Young and too full of life to face death.

'Take your dress off, Ellen.'

She shook her head, not to say no but to chide him for asking such a thing, yet, smiling, she began unbuttoning it. He watched, leaning back and resting his hands on the bed.

She undressed slowly, then turned her back to him so he might unlace her short corset. The moment it fell away there was a knock on the door.

'Your dinner, ma'am, Captain,' Jennifer called, scarcely more than a quarter of an hour after she had left.

'Thank you, Jennifer. Would you leave it outside the door!' Ellen turned away from Paul. She wore only her chemise. She listened as Jennifer walked away before opening the door to collect their food. The smell of hot, cooked mutton filled the room as she carried it in.

'Well, now my stomach is rumbling,' Paul said, standing up.

They ate at the small table in their bedchamber, facing one another, she only dressed in her chemise, he in his pantaloons. She had shared many moments with him in the past six months, but none had felt as intimate as this, as he sat shirtless before her, eating hungrily and speaking of his day. At the end of the meal his hand swept his hair back from his brow and his gaze settled on her.

She got up. 'Let me rub your shoulders, you look tense.'

'That would be nice.'

She stood behind him and her fingertips and thumbs pressed into the tightly bunched muscles across his shoulders and lower neck. 'Relax.'

He leaned his head back against her bosom, his breathing slowing as he shut his eyes. She kneaded his flesh as he had done for her on days when they had travelled for relentless hours, during their journey to Brussels. It took a few minutes, but the muscles beneath her fingers softened.

'I love you,' she said to the air above his head.

'And I you,' he answered, his eyes opening and looking up at her. She smiled. She had never been in doubt of his affection. It was constant, solid, and assuring.

'May we go to bed now?' he said. 'I know it is early, but I ache for you.'

'And how can I deny such a request...'

His smile widened, and then he stood suddenly, turning to kiss her, his fingers combing into her hair and bringing her mouth to his.

He made love slowly, just touching and kissing her for a long time, before moving over her. She opened her legs so he could come between them, and held his gaze, offering comfort with her eyes as well as her body. His gaze clung to hers as he moved, pushing in, and pulling out, over and over, in the pattern which drove her senses towards delirium. Her fingers lifted and stroked through his hair.

It was precious, what he did to her – precious and beautiful. She would hold on to this moment for the rest of her life.

His movements stayed slow and deliberate as her fingers clung to his shoulders and she looked into his blue eyes.

He was hiding from reality. But she wished to hide with him and keep it at bay for as long as they could.

She pressed back against his movement as he continued. An animalistic sound left his lungs, before her name... 'Ellen.'

She moved more forcefully against him. Wishing to help him escape and escape too.

'You are a wonderful wife.'

She laughed, clasping his shoulders. 'You are the perfect husband.'

His gaze became matt for a moment. 'I will try to continue to be, Ellen.'

Damn it, she had let reality into the room. She did not want to think of the approaching battle, or Napoleon, or anything beyond their bed...

'You *will* continue to be.' She filled her voice with strength, as her hand braced the back of his head and pulled his mouth to hers. She slipped her tongue across his lips.

His movement became more urgent in reply, his hips working swiftly. Her hands dropped to hold his waist, where the muscles worked beneath his skin.

Oh, he made her feel so... so...

He broke within her in a flood of warm sensations, and his weight came down on top of her, pinning her onto the mattress. She did not mind. She liked the feel of him lying over her, and his presence between her thighs. But then, after a moment, he rose and rolled on to his back.

She rolled to her side, pillowed her head on his shoulder, her hand resting on his chest.

His arm came about her shoulders and held her close.

She fell asleep thus.

* * *

It was warm the night of the Duchess of Richmond's ball, so they walked rather than try to hire a carriage with no payment. Paul had purchased a new dress for her, though, on goodwill and an I-owe-you payment. It was in the style of the new fashion, a very finely woven white muslin, so fine, the fabric was virtually translucent, and light and fluid. It was cut close to her body, and clung to the curve of her bosom, falling to lay flat over her petticoats. She felt beautiful in this dress, walking beside him, holding his arm.

Nearly every hour he had spent at home, since they had the conversation about the possibility of his death in the park, had been spent in bed together. He wanted to love her constantly, and they lay in bed, kissing, talking and laughing, and acted as though fate could never throw them a fatal hand.

And here they were, attending a grand ball, as if it were something normal in their lives. Of course, for both of them, it could have been, if he had not become a soldier and she had not chosen to marry him and follow the drum.

She and Penny had once crept downstairs and watched a ball at her father's house, peering about the door which opened onto the musicians' gallery. The images spun through Ellen's head.

Her parents' world, her childhood, seemed as if it had been a fairy tale now.

Her fingers held Paul's arm as they climbed the steps to the door of the Duke of Richmond's house, amongst others who had arrived on foot, or in carriages.

'This way, sir, madam.' A man in livery bowed to them, and then held out his arm, pointing towards the back of the entrance hall. 'The ball is being held outside.'

'Outside...' Paul whispered, his eyebrows rising, as they followed the trail of guests walking across the hall.

Ellen smiled, wondering where on earth the ball was to be held. It was warm but the weather had been temperamental for weeks. *What if it rained?*

'This way, please.' Another footman held out a hand, directing the guests towards a narrow door.

As they stepped outside into a small cobbled stable-yard, she could hear music and conversation and laughter.

Another man in livery directed them towards a long building; the tall, wide, arched doorways made it look like a coach house.

A servant held a door open for guests to pass through.

Inside, the building looked nothing like a coach house. The walls were papered with an ivy print, there was a wooden floor for dancing upon, and the room was illuminated by hundreds of candles in the chandeliers hanging from the ceilings.

The music she had heard outside was a jig. When she passed through the crowd talking about the edges of the room with Paul, she saw the soldiers of the Highlanders Regiment in their kilts, dancing about and leaping over their swords.

She looked at Paul as he glanced at her. 'A worthy entertainment,' he said. 'But do not expect to see me dancing about a rifle to amuse you.'

She laughed.

'Come, let us find a drink and others we know.'

It was an exclusive company they walked through. Paul acknowledged several people and introduced her to a few. Then he whispered, 'The Duke of Wellington,' as he leaned towards her.

'Oh.' She turned and looked. The Duke of Wellington stood across the room speaking with a number of women.

'And there is the Duke of Brunswick.' Paul nodded in another direction. Her gaze turned to the second commander. She knew Paul revered these men.

'Sir Thomas Picton is here too, look.'

She did. They all meant very little to her, but they were the men who would be responsible for making the right choices to keep Paul alive.

She looked at him. 'Do you hope for promotion if the Allied army wins?'

He smiled. 'I would not be averse to it.'

'Then I will one day be a Colonel's wife.' She proudly tilted up her chin. After their conversation in the park, neither of them had spoken of the possibility he might die. They were denying it. Ellen was glad.

'You may hope.' His smile filled with warmth.

'Do you think my father might receive us then?'

'I would need to be a General and have earned myself a dukedom like Wellington for your father to accept me.'

She faced him as the music changed tempo and the Highlanders cleared the floor, and searched for partners among the women.

'Dance with me, Captain Harding, before anyone else might spot us and ask me.'

'Of course, Mrs Harding.' With that she was swept away into a waltz. The dance was its most beautiful when she danced it with her husband, holding his gaze and feeling the gentle pressure of his hands as they spun. She was glad they had come to this ball. This night felt precious. She would hold on to the memory of it – of dancing in a room amongst Paul's heroes.

When the dance came to its conclusion, Captain Montgomery appeared beside them and held out his hand. 'May I claim the next, ma'am?'

She smiled and agreed, though as she moved away she looked back over her shoulder at Paul. It wrenched her heart to walk away from him. '*Have fun*,' he mouthed. She did not feel as though she could have fun without him. But then she remembered Captain Montgomery would be fighting soon too, so she focused her attention on him. He deserved that much when he might never dance again.

He smiled at her over-brightly, not at all his usual jovial self.

When the dance ended, the lieutenant colonel came to ask for her hand. He could not play cards here, as there were no card tables because the ball was only in this one long coach house. She even felt more disposed to be kind to him. After all, everyone was at risk on a battlefield, and he was not so bad, he was polite when he did speak to her. It was just his constant stares she did not like. As they danced, she looked across his shoulder, while his gaze seemed to hover on the curve of her jaw and her neck.

She was glad, though, when the dance was over and she could go back to Paul. She clung to Paul's arm and lifted to her toes to whisper in his ear. 'If anyone else asks me to dance, say no, say you wish to keep me for yourself.'

He looked down at her with a question in his eyes. 'But there are a couple of hundred men in here, Ellen, all seeking partners and a moment to escape.'

He made her feel guilty, and as she glanced around the makeshift ballroom, she realised there was a forced feeling to the exuberance of the dancers. All these men were a little afraid but being brave and forcing fear aside.

She faced Paul and knew he was too. That was why they had spent most of the week in bed. 'I am sorry. I shall dance again if anyone asks me. Shall we seek a cup of orgeat? I am hot and thirsty.'

There was a lot of high-pitched laughter in the room, from both men and women, and many of the young officers were drinking glass after glass of the punch that contained liquor.

She was sorry for the men. All of them.

When they reached the refreshment table, Paul accepted a sculpted glass in the shape of an open tulip and handed it to her, then accepted another for himself. The cordial made from almonds and orange was sweetened with sugar that she and Paul could not afford, and it was cooled by ice, which was needed in the room that had become overly hot with so many people gathered.

They turned as the orchestra struck up another jig to jubilant calls from the crowd, their glasses in their hands. The Highlanders came forth again to entertain.

Paul sipped the orgeat; he would normally drink wine, or the punch.

She looked about the room – most of the senior officers were drinking orgeat, or not drinking at all. She knew that ever since Napolean had paraded through Paris, before departing to seek out the Allied forces, Paul had been waiting for the moment he would be called to fight. As each day had passed, it had become more likely it would be at any moment. She could see here, many others had been waiting for the grains of sand she had imagined in the hourglass to fall – and time was running out.

Paul's fingers touched her elbow. 'Let us watch.' He drew her forward, among the people who had gathered at the edge of the dance floor. The Scotsmen stepped and danced over the crossed swords they had laid on the floor. The crowd clapped to the rhythm of the jig, gasping and then laughing as the Highlanders' feet moved across the blades.

Again, she felt a false exuberance in the atmosphere.

She leaned into Paul's side, and his arm unusually came about her, his fingers bracing her waist. She rested her head against his shoulder too, as they continued watching the men. With no force, or falseness, she felt happier than she had thought it ever possible to be. A wave of love swept through her blood.

When the jig had finished, she would have asked Paul to dance with her again, but one of the Highlanders asked for her hand. She could not refuse, not now she had realised what tonight meant.

After dancing with the Highlander, Paul's lieutenant colonel asked for her hand for a waltz. Her heart longed to return to Paul through the whole dance, but she tried to smile and speak brightly. These men were willing to give their lives for her and others.

She was breathless when the lieutenant colonel returned her to Paul, his hand holding her elbow. His fingers clung and held her for longer than necessary, as they stood facing Paul. 'Your wife, returned, Captain.'

Paul saluted, then bowed a little. The lieutenant colonel's hand released her, then he walked away.

Ellen wished it was time they could go home but the ball was nowhere near ready to break up and it would look odd if an officer left so early.

'May I dance with you?' Paul asked.

She smiled. 'I would love to dance with you.'

'Come then.' His embrace was firm as he took her waist and her hand then spun her into another waltz. Paul had said London society would be shocked to its core by the army's addiction to the waltz, a dance that meant couples remained close together for the whole melody. But every society rule was different here, because people had less fear of consequences when death hung on the horizon. When Ellen danced waltzes with Paul, it felt like flying in heaven.

When the dance finished, heat flushed her cheeks. She smiled at Paul, laughing, as he breathed more heavily, his blue eyes clinging to her. 'We shall leave soon,' he said, implying that his thoughts on where he would rather be were the same as hers.

Directly behind him there was a flurry of whispers. Ellen looked across his shoulder. The group of people about the Duke of Wellington were turning to others and passing some message on. The Duke of Wellington spoke to the Duke of Richmond with a concerned expression. Then both dukes walked from the room, at pace.

'Paul...' She touched his arm.

He turned to see what she had been looking at.

When he saw other officers gathering in that corner of the room, he did not hesitate but crossed the room with quick strides to join them. She followed, hurrying to keep up. Captain Montgomery was there.

'What is it, George?' Paul asked him.

'Word has come,' he answered.

As Captain Montgomery answered Paul's question, Ellen saw a man in a muddy uniform standing among a huddle of women, who were offering him food and a glass of something to drink. Behind him the orchestra still played, and people were still dancing, as the news passed about the edges of the room from one person to another.

'Napoleon has struck our left side,' Captain Montgomery continued. 'He caught the Duke of Wellington off guard. We are to march. There will be a battle within hours.'

Ellen's heart dropped to the soles of her dancing slippers. *No!* The denial screamed inside her. She did not want to face this...

* * *

Ellen had known the battle would come. But knowing, and accepting it was a reality, were two very different things. At the ball Paul had left her sitting in a chair for nearly an hour, as he had found the other officers of the 52nd, then disappeared with the lieutenant colonel in search of the Duke of Wellington. When he had returned, he had an air of determination – the soldier. His jaw had been taut and the grip on her arm firm, as he told her they must go home.

She knew they were not only leaving the ball, but he was also about to leave her.

Yet what could she do? Nothing. It would be wrong to plead with him to stay; it was his duty to go, and it was honourable and right. But the thought of him walking into a battle made her heart hurt.

What if he never comes back?

Ellen pushed the thought away – she did not want to even think it.

As they walked back through the shadows the moonlight cast across the streets, she did not speak, afraid that if she did, she would sob.

He was silent too. She could tell from the tenseness in his

muscles and the intent look in his eyes as he stared ahead, his mind was on war.

When they reached their rooms, he changed immediately, stripping off his best uniform coat. Then he put on another. When he strapped his sword on, something tumbled over in her stomach. Horror. Fear.

He picked up his canvas bag that he could hang from his shoulder, and packed his razor, a clean shirt, and little else.

'May I do anything to help you?' Her voice came out at last. She could not let him leave without speaking.

He looked at her, as though only now he remembered she was there. 'No, Ellen.' He straightened, his eyes glowing a beautiful heated blue, and opened his arms. 'Come here.'

She went to him, her arms slipping about his lean waist. She could not hold the tears back.

'You will manage, Ellen, whatever happens, because you must. Do you understand?'

She nodded against his chest. She knew she would; he had told her what to do if he did not return. But... her heart could not endure it... how would she breathe if anything happened to him?

His fingers stroked through her hair, knocking out pins as she wept against his uniform which smelt of soap and starch from washing.

He had it washed to wear into battle... She felt like laughing and crying all at once.

Paul held her away a little, looking into her eyes. His eyes burned with a word he did not speak. *Sorry*, his eyes told her. *I am sorry I brought you here.*

She wiped the tears from her cheeks. She must cease crying. It was making this worse for him. 'I do not regret marrying you, not at all. You have made me happier than I ever thought it possible to be.'

He pressed a quick kiss on her lips, a chaste kiss.

'And you will fight for our country,' she said, 'and I shall be proud of you, and you will come back and make me even happier.'

He nodded, then his head bent and this kiss was not chaste at all but searing with intensity. 'I love you,' he said in an earthy voice when he broke it.

'I love you too.'

His eyes still looked regretful, yet he smiled. 'I had better finish packing.' He let her go and turned to the bag he was packing. 'I have told you what you must do,' he stated as he pushed spare items of uniform into the bag. He did not say – *if I die*.

She knew. 'Yes.'

'And you remember...' He glanced over his shoulder meeting her gaze for a moment.

'Yes.'

He looked towards his packing. 'Swear to me, again, if there is any news that we have lost, you will do everything possible to get out of Brussels and travel to Ostend, with anyone who will take you. When you reach there, sell whatever you have to get a passage back to England and go to my father. If I survive, I will come and find you there.'

She caught hold of his arm to stop his hurried packing. 'You will survive.' She wanted to say, *swear to me you will survive*.

He straightened, looking at her. 'If fate and God are on my side, yes, but I have long ago learned there is no ordering either of those things. As I have said before, Ellen, what will be will be, and we must make the best of it.'

His fingertips brushed her cheek. 'You are so beautiful. I

have been a very lucky man these last few months. I do not
regret marrying you either, though, I feel that I should.'

'You should not,' Ellen answered vehemently.

He smiled, then turned back to his packing.

* * *

It took Paul more than half an hour to walk back from the ball,
it was taking him longer than it should, as he pressed what he
needed to take with him into his bag. His mind was only half on
his duty; the other half was focused on his wife, who hovered
close, like a fearful butterfly drawn by the colour of his scarlet
coat but not daring to come too near.

When he had put all he needed in the canvas bag, he pulled
the drawstring closed and tied it off. His men were to march at
three hours past midnight; much of the army was being moved
to defend the critical crossroads of Quatre Bras. His regiment
was to form part of a screen to the west and south west of Brussels. The Duke of Wellington's orders were to be in position
before six o'clock, as Napoleon's army were as well known for
attacking early as they were for marching long distances at
pace.

Paul straightened and turned.

Ellen's arms hung limp at her sides.

Now the last moments were here, he did not know what to
say. Sorry? But sorry was a useless, pointless word – he had
done what he had done. There was never any going back, only
forward. Yet this could be the last time he looked at her face,
and those perfect pale eyes. 'I love you.' He opened his arms to
her once more, fear gripping cold and hard in his stomach. His
hand stroked over her beautiful hair, which was a mess from his
earlier embrace.

'As I love you.' Her words were warmth and vibration seeping through the fabric of his coat.

Should he wake Jennifer before he left, and ask her to sit with Ellen?

He held her tightly for a moment more, as her breasts pressed against his chest with each breath.

He did not in general pray before a battle, he was never convinced that God would take sides in war, but he prayed now, not for himself, but for her sake. That she would be safe. That he would come back to her. *Let me return.* The words whispered through his thoughts as he looked up to the ceiling, as if God really lived upwards within their room and he might see Him.

Sighing when there was no immediate echoing voice announcing that God had heard, Paul lifted her chin and kissed her, deeply, slipping his tongue into the haven of her mouth and wishing he could slip into the haven of her body too. But there was no time.

He broke the kiss. 'I must go.'

She nodded. He saw the sheen of tears glittering in her eyes, and he knew she was fighting them.

'Goodbye,' she said in a quiet voice, as he threw his bag over his shoulder.

He turned back. The tight feeling in his stomach was excruciatingly painful. He had never imagined when he had decided to take her as his wife, that it would feel like this when there was a time to fight. But he must leave her behind... This woman who had become his whole world.

'Goodbye,' he said. What a final word. He would not have it be his last to her. 'My beautiful, precious wife, I shall hold you in my heart as I fight. I shall not be alone on the field.'

Tears sparkled even more intensely in her eyes as she nodded – obviously unable to reply in words.

When he left the room, she followed him outside. On the step outside the door, when he turned to say a final goodbye, she threw her arms about his neck and sobbed against his collar.

'Come now, Ellen. This is not how I wish to leave you.' His voice sounded as though it rolled through gravel as emotions welled in his throat. 'Let me remember your smile as I leave.'

She stepped back, nodding, swallowing and wiping away the tears. 'Sorry.' She bit her lip as she fought to control her emotions.

'I must go.'

'I know,' she said in a rush. 'I will be thinking of you, and praying for you, and waiting to hear word. I love you with all my heart.' She gave him a quivering smile, a pretty smile, though there was still moisture in her eyes.

He smiled too. 'I will do my very best to come back to you.'

She nodded.

He pressed a last kiss on her lips. But as he did so, the feeling of love within his chest swelled. His hand lifted to brace her head as his tongue swept over her lips to part them, and he showed her with his last kiss how little he wished to leave her, even if he would not admit such dishonour in words.

Her arms slipped from his neck as he pulled away.

'God go with you,' she whispered.

But he wished God to stay with her. Could God's grace be in a hundred thousand places at once? Every man on the battlefield probably prayed for divine protection.

His hand stroked over her hair. 'I love you. I will always be with you, Ellen, no matter what.' He turned away then, because he had to. If he did not, he would never leave.

15

Having watched him from the door until he turned the corner at the end of the street, Ellen ran back upstairs, scared and hollow inside, and threw herself onto the bed, then turned, her arms cradling her stomach, and she prayed as she cried, whispering the words aloud.

'Protect him. Save him. Bring him home. Bring him back to me...' Tears rolled onto her cheeks and dripped onto the mattress as she lay there enfolding the child she thought was inside her in her arms.

* * *

The call of a bugle woke her, the familiar sound that had woken her each day the regiment had marched towards Brussels. A loud piercing sound rang ominously through the streets outside. She rose, she had not undressed, she still wore the precious ball gown Paul bought for her. She must have fallen asleep as she cried. The sound summoned the military men, *rise from your bed and report for duty.* She looked through the window as another bugle call rang out.

Leaning her shoulder against the edge of the window, she watched the street, listening out to the calls. She could not imagine that any soldier was still abed, the news had raced through Brussels like wildfire last night, sweeping into every street and alley. No one came from the houses around her.

She returned to the bed, lying on top of the covers, curled on her side, looking at the stars in the night sky beyond the window and hugging the child in her stomach with both arms.

At a little after three o'clock, when it was still dark, she heard the beat of a drum. She hurried to the window. It was another sound she had become so used to on their journey here. It paced the men's steps. There were the brighter sounds of tin whistles too. The sounds grew louder, coming closer. She heard their steps on the dusty street long before she could see the soldiers.

Many men came marching along the street, rifles clutched in their hands and balanced on their shoulders. Windows opened along the street, it seemed that everyone in every house was at their window.

'Good luck!'

'God bless you!' people shouted from the windows.

More men marched past, a long stream, it was not one regiment but many. Some women hung out of their windows in their nightdresses, waving and blowing kisses at the men below. A soldier looked up in her direction, and his gaze caught Ellen's through the glass. She heard Paul's voice; *Let me remember your smile as I leave.* This soldier was younger than Paul, he looked younger than her, and she saw fear in his eyes.

She lifted her hand and waved, smiling for his sake, mouthing silently, *Good luck.*

He smiled, then looked away as he marched on with his rifle on his shoulder.

She opened the window as the men kept coming, shouting out, 'May God bless you.'

Some people had hurriedly dressed and were now lining the edges of the street. She did not go down.

When the last man walked past, it was almost an hour after the first had passed.

Her heart bled like an open wound and her stomach churned with a bilious feeling as she shut the window. But she was resolute, she would not fail her husband. Misery would not help the army win the battle. Paul had told her she was strong, she was. She would change and go for a walk in the park. A walk would make her feel better, and if she was outside, knowing Paul was outside somewhere, she would feel closer to him.

'Jennifer!' she shouted for the maid.

It was at one o'clock in the afternoon that she heard the first cannons firing. Deep, heavy, booming sounds which rumbled over the city.

When Ellen had walked through the streets to the park earlier with Jennifer, she had seen some people packing their belongings onto carts to leave the city. She thought it was deser- tion, leaving behind the men they had cheered only hours before. But now, as they walked, seeking to buy something for their evening meal, the exodus had swelled, and just like the moment when the news had come of Napoleon's parade through Paris and people had known a battle would come, there was now at least one cart being loaded in every street. It was cowardice.

They purchased freshly baked bread and milk, and eggs and cheese that would last a week or so, and bacon; Paul liked the thinly sliced mutton when it was fried in a pan. The increasingly loud sounds of the cannons, shaking the sky like thunder, chased them quickly back to the house.

At the house, Ellen found her sewing, as did Jennifer, and they sat in the small parlour.

The sound of one cannon firing resonated through the window, so loud it rattled the glass in the frame.

Jennifer looked at the window, her expression anxious.

The next boom shook the window too.

It became constant, the sound rumbling like a persistent thunderstorm. At least with thunder she could make a guess of how far away the lightning was by counting the seconds between the light and the sound. There was no way to guess how far away the cannons were, or whose army the sounds were made by.

Ellen's heartbeat hesitated a little each time as she worked on a new shirt for Paul. She refused to think of him fighting amid that cannon fire.

Another boom rattled Ellen's nerves, along with the sheet of glass in its frame, and a quiet, frightened sound escaped Jennifer's throat.

'What are you sewing?' Ellen began talking. They hardly ever shared a conversation, as Jennifer had made it clear, with short, stilted, answers, that she preferred it if Ellen did not try to talk with her. But today; they both needed to preoccupy their minds with something.

'A new nightdress, ma'am.'

'If you would like some lace for the cuffs, I have enough spare from the collar I replaced on my blue dress.'

'That would be kind, thank you, ma'am.'

'Shall I tell you about the Duchess of Richmond's ball that

the captain and I attended last night, would you like to hear about it?'

'That would be nice, ma'am.'

'The oddest thing,' Ellen began, 'was that it was not in the house...' As she related tales of the room and the Highlanders, and the atmosphere when the news of Napolean's attack came, she had a feeling the ball would still be talked about for a long while – certainly there would never be another like it.

At just before two o'clock, the cannon fire ceased as abruptly as it had begun, and an ominous quiet fell.

What was happening? Ellen's desire was to look through the window, but all she would see was the carts of the last cowards to leave the city. The ticks of the mantelpiece clock's mechanism marked each second as she and Jennifer worked in silence, their conversation now dry.

When the clock chimed three times, she put aside her sewing and stood. 'Let us go out for another walk.'

It was not for the sake of being outside this time; it was for the possibility of hearing any news.

After the earlier exodus, the streets were eerily empty. Only one or two others walked along the dusty roads and cobbled pavements. Ellen led the way to the park, and they walked all about it in silence, again, as Ellen could think of nothing to talk about. She saw no one she would have the courage to ask if they knew what was happening.

It was different when they walked back towards their lodgings, though. The previously empty streets all now contained huddles of people, some moved from group to group, others knocked on doors, seemingly announcing something to the occupants.

This must be news... Ellen walked towards one man dressed

in livery, who had knocked on a door and spoken to a woman then moved to knock on the next.

She stood in his path, so he had to face her. 'Is there news?' she asked.

'The Allied army has been overcome. We are to leave the city. Everyone must leave.' He walked around her, moving onto the next door.

She had no idea who he was or where he had come from. Or most importantly whether she should believe what he had said. So many thoughts fought for attention in her head as her heart kicked. Paul said she must leave if such a message came; he had made her promise – and yet... *How can I go?*

Some people in the street were turning and hurrying away in different directions, as the conversations of those that remained grew louder with agitation. They all discussed what to do.

'We must get home,' Ellen said to Jennifer.

When they reached their lodgings, Ellen returned to the parlour, but she could not sit and sew with so many thoughts spinning in her head, weighing up her choice – stay or go. She went to the window and looked down on the street as Jennifer hovered by the parlour door. People hurried past. Some doors were open, as people stood on their doorsteps with arms crossed and chins high, talking hurriedly to people in the street. Others were rushing to somewhere, perhaps to hire carts or carriages, or horses. What would be left after so many people had gone this morning?

She sat on the parlour's wooden window seat and watched the street. Some carts arrived, hand carts, some pulled by horses, then as items were taken from houses and loaded, people from other streets walked past, some with their belongings wrapped in bedding on their backs. The numbers walking through the street increased slowly, until it was a crush of people running away from the city.

A carriage tried to pass through the crowd. Some men sought to free the horses, presumably to steal them for their own escape. The driver raised his whip and brought it down on the men. The people she quietly watched from her window seat were panicking, pushing each other to force their way through as they tried to get out of the city. She was waiting. She believed in Paul. She would not give up on him.

There had been no sign of any soldiers, but these people were behaving as though Napolean and his army were nearly at the city gates.

As the carriages and carts slowly progressed at the pace of those on foot, people waved watches, money and jewellery towards the drivers, and she heard their shouts.

'Let me embark, damn you!'

'Come on, it is a pretty ring! These are diamonds!'

'I will pay you anything you ask for just one of your horses!'

It was a melee, a nightmare – *and it was disloyal.*

Paul would have had her doing the same, but she could not bring herself to go. What if half an hour after she had fled, Paul came looking for her here, injured and needing her care?

'What do you want to take with us, ma'am?' Jennifer asked. 'I can go upstairs and pack your most precious possessions in the sheets, so we can carry things ourselves.'

It was the fourth time she had suggested they pack.

'I honestly think nothing, Jennifer. I am waiting. I cannot believe Napolean will reach the city.' Four times Ellen had denied the suggestion that they should leave.

Her stomach was tied in a tight knot, full of fear – not for herself, but for Paul. Her mind's eye continually saw the high-wayman's bloody body – but the body had Paul's face. He could not be dead; she would feel it.

She looked at Jennifer, her heartbeat pacing out the seconds. 'Let us go outside and see if it is like this all over Brussels.'

'Ma'am, we should not go out, we should leave with everyone else. If the city is overrun we shall be...'

Raped and murdered; Jennifer did not have to say the words. They had both heard rumours of the Peninsular War on their journey here, and Ellen knew that was why Paul had told her to run.

But how could she abandon him? It would be treacherous to leave him behind, it would imply she believed he was dead, and she refused to believe that.

'Please humour me, Jennifer, let us go out into the streets.'

For the fourth time that day, Jennifer held Ellen's pelisse for her to put on, but Jennifer's expression was not happy.

Immediately after stepping from the door, Ellen was jostled by the crowd, everyone was forcing their way towards the edge of the city to escape.

'Ma'am, we should go back inside and pack,' Jennifer said urgently.

'Let us see what is happening first,' Ellen denied, refusing to give in.

At the very edge of the crowd, one shoulder against the walls of the houses, she pushed her way through, walking against the tide of people. She did not look to see if Jennifer followed. She worked her way slowly along the street to the corner, believing that in the side street it would be quiet. Of course it was not, it was the same.

Ellen saw a woman in the crowd, beside a carriage, holding

her wedding ring out towards the carriage window. Ellen had seen her a dozen times, walking along the streets on the arm of a soldier. 'Give me a seat on your carriage, sir. I only ask to sit beside the coachman?'

'Get back,' the coachman yelled at her. 'Or I'll rear the horses and 'ave them crush you!'

People were doing anything today, at any cost, to escape the city.

Paul had urged Ellen to do the same as this woman, but she had been denied anyway. It was better to stay, she decided.

'Ma'am!' Jennifer's hand gripped Ellen's arm, holding her still. 'If you will not leave the city, then I must leave your service. I shall find my own way back to a port.'

Horror struck Ellen full force, she would be alone. But she could not insist Jennifer stayed. 'Of course. Go if you must. We will go back, and you can quickly pack your belongings.'

Paul would shout at her when he discovered she had chosen to remain here. He would call this foolish. But the warm light that burned in her heart for him could not leave.

'Come with me, ma'am.' Jennifer's grip firmed on Ellen's arm, urging Ellen physically as well as with words.

'No, I will stay and wait for the captain.'

'And if he does not return?'

'He will.'

Ellen let the flow of people carry her back to the property she and Paul had called home for weeks, with Jennifer in front of her.

As Jennifer went upstairs to pack, Ellen went to her bedchamber and found out the money Paul had left for her, then took it to Jennifer. She had not been paid for four weeks; the money would be compensation. It would be unthinkable to let Jennifer go without the means to obtain a passage home.

'Ma'am, you need not give me all of this.'

'Just take it, Jennifer.'

'But you will need some for yourself.'

'I shall be fine, once my husband returns.'

Jennifer stopped packing. 'Ma'am, come with me? You should not stay. If the captain lives, he will find you. It is better to leave.'

'I cannot.'

'Ma'am...'

'Jennifer! I will not. There is no point in urging me. I cannot leave.' The words came out in a cross voice, but only because she was afraid. She had no idea how she would cope on her own.

'Very well.' Jennifer folded the sheet she had packed hurriedly and tied the opposing corners.

Ellen watched, the scene feeling unreal. This could not be happening.

Jennifer already wore her bonnet and cloak, so once she had packed, she lifted her makeshift bag to her shoulder. 'You are sure you will not come?'

Ellen nodded, as inside uncertainty roared, rising as a screaming sound in her inner ears.

'Very well then, ma'am.'

Ellen followed Jennifer downstairs, to the front door.

'I wish you luck,' Ellen said.

'As I you, ma'am. Goodbye.' Jennifer opened the door and stepped out.

Ellen closed the door, a sigh slipping from her lungs. Her limbs shook a little. Almost collapsing, she sat on the second step of the stairs, fear hanging like a lead weight on her shoulders. She stared at the door.

The she remembered, she was not completely alone. The

woman who owned the property lived next door, and Ellen had not seen her leave. It was mostly the British who were fleeing.

She covered her face with her hands. But she did not cry. She was beyond crying. She just wanted to know if Paul was alive.

16

'Rise up!' The lieutenant colonel's voice reached through the trees, strong and definite. 'Rise up!'

The cannons had begun pounding at about one o'clock, but Paul, and his men, had not been among the fighting yet. His orders had been to remain in the woods, on the Namur road, just north of Lac Materne. The regiment's role was to defend the road in case the French broke through.

Paul had been lying down amongst his men for hours, beside the sunken road, hiding among the trees, to avoid becoming targets for the cannon fire. He had not been able to see over the brow of the hill. He had lain here listening to the battle unfolding a short distance away from him, rejecting every urge to stand up without an order. They might be the last defence; if the French got this far, they would not expect a whole regiment hidden in the undergrowth not already a part of the battle that had been raging for hours.

'I said rise up, men!'

Now the order had come, Paul moved instinctively, getting onto his feet.

A moment later, the French riflemen poured over the brow of the hill, and in the next instant, after hours of waiting – no, after months of waiting – Paul was ready to fight. It was kill or be killed – for every single one of his men who had stood up on this ridge.

'Rifles! Present!' Paul called to his men to make ready. Then having given them a moment to prepare, raise their rifles to their shoulders and get a man in their sights, he yelled. 'Fire!'

The front row of men charging forward fell, with screams of pain as they clasped at wounds. A man looked at Paul with horror, in the moment before he dropped to his knees and died.

The stench of gunpowder, blood and guts – death – dragged Paul back to the battles he had forgotten in Ellen's bed.

'Make ready!' he called, raising his arm. The second line of his men stepped through the first, while the men in the first line began reloading.

The sounds of his men moving, firing, reloading and firing again, always stirred the patriotism in his blood. *For Britain and for victory!* 'Present! Fire!' The second line fired their rifles. More of the French who came over the brow of the hill collapsed to their knees. Smoke, from the explosion of gunpowder in the rifles, drifted along the British line. The caustic smell burned at the back of his throat, making his stomach lurch, as Paul's third row stepped forward.

A volley of fire was released by the platoon beside theirs.

'Prepare!' Paul yelled over the noise. 'Fire!' Rifle shots rang out all around him as the third line of his men blasted the French.

He knew every inch of this terrain, and he had calculated in strides how long it would take the survivors to run and reach the British line. There would be time for two more rounds. Two more.

'Ready!' he yelled again, as the first row stepped through the third. 'Fire!' So many French men were charging over the brow now, they could not shoot them all.

They could fire one more round before the French would be upon them. He held his nerve, willing his men to do so too. They trusted him implicitly; he knew they would. 'Prepare!' The sound of rifles being lifted to shoulders and aimed repeated along the line either side of him. 'Fire!' The final shots were deafening, ringing in his ears. Paul looked into a man's eyes and watched the man's gaze shutter with pain, the light within his soul dying out. He fell.

There was no time for compassion. None for thought. Breathe and fight. That was all he must do. He lived as part of a whole on a battlefield. He was a soldier. A British soldier. Nothing else.

'Draw arms!' Paul yelled for his men to lower their rifles and present their bayonets. The enemy were too close now for bullets.

The French shouted, 'Vive l'Empereur!'

'Attack!' Paul shouted.

'On to victory!' his men yelled. 'Give them the bayonet!' The words echoed over the cries of the wounded men they ran across, and blood streamed in rivers through the mud that squelched beneath Paul's boots.

An unearthly cry came from behind Paul's men, along with shrill hollers and whoops.

Paul looked back, as Picton's Highlanders, the men who had been dancing jigs last night, came charging through the lines of Paul's riflemen at a run, swords drawn.

The fighting was fierce. Paul held back, rather than waste himself by getting caught up with Picton's men, he prepared to fight if the Highlanders failed.

Paul watched the Highlanders fight with a vicious energy in an unrelenting onslaught; they hacked and parried, pushing the French back, away from the 52nd riflemen. But then the sound of thundering hoof beats vibrated through the ground.

'Form a square!' Paul yelled to his men. 'A square! Now! As swift as you can!' The men ran about him. They rehearsed this manoeuvre over and over again, but in a battle, leaving any space in the square open would allow the horses through and from within it the cavalry could kill many men.

'Retreat! Move among the 52nd!' Picton called to his high-landers.

It was the turn of Paul's men again. He shouted, 'Make ready!' Even as they moved into the square, the Highlanders ran into the middle of them for protection.

The men either side of him dropped to one knee, their rifles already raised to their shoulders ready to fire and bring the horses and their riders down. The brutally sharp bayonets on the end of the guns would be used to stab any cavalry man who dared to come closer.

Above Paul's head, the regiment's flag caught on the wind, held aloft by their pole bearer.

On all four sides of the square his men had formed, there were now men on one knee at the front of the square on every side. The last straggling Highlanders ran through their boundary as the cavalry came over the hill, their horses' hooves trampling the dead and dying French soldiers.

Standing with a rifle, facing a man on a horse, was terrifying, if that man got too close there was no certainty you would survive... 'Fire!' Paul yelled. The cavalry were only paces away. Horses screamed and fell, writhing on the ground as Paul called his second line forward.

'Present!' Paul's second line of soldiers lowered to one knee.

There were French men trapped beneath their horses, buried among the corpses already strewn across the ground, crying out to be saved.

'Fire!'

Another volley, more men and horses fell. But there was no time for another, as the cavalry thundered into the front of his men. Swords slashed and hacked, while his men presented a boundary of lethally pointed bayonets. The metal glinted, catching the sunlight, trying to protect the Highlanders hidden within the square.

Two of the Highlanders had not made it to safety; Paul watched them be cut down on the field.

'Present!' Paul yelled, speaking to his third line. Those at the front were still kneeling, jabbing at the horses with the tips of the piercing blades on the ends of the rifles.

'Fire!'

More horses and cavalry went down, some falling onto his men.

'Make ready!' he called again, determined to keep as many men as possible alive. Determined to win. 'Fire!' His mouth was dry and his voice hoarse from breathing in the gunpowder.

The French cavalry turned their horses and drew back. But he knew in a moment they would charge at his surviving square again. But his men were not alone. Along the brow of the hill, Paul could see other regiments also formed into squares, fighting just as hard.

The bombardment went on for hours, as they repelled line after line of the French, and after a while he heard the cannon booming to the north of them again. But there was no time for fear. No time to wonder if they would survive – if the French would tire before he did. Only time to fight.

'Fire!' he called again, his throat painful with thirst.

They would run out of ammunition soon.

'Fire!'

He could see his men were pale and worn.

'Fire!'

How many more men did the French have?

'Fire!'

Another charge of cavalry came over the hill, a fresh wave. But there was only a single battalion charging against Paul's square and the others that he could see.

There must be many more Allied squares he could not see along the line of the hill.

'Fire!' he yelled.

The volley rang out, denying the yells of those charging towards him, their horses' hooves pounding over the dead and wounded at a gallop. The horses were already blowing, they must have been raced at a gallop all the way up the hill.

'Make ready!' Even with another wave of cavalry charging towards them, even though they must be tired to their bones, Paul's men did not falter. They stayed steady, bayonets held upwards and rifles hurriedly recharged.

'Present!'

'Fire!'

More French went down.

'Make ready!'

Paul prayed for it to be over. His men could not hold much longer, but this new French charge was already thinning.

Instead of attacking directly, the French sought to pass between the squares of the Allied lines and ride on over the hill.

'Present! Left! Right!' he yelled. The same call came from the squares beside his. Shots rang out, bringing down a dozen men or more from their horses.

The next row of rifles rose. 'Fire!' Another volley and a

dozen more men and horses went down as other horses reared and their cries reverberated on the air.

'Make ready!' Paul called again; the French onslaught had slowed, though. Those remaining turned their horses and raced away.

His heart leapt, and energy – which had been non-existent a moment before – flooded into his arteries, as adrenalin pulsed into his limbs.

'Attack! Attack!' The cry came from a man on a horse racing at a gallop behind the lines. 'Wellington bids you attack!'

The square closest to the rider was already breaking up, men rising and dispersing – men who had knelt for hours at the front with bayonets, stood, and were now charging forward on unsteady legs.

'Attack!' Paul took up the cry, beckoning his men to move forward and release the Highlanders from within. 'Attack!'

In moments, they were running, with energy only a quarter hour ago he would not have thought they had. 'Attack!' he yelled again to keep his men on their feet and moving. 'Attack!' The cry came from the right of his regiment now too, as the British army raced forward, running over bodies, as though bodies were no more than mud or grass, forcing the French to withdraw further and further back.

Within an hour they were no longer charging but walking, claiming more ground, as the French continued pulling back. The light turned from day to early dusk then twilight, before slipping further and further towards night. It was then the call came to camp. But there were no tents to be put up. Small fires were lit from gathered wood, and he and his men, and others further along the line crowded about them, exhausted from battle, and haunted by death, and lay down on the cold hard ground.

It was only then he thought of Ellen, left behind in Brussels. Dread ate into his empty stomach. *She must be afraid for me.* He whispered silent prayers for her and for his return to her before his eyes closed. When they did, he thought of her soft, beautiful body, of sleeping with her warmth and softness against him. Even thinking of her soothed his soul and freed him from the memories of the fight and the faces of the dead men.

Exhaustion and darkness claimed him.

A hand shook his shoulder, waking him. It was light. The man who had woken him walked along the line of soldiers, shaking every man's shoulder. 'We are to move.' The words were whispered to him by a stranger. 'The Duke of Wellington's orders are to pull back to the ground by Waterloo.'

Paul knew the ground. It was the point the Generals had considered the best place to fight. It was more defendable, there was another ridge and a larger wood, the Forest of Soignes, where men could hide if need be. Every officer had been ordered to become accustomed to the terrain in the months they had spent in Brussels.

Paul sat up and rubbed his face, urging himself to wake, as the men around him stretched and yawned, rising slowly. 'Eat and drink,' he whispered. They looked at him. There was only limited water and dry biscuits in their provisions, but they needed some sustenance before they fought again.

It seemed this second day they marched for hours. But it was not very far. Within a day they had re-camped and positioned themselves on the Duke of Wellington's chosen ground to take the enemy. The losses of the day before had not been as bad as Paul feared, only a couple of thousand, some of the wounded had been moved by cart back beyond the lines, but many were bandaged and ready to fight again.

17

When Ellen woke the day after Jennifer had left her alone, it was to a quiet city. She did not even hear birdsong penetrating the windowpane. She looked through the window. No one was in the street, and there was not a single sound in the air. Those who were the sort to run had gone, and those who had chosen to stay must be in their homes, waiting to hear more news – or cannons.

Ellen's stomach suddenly turned over, she pressed her hand to her mouth then turned to the chamber pot and was sick; probably because she had not eaten anything for dinner.

Her stomach felt like a whirlpool, swirling with fear. She dressed, though, went to the kitchen and ate some of the bread they had bought yesterday.

She tried to sew but her fingers shook too much to thread a needle. She tried to read but her mind would not concentrate on a single word. When it reached two past midday, she went for a walk outside, alone, which as a genteelly bred woman she should not do, but with Jennifer gone she had no choice.

The streets, which yesterday had been crowded with

people, were entirely empty. She walked for an hour and saw no one.

When she returned to their rooms, she sat on the window seat with her knees lifted to her chest and embraced in her arms. She had sat in her room like this as a child, when she had been scolded and experienced her father's wrath. Her chin rested on her knees as she watched the street, silent and praying, her heart beating to the rhythm of the mantelpiece clock.

Where are you, Paul?

She remained where she was, watching.

Even when dusk fell, she had only seen the odd servant passing through the street.

As darkness claimed the city, falling like a shroud, Ellen moved to the bed. She was so exhausted by worry her eyes closed.

When Ellen woke the next morning, she was sick before she had even risen from the bed, cramps pulling at her empty stomach as she vomited bile.

Paul would be angry when he discovered how poorly she had been taking care of herself. She must eat. What would he say when he found her still here? But surely if the French had won, as they were told yesterday, Napoleon and his army would be in the city. She had made the right choice.

Ellen went in search of the bread. She ate it with cheese and drank some of the milk.

Clunk.

Someone struck the knocker down on the door.

Clunk. Clunk.

It was not an urgent knock. But it would not be Paul, he had a key to get in.

She opened the door cautiously. It was Mistress Peeters who

owned the house. She stood in the rain, holding a shawl over her head.

'Good day, Mrs Harding, I saw your maid leave yesterday, so I thought I would pop in, say hello and ask if you need anything.'

'Would you like to come in? I could do with some company.'

The woman smiled and nodded. 'I could do with some as well. Do you have any tea?'

'I do.'

'Then shall we get a pan of water on the boil.'

'Have you heard any news of the battle?' Ellen asked as they made a pot of tea.

'No...' But Mistress Peeters held a hundred opinions upon the French and proceeded to share them as they sat down to drink. After Jennifer's constant silence, Ellen was relieved to listen to another woman's voice as she drank the milky tea.

A loud, thunderous boom interrupted their conversation. Ellen looked at the clock, it was half past eleven. She rose and looked through the window, as though she might see the cannons and know what was happening. Another distant boom could be heard. The cannons sounded closer than the other day.

18

On day three of the fight, the first cannon fire rang out at twenty-five minutes past eleven in the morning. Paul's regiment were prepared; they had their orders for the battle, the best position to defend, and a day's rest.

But an hour and half later, the cannons were still pounding, and Paul and his men were on the ground, lying still and silent, hiding behind the ridge on damp bracken, as the rain seeped through the cloth of their uniforms. He was cold, but not because the day was cold, it was warm. The chill in his skin was fear. It would ease when it came time to fight, but while they waited for their moment it was always like this.

In the hours he had lain here, he had thought a hundred times of Ellen in Brussels; she must be able to hear the cannons and would be thinking of him.

He had survived one battle; he only had to survive one more. Today, they all believed, would bring success or failure. Whichever army won this fight would win the war.

All of his men about him lay still and silent, listening, waiting.

There were encounters taking place only yards away over the ridge, on the hill. He heard rifles firing in the rhythm of three rows, horses, swords clashing, screams from the wounded and battle cries, men exerting their strength to stay alive. But the battle was not close enough for Paul and his men to be called in to fight. The Duke of Wellington was holding back Paul's regiment, along with others, so if the French prevailed in this initial fight, there would be a second wave of Allied forces.

Paul was aware of every beat of his heart, and every breath he took.

Another long hour passed, then the call to 'Rise up!' was shouted a hundred yards away. It was not an order for Paul's regiment. It was Picton's Highlanders who were called forward. The sounds made by a hundred men rising followed.

Paul watched Picton's Highlanders silently creep towards the brow of the hill, swords drawn.

Shouts of '*Vive l'Empereur*' rang from the far slope.

'Charge! Hurrah!' Picton yelled out, calling his men over the top.

Paul's heart pumped hard, waiting for his moment, certain it would come soon, as he looked right and left for the lieutenant colonel. His commander was holding back behind the ranks. He rode the horse so he could see over the heads of the soldiers and see along the battle line for a signal, for orders.

The sounds of the fighting increased; screams, shouts and rifle fire as the cannons still boomed. The British would be firing at the French cannons. With the French on the hill, they could not fire their cannons without risking their own men.

Every muscle in his body burned to rise and take part. But he had been a soldier long enough to know how crucial it was to await orders from the men who had the oversight of the whole battle. He simply needed to hold his nerve.

Hollers of another charge came from beyond the ridge of the hill, and amid them more cries of '*Vive l'Empereur!*'

Instinctively, Paul looked back at his lieutenant colonel. He had received a signal that had come along the line from the right. His head turned sharply and he looked at Paul first and lifted his hand without a word, bidding Paul to rise. Paul urged his men to follow the command, his palm up, his hand lifting, displaying the same signal.

'Up,' Paul said in a low voice, the word swept along the row, repeated in a quiet wave of sound.

The lieutenant colonel waved his hand, urging them forward.

'Forward,' Paul ordered as quietly as before, taking a step himself that the men followed a step after, and so, silently, they paced forward through the bracken.

'*Vive l'Empereur! Vive l'Empereur!*' The cries of the French became louder.

From the sounds, they were running up the hill, believing they were about to claim the point of advantage.

Lieutenant Colonel Hillier rode past Paul at a canter, leaning low in his saddle. 'Halt, raise your rifles.' He repeated the order as he rode along the line as quietly as possible.

The men's rifles had been ready to fire for hours.

'Present,' Paul said firmly.

A couple of hundred rifles were lifted to press against shoulders along the line of the 52nd. The men were not in rows of three but stood as one long line.

Lieutenant Colonel Hillier's palm lifted – *wait*.

Paul could hear the French army approaching, a mass of sound beyond the brow of the hill. Surely they would see the colonel on his horse soon.

His heart pulsed.

The colonel's arm dropped and he rode through the middle of the line of men, out of harm's way.

The French rushed over the top, in reams. 'Fire!' The cry rang out from half a dozen commanders along the line. A look of horror flooded the eyes of the French as the volley of shots scythed them down. They had not known the British soldiers had lain hidden over the hill.

'Forward!' the lieutenant colonel shouted over the sounds of battle. Paul raised his arm, calling his men forward, winning back the ground one step at a time, pushing the French down the hill.

When he was over the brow, in the fray, Paul could see thousands of dead and dying spread over the fields below.

Now they were in full sight of the French, it was only a few minutes before a cavalry regiment charged towards them, forcing Paul to order his men into a square behind the Allied cannons. This time it was the gunners who manned the cannons who ran to shelter in the middle of the square his men had formed. When the cavalry failed to break the square and withdrew, the gunners ran out to load and fire another round at the French.

A thunder of hoof beats came from behind Paul, a regiment of British cavalry charging through the riflemen. They were mounted on huge grey horses. The charge forced the French foot soldiers further back. The regiment carried on riding, chasing the fleeing men to the far side of the field.

There, they used their swords to strike down the gunners who were firing the French cannons.

The British lines cheered as the French were called back to the far edge of the field to regroup.

But it left the British cavalry trapped.

They were pulled from their horses and killed.

An eerie silence fell on the fields they fought over as Paul glanced back to check his men.

None of the Allied lines were called to move forward; instead, orders reached Paul to say that Wellington was taking the opportunity to break the soldiers from their squares. As Paul and his men rested and drank water from canteens, messages were passed along the line, checking casualties and positions.

When the battle began again, Paul was on the hill, and like the whole Allied army, his men had reformed their square.

'Move forward!' the lieutenant colonel shouted, as Paul heard others call the same order.

His men stepped carefully, holding their rifles in a forward position, bayonets ready to pierce, moving as all the squares moved, claiming more ground. French cavalry continually assaulted them, but his men repeatedly repelled them, and each time more of the French fell to the ground.

Late in the day, a new wave of French soldiers poured onto the field.

The fight could not go on much longer; men could not fight forever. Yet the French were not conceding, and the Allied forces would not.

Weary but determined, as the French foot soldiers charged again, Paul received the order to have his men form a line four deep. The line was repeated by all regiments along the hill.

He called for his men to make ready and fire, as others shouted the same call.

Volleys rang through the air, and smoke from the gunpowder rose in clouds.

19

Not long after the clock had chimed four times, Ellen's gaze lifted from the sewing she was attempting. A movement outside had caught her attention. Speaking with Mistress Peeters had calmed her nerves, and since then she had tried to distract her thoughts by keeping her hands busy.

She put down the sewing and went to the window. A few women were running through the street.

Ellen did not hesitate, she ran to the front door and pulled it open, hoping to stop one of the women. 'What is happening!' she shouted at a young woman, who was probably her own age. 'Tell me, please!'

The woman slowed and looked at Ellen, 'They are bringing wounded soldiers into the city on carts.' Her breathing was ragged from running. 'They have not lost! I am going to look for my husband.' The woman did not wait for acknowledgement but ran on.

'Thank you!' Ellen called after her.

Ellen rushed to follow, hurrying upstairs to the bedchamber and pulling on her pelisse, images of Paul in her mind. Then she joined the women in the street and went to the gate leading onto the Nemur road.

There were wounded men everywhere, they lifted them onto the ground as the carts full of men with limbs missing or torn open were emptied. She watched an emptied cart leave the city, she presumed to gather more wounded.

Dear God. Her gaze scanned the men as women and servants, and the men of this city, carried them into houses, her heart pounding as she looked for Paul. She did not see him. But as she glanced over the men, she was drawn forward. She remembered the young soldier she had waved to from her window. So many were young.

She knelt beside one young man who was crying with pain, holding his damaged leg. 'What do you need?'

'Water,' was all he asked for.

'If you can help, I have a dozen things you might do...' Ellen turned as a woman spoke. 'There is water, and bandages, and we are looking for people to hold men who require treatment. Will you come?'

Ellen rose, and turned. 'Of course, but let me bring water to this man first.' Like so, she was swept into the mayhem of war. It was beyond anything she might have imagined as hundreds of men were brought back into the city, and as she worked, she constantly looked for Paul in each new cartful.

It was early evening when the first men arrived at the city gates on foot, hobbling, exhausted and bleeding.

Her heart beat out a steady rhythm, the pace of the drum the men had marched to, a beat or two away from panic as she waited for Paul to come back and helped those who had made it. Her panic was held at bay only by the need to do something for these men who had survived but were in agony.

'Madam!' The doctors and surgeons worked at the far end of the drawing room, where two dozen men lay on the floor.

She was kneeling beside a man with many wounds, holding his hand.

'Madam!' As the shout came again, and the doctor waved a hand, beckoning Ellen, the soldier's hand fell slack in hers. She looked down. His eyes looked at nothing.

Her heart missed a beat, and sickness threatened, as she pressed a hand over his bloody coat. There was no sense of his heart beating, and no feeling of movement in his lungs.

'Madam!'

She stood, not knowing what to do, and walked to the doctor as though she were sleepwalking. 'I think the man I was with is dying.'

He looked over but when he looked back at her there was no hope in his eyes. 'There is nothing I can do. I must help those who have more chance of survival. This man needs his arm taken off, and I need someone to hold his shoulder while I cut. Will you do it?'

A soldier who had a bloodied bandage over one eye but in all other ways seemed well, was already kneeling, holding the man's legs down. Their patient looked up at them with wild terrified eyes. But the bone in his forearm was protruding from an open wound, shattered and in splinters.

Ellen's stomach turned again, but she bit her lip and nodded. She would do anything to help these men – in the hope that someone would do the same for Paul if he was wounded, somewhere, needing help.

20

As the last sunlight painted the clouds above Paul orange, the battle could still go either way. Neither side had gained an advantage.

Napoleon's force made another push to break through the centre of the Allied lines, trying to cut Paul and his regiment off on the left. The fight continued as daylight turned to dusk, and then edged towards night, and once again Paul was on the defensive, in a square, watching as a British troop charged past to push the French back down the hill.

A call rang from the left. Paul's lieutenant colonel raised his sword, calling Paul's square to break and move about.

Something was afoot.

Paul lifted his sword high, calling his men to break from the square and move. Then he saw the risk. The riflemen of the French Imperial Guard were running up the hill, seeking to break the Allied forces once and for all.

Paul ran ahead of his men, calling them on, his sword raised. The pole bearer ran beside him, holding up their colours, and the flag flew out on the breeze. 'Halt and kneel!'

Paul bid his front row when they were in close range. 'Present all!' Three layers of men at varying heights all raised their rifles a moment before the French line formed into the same position.

'Fire!' he shouted.

'*Feu!*' the French officer called.

There was a sudden vicious volley of bullets, back and forth.

A force ripped through Paul's stomach; a solid mass, tearing through his flesh and pushing him backwards off his feet, slamming him down onto the muddy ground as the air about him filled with the bitter smell of gunpowder and blood. There was no pain, only shock. Cold, disbelieving, shock.

My God!

'Captain! Captain!'

One of his men was beside him, and Paul saw him for a moment before the world went black. 'Captain!'

There was a foul smell in the air. Death. His death. The smell of a gut wound.

Ellen...

He had no feeling in his arms or legs, though his heart beat even in the darkness, but his blood and energy drained away. *I am going to die.*

'Tell my wife...' He forced the words from his dry lips into the emptiness beyond him, and felt a man's hand touch his face. Then... the last image in his head was Ellen, her face, as around him shots still screamed above his ahead, and swords and bayonets clashed.

Life ebbed, creeping away into nothing.

'Captain! Captain!'

21

Ellen moved from man to man, and each time she knelt down beside another she prayed it would not be Paul. They were all so bloody and mud-stained she could not tell until she was close. This was hell on earth. So many men. So many wounded, and for every man here, they were saying there was a dozen left on the field.

Please, God! Please, God! Her mind called a constant prayer that Paul was safe.

'Would you like water?' She knelt beside another man. The lower half of his leg had been torn off by cannon fire. The rags he lay on and his clothes were covered in dried blood. The doctor had stopped the bleeding with a tight tourniquet around the man's thigh, but he would need the upper limb amputated, he may have survived the battle and die from infection in a day or two.

Nausea twisted through the knots in Ellen's stomach.

She would hold Paul so tightly when he came back and love him even more.

He nodded, a look of terror hovering in his gaze. The man's

skin was starkly pale beneath the stains of gunpowder, mud and blood, and his eyes were whiter from blood loss. She smiled, trying to ease his fear, though she was terrified herself. She filled the ladle in the bucket with water and held it to his lips, letting it trickle into his mouth. He caught the ladle with both hands and drank more thirstily. She refilled it and let him drink again. Then he sighed and lay back, closing his eyes.

As she stood, to offer the next man water, a surgeon waved her over. 'I need bandages. Have we more bandages?'

The women had been ripping up sheets for hours and she rushed now to fetch some of the strips that were left; there were not many.

Paul's image was constantly in her mind, as her heart continued praying for his safety.

She handed the bandages to the doctor and watched him wrap them about a wound he had just removed a bullet from. Behind her, another man was brought into the room, shouting out in agony. The doctor looked at her. 'Carry on here.'

'*Tie a tourniquet,*' Paul had said months ago, when she had mourned a single highwayman. She could not have imagined this then.

22

When it was dark, the sounds of cannons suddenly ceased.

Everyone helping in the house in which she worked stopped and looked at one another as the world fell silent apart from the groans of the men in the room. Her heart skipped a beat. *Was it over? Had the Allied forces won? Was Paul alive?*

But she had no time for such thoughts – the men here needed help, and more wounded came every minute.

It was very late at night when an uninjured rider raced through the city gate. 'Napoleon is defeated!' he shouted repeatedly as he rode. Ellen rushed to look from the window, as did all the women in the house as people cheered in the street. Even the wounded men lying on the street, waiting to be moved to houses, hollered with joy.

Ellen's heart filled with hope.

'Back to work, ladies,' a doctor called. 'These men need us.'

The first light of dawn showed on the horizon when Ellen heard the footsteps of the first regiment marching back into the city. She looked from the window; it was not the 52nd.

Numerous times she rushed to the window to see another

regiment arrive, to the cheers and applause of the occupants of Brussels. None were the 52nd, and each regiment brought more wounded with them.

She asked soldiers who were brought into the house for wounds to be cleaned and bandaged if they knew where the 52nd were. But the numbers of men fighting were so many, no one she asked had seen or knew the fate of the 52nd Oxfordshire Regiment of Foot.

'Mrs Harding, go and rest.' Ellen turned to face Mrs Beard. She was the wife of a Colonel from another regiment. It was her house that had become a makeshift hospital in the last four and twenty hours, like a dozen more along the street.

Now Ellen wished she had socialised more during their time in Brussels. Not at the parties but among the officers' wives.

She had judged all the women by those who'd fled, but now she had discovered another society. These women were also resolutely waiting for their men, while fighting to save those who had served beside them.

'You have done enough now, and you will only be able to do more if you sleep.'

Ellen looked at the woman. There were no beds left in the house and there was no space to rest. If she was to sleep, she would have to go back to the lodgings she shared with Paul – *perhaps he would be there, waiting for her.* She had not even thought of that. 'Yes. I will return when I can.' She turned away to fetch her pelisse, leaving Mrs Beard to help the wounded man she had been attending.

Ellen's heart pounded hard as she hurried through the streets full of men in filthy and bloody uniforms. As she opened the front door, though, she knew he was not within. She did not feel him here. Desolation struck her, and with it came the exhaustion from the hours she had worked.

Too tired to stand anymore, she climbed the stairs to their bedchamber, and washed her hands and face in the warm water that had stood in the jug for days. She took off her pelisse but did not lie on the bed; instead she took up her vigil on the window seat, clutching her knees. Her head rested against the windowpane as sleep crept closer.

She woke to the sound of someone knocking on the door below the window, her body jolting awake. She stood hurriedly. But it could not be Paul. Paul would not have knocked.

She heard a man's pitch. Outside she saw a horse and two men in the uniform of the 52nd. In an instant she was running from the room.

When she opened the door, the lieutenant colonel stood before her. Behind him the two soldiers stood beside his horse. They all looked weary. Even though she had never liked the lieutenant colonel, compassion burned in her chest. 'What is it?' she asked. 'Where is my husband? Where is Paul?'

She saw the answer in his eyes before he spoke. 'Captain Harding died on the field.'

'*No!*' The word was screamed; she was unsure if it was aloud or in her head. '*No!*' She would not believe. She could not... Darkness crowded in on top of her, stealing her vision, then she dropped.

When Ellen woke she was lying on her bed. The lieutenant colonel was sitting beside her, while the two men dressed in the uniform of Paul's regiment stood across the room with Mrs Peeters. The room stank of burning feathers. The lieutenant colonel held her hand and rubbed the back of it with his other. 'Madam...' he said quietly.

Ellen's heart raced as the memory of what had been said rushed back. *How? How had it happened? How would she live?*

'You have no relatives,' the lieutenant colonel said. 'Am I right?'

Ellen nodded. Paul had always insisted they did not speak of her father.

'Have you some money?'

She shook her head. The lieutenant colonel must know Paul's wages had remained unpaid for weeks.

'Do you have anywhere to go then?'

Emptiness and loneliness opened a void inside her. There was not even grief – just an empty space that belonged to Paul.

'You must come with me then, Mrs Harding.'

Ellen looked at him, unable to think. But then her mind filled with the images of the wounded she had seen over the last few hours. 'How did Paul die?'

The lieutenant colonel let go of her hand. 'At the end of the battle the 52nd broke the last surge by the French. In only four minutes of gunfire, I lost one hundred and fifty men. Captain Harding was among them, shot by the French. I believe his death would have been quick.'

She needed to hold Paul – she wanted to feel his strength and warmth, and breathe in the scent of him. But she would never be able to.

'Paul said I am to seek Captain Montgomery's help.'

'I am afraid Captain Montgomery also passed away,' the lieutenant colonel answered.

Cold horror chilled Ellen's chest. So many men dead, and – *Paul*. He was alive in her head, saying goodbye to her, kissing her. *How could he never come back?* His face hovered in her mind's eye, youthful and smiling, alive and elemental...

'Let me take you to my accommodation. Where is your woman? She should pack your things.'

'She left.' Ellen's voice had lost its strength.

'Then I shall find you another. But for now...' He looked at Mrs Peeters. 'Would you pack Mrs Harding's possessions? I will take her with me and send for them later.'

'I shall. I will be happy to help you, Mrs Harding.'

'Come, Mrs Harding. Let me take you under my protection.' He held out a hand.

Ellen rose, but it was in the guise of a ghost. It was not her who moved. She walked outside with him as though she were in a dream – no, a nightmare.

She was leaving the place she and Paul had lived for weeks – their home. She was deserting him. In the street, she looked back, longing to refuse to leave, but if she did not go with the lieutenant colonel, what else would she do? She had no money.

'Let me lift you onto the horse, you need not walk.' The lieutenant colonel's hands embraced either side of her waist, not waiting for her consent. He lifted her onto the saddle, so swiftly, she had to grasp his shoulders. He smelt clean, and she noticed for the first time he was clean. He must have washed and changed his clothes before he had come with his hideous news.

The lieutenant colonel led the horse through the streets himself, at a walk, as Ellen held the saddle's pommel and tears flowed down her cheeks. The two soldiers walked beside her, at either side of the horse, making this an odd sort of procession.

When they reached the house which she and Paul had visited several times over their weeks in Brussels, he lifted her down, his eyes asking questions he did not speak. When he did not release her waist, she stepped away, pushing his hands off her, her emotions in turmoil.

'Forgive me,' he said. The front door was opened by a

servant. The lieutenant colonel held back, his hand gesture encouraging her to enter first. 'Find the maid and ask her to help Mrs Harding,' he told the servant. 'She is to stay.'

'You may go,' he told the soldiers who had accompanied him.

He led Ellen into the drawing room where she had stood with Paul when they had attended a dinner or a party here. Memories wrapped about Ellen's heart, strangling it with pain. She did not believe he was gone. The lieutenant colonel spoke, but she did not hear what he said as he moved to pour a drink; she could think of nothing but Paul now.

When the maid came, after only a few minutes, Ellen went willingly, following her upstairs to a room at the rear of the house. It was a small suite of two rooms. A sunny sitting room decorated in pink, with a door into the bedchamber beyond it.

'May I do anything to help you, or fetch you anything, ma'am?'

'No. You may go.' Nothing could bring Paul back, and that was all she needed.

When the maid had gone, Ellen walked into the bedchamber, climbed on to the bed, crawled into the middle, curled into a ball, and wept, with her knees hugged tightly to her chest as her heart broke.

23

Ellen stared at the window. She had remained in this room, on this bed, watching the sun travel across the sky, then the moon rise, and now the sun was appearing again. She must get up and return to those who were wounded. That was what Paul would wish her to do, he had told her at the Duchess of Richmond's ball to think of other men.

She rose from the bed, still clothed. She had neither eaten nor undressed since arriving here.

A sharp knock struck the door of the sitting room beside her bedchamber. It was not the maid, the maid would have knocked on the narrow servants' door that opened into that room.

'You may come in!' she called as she walked into the sitting room.

When the door opened, it was the lieutenant colonel. He stepped into the room.

Instinctively, Ellen took a step back.

He raised a hand as Ellen might have done to soothe a

horse. 'Mrs Harding, I have come to see how you are. The maid said you have not eaten…'

'I am as well as I might be. I am returning to care for the wounded today. I was helping in Mrs Beard's house. She has taken some of the wounded in.'

He walked towards her. This time Ellen rejected the instinct to back away; it was rude, when he had been kind enough to give her somewhere to stay.

When he reached her, he took her hand from her side. Ellen recoiled, she could not prevent the reaction, she was too heart-sore for Paul. She did not want the touch of anyone else, but his clasp firmed and would not release her, though it was not painful.

'My dear Mrs Harding, you should not leave the house, not yet. I refuse to allow it. You are in shock, and suffering grief. It is not sensible for you to go to help others. For now, you must look after yourself, I insist upon it. I cannot allow you to go. You must stay here and let me care for you.'

What could she say? She had no heart or will to argue. Her spirit just wished to curl up in a ball and be with Paul. Tears filled her eyes, clouding her vision, then spilling onto her cheeks, rolling downwards in a trickle to drip from her chin. He released her hand so she might wipe them away.

The lieutenant colonel's arm came about her. He led her to the small sofa and sat beside her. 'You must not distress your-self, I shall protect you now. You may stay with me for as long as you wish and I will keep you safe.'

Ellen nodded, wiping away more tears. She felt uncomfort-able with him, but she had nowhere else to go. She needed somewhere to stay.

'Let me send up some food to tempt you to eat, and I shall buy you some pretty dresses to cheer you.'

'I do not need them...'

'But you should have them. You should have beautiful things. I have hired a lady's maid for you, one who knows how to style a woman and such. I shall send her to you now so she might help you change. Then would you come downstairs and eat your breakfast with me?

'No.' Ellen's answer was vehement. She could not sweep Paul aside and dress and dine... She looked at the lieutenant colonel and said more quietly, realising perhaps she had been disrespectful, 'No, thank you, I would rather remain alone...' She left a pause after her words, a pause asking him to leave her now.

He stood, bowed, lifted her hand from her lap and her fingers to his lips, pressing a kiss there. When his head lifted and he straightened, his gaze looked deep into her eyes. 'Believe me, Mrs Harding, I shall do my utmost to make you happy.'

He gave her a stiff nod, before letting her hand fall, and then he turned away.

Discomfort skimmed up Ellen's spine.

Once the door had shut, she returned to the bedchamber and climbed back up on the bed as tears traced a path down her cheeks.

24

The maid the lieutenant colonel had employed stood before Ellen, holding the chamber pot Ellen had recently vomited into. 'But you have been sick almost every morning, ma'am,' she argued against Ellen's protests that it was grief making her ill. 'It is not normal. When did your last bleed come?'

Three weeks had passed since the Battle of Waterloo. Ellen tried to remember, but she had not been able to think properly since Paul's death.

She could not remember. She had been sick a few mornings in the last week of Paul's life too. Before then... Whenever she thought of Paul, an overwhelming pain absorbed her heart and a burning emptiness opened a chasm in her chest.

It was possibly two months since she had bled...

She looked at the woman with bewilderment. Megan had asked a few moments ago, *'Are you with child?'*

'Shall I send for a doctor, ma'am?'

In the first days, every day she sought to leave and help the wounded, and every day Lieutenant Colonel Hillier persuaded her against it. Then she had become increasingly listless with nothing to do but think of Paul, and she had not even tried to leave her rooms.

She had cried so many tears there seemed none left within her. Yet she thought the emptiness inside her would never leave. *A child? Paul's...* Was she carrying a part of him inside her? He might live on through her body...

Ellen looked at the woman and nodded.

When the doctor arrived, he pressed her stomach a few times, then looked up and nodded. The verdict was swift. 'You are indeed with child. Have your breasts felt tender?' Ellen nodded, but she had thought that merely a part of her aching heart, and longing for Paul's touch. 'That is all a part of it. I would estimate the child is due in February.'

Ellen's hand lay on her stomach as she sat upright. *A child.*

The doctor watched her. 'Who should I look to for my fee?'

Since the battle, with so many men lost, and so much debt dying with them, she had heard from the maid that no trades accepted credit.

'You must speak to the lieutenant colonel,' Ellen answered. He had supported her since the battle. He had bought her the new dresses she did not want, and sent the best food up to her rooms, though she ate little more than a couple of spoonfuls.

'Is the child his?'

A blush rose through Ellen's skin as she looked with disgust at the doctor. 'Of course not. My husband is... was a captain in his regiment... He died during the battle.'

'And you are living with the lieutenant colonel now...' His words carried judgement as though it was wrong for Lieutenant Colonel Hillier to help her.

But he was being kind to her...

'Very well.' The doctor turned away and Megan followed, to escort him downstairs.

A child... The thought grew like a planted seed in her heart. Her fingers spread over her stomach. Paul was not here but there was another reason to live now. *A child.*

She thought of telling Paul he was to become a father... The tears she thought had dried up forever flooded her eyes.

* * *

A knock struck the sitting room door.

Ellen climbed from the bed.

Lieutenant Colonel Hillier. She knew his knock; it was always the same. The door opened without her calling as she entered the sitting room.

'Ah, forgive me, I thought you may be sleeping. I wished to know how you fared. I have paid the physician. He says you are with child.' He stared at her, his eyes questioning her as they had always done.

A shiver spun up Ellen's spine – his stares still unnerved her. But she ignored it. It was just his way. She was used to it now.

To hide her discomfort, Ellen clasped her hands before her stomach. She was in awe of the news. *Paul's child grew inside her, even though he had gone.* Jubilance, fear and love filled her heart in equal measures.

'You need not fear,' Lieutenant Colonel Hillier said in a tight voice. 'You may continue to reside with me. I shall keep you, and protect you while you carry the child, and I am willing to look after you once the child is born.'

It had never occurred to her that he may not allow her to stay, because if she did not stay where would she go? Yet she ought not to stay forever. She should apply to Paul's family, and her own, as Paul had asked her to do.

'Will you dine with me tonight, Mrs Harding? You cannot remain in these rooms forever.'

'I will dine with you, yes.' He was right, she had to create a life for her child.

He stared at her, his gaze intense and questioning, then turned away and left the room.

He was a difficult man to understand, and yet he was being kind to her, taking her in and protecting her. *'Any of the officers would help you, you may appeal to any of them,'* Paul had said when he had told her what to do before the battle. But he had also told her to look to his father for financial support...

An hour before dinner, a new dress was sent to her rooms. It was a very pale blue, almost the colour of her eyes. The muslin was thin, and very fine, and the white lace that adorned the neck and the hem of the short sleeves was exquisite. It must have cost a good sum; more than Paul could have afforded.

The maid of all work who had delivered it bobbed a curtsy. 'Ma'am, Lieutenant Colonel Hillier said he wishes you to wear the dress tonight, so you might look pretty when you dine with him.' The girl looked at the floorboards, not at Ellen, with a blush rouging her cheeks.

'Say thank you to Lieutenant Colonel Hillier,' Ellen replied, bluntly.

She had no desire to dress prettily. She did not feel like dining with him or even eating. She walked within a nightmare that would not end. Perhaps, in a moment she would wake, and Paul might walk through the door, come to take her home. She imagined the kiss he would give to her. Her soul ached desperately for him.

As her ladies' maid helped her dress for dinner, Ellen was silent, allowing it, not really thinking or focusing, and then she sat before the mirror not at all aware of what the maid did with her hair.

'There, ma'am. The lieutenant colonel will be waiting.' Megan stepped back, admiring her work. Ellen did not even look at the mirror. She turned away, a dark fog surrounding her as she left the room.

It was the first time she had gone beyond the door of her sitting room since coming here. It was odd; everything felt surreal and out of place. She lived with a stranger here – she was a stranger to herself.

Her fingers ran along the oak banister as she walked down-stairs. Two footmen waited in the hall; neither of them looked at her but at the polished floorboards near her feet. One opened the door leading into the dining room.

A sharp sudden pain pierced Ellen's breast.

The last time she had entered this room, it was with her hand on Paul's arm, and the last time she had sat at the table was when she had been beside Paul. She heard his voice as he talked animatedly with his peers, while she had been absorbed watching his expressions, not following the men's conversation.

Tears distorted her vision as she walked to the table. She blinked them away.

Lieutenant Colonel Hillier stood. 'Let me draw out a chair for you.' He slid back the chair next to the one he had risen from at the head of the table.

She looked at the chairs she and Paul had previously occu-pied at the lower end of the table as she walked past, her heart aching for him.

'Do sit,' Lieutenant Colonel Hillier said, ignoring any evidence of her distress.

Ellen bit her lip and swallowed several times, fighting tears.

She shut her eyes to dispel them, but as she did so, she saw Paul, smiling at her.

She opened her eyes again and took the seat Lieutenant Colonel Hillier held out for her. She thought of Paul doing the same on their wedding night.

'The dress looks very beautiful upon you.' He sat too.

Ellen looked up and nodded. 'Thank you.'

'You are a very remarkable woman, but I am sure you are aware of that.'

She did not know how to answer.

'Do you like my gift?'

Ellen nodded again, feeling dazed. 'Yes, thank you.'

'I picked the colour because it is so like your eyes; though I think no man-made colour could match their quality...'

Again, Ellen did not know what to say.

He looked at the servants. 'Go ahead then, serve.'

A footman came forward to serve her soup, then filled her glass with wine.

Ellen ate. The oxtail soup was warm, sweetened, and full of flavour. She was not hungry but she ate now for the child's sake.

When she had finished the soup, the footman took the bowl from in front of her, then the lieutenant colonel reached across the table and his hand lay over hers as it had rested on the table. The sensation made her jump. She had forgotten to wear gloves. How foolish!

He had been speaking of something, and she had not listened. She could not put her thoughts in any order to hold a conversation.

She thought of the white satin gloves Paul had bought her for the Richmond ball. Where were they? Then she remembered the lieutenant colonel saying he had disposed of the items left behind at her former residence... She had not cared in that moment; she had not been able to take in what that had meant – all of Paul's possessions were gone. The lieutenant colonel had disposed of her clothes, and all the things that would have reminded her of moments with Paul, without her permission.

I should be wearing black... The thought struck her with horror.

She looked at Lieutenant Colonel Hillier. 'I should be wearing black. I am in mourning.' How ridiculous not to even remember something so simple. But why had he not remembered? Why had he bought her colourful dresses?

'Would you purchase me blacks?' Her words rang about the silent room. His gaze searched and questioned again.

'Of course.'

The hand that lay on top of hers became heavier. She pulled hers from beneath it.

'Ellen.' She had not given him permission to use her given name, and yet she was too tired and hurt too much to care to correct him. 'I think much of you. You are a charming woman. I have always thought so. I can be patient. You need not worry. I understand you are grieving for your husband, and I shall allow you to do so...'

Ellen nodded. 'Thank you.' She wished to return to her rooms, to cry over Paul. There were too many memories of eating with him here crowding into her head.

She did not ask to withdraw though; it would be too rude, when he had been kind enough to give her a place to stay and food and clothing. So she remained at the table, picking at her food, and eating what little she was able while he watched her, smiling and talking, as though the woman beside him did not have a broken heart.

She did not listen; her mind was too absorbed with memories of Paul.

* * *

Ellen sat at a small desk in the sitting room, a quill in her hand.

A week had passed since she had discovered she was with child, and now, the lieutenant colonel had received orders to go to Paris.

Napoleon had given himself up on the 15th of July, in the process of trying to escape to America.

The 52nd were to follow the Prussian army across France as part of the Allied forces, ensuring the peace they had fought so hard for, and so many had died for, lasted.

Ellen stared at the blank sheet of paper.

Paul had said, '*Write to my father,*' if he died. But she did not know what to say. The army administrators would have written and told him Paul was dead.

A sharp pain cut into her chest, the pain that could still not believe those words.

What to write? *My name is Ellen, you do not really know me, but we did meet last summer, I am your deceased son's wife.* Every word she thought of sounded so much like begging. And she could not bring herself to write the word deceased anyway.

My Lord,

She began. The nib of the quill hovered over the paper.

Paul asked me to write to you, and seek your help, should he...

The words halted as a tear dropped onto the paper, then she wrote.

...die. I am to move to Paris with his regiment. I thought I should do as he said and let you know I am with child.

There was no more to say.

Yours sincerely, Eleanor Harding, your daughter-in-law.

She had met Paul's father when he had come to the house party with Paul. She had no idea if the man thought kindly of her. Paul had said very little about his father following their marriage.

Ellen understood that now. Her sisters' images crept through her thoughts. Her father's house was another world, they would never be able to imagine this one. She would have nothing to speak to them about.

Still, Paul had told her to write, and he seemed confident the Earl would help her.

Having folded and sealed that letter, Ellen began another, to her father.

Father, I do not know if you have heard, but Paul died in the battle of Waterloo.

Again tears ran over and spilled onto the page.

His Lieutenant Colonel is taking me as far as Paris. But I have nothing of my own, no money or items left. Would you send me the money for a passage home? I am with child. Yours affectionately, Eleanor.

Surely her father would know how hard things were here. Surely he would understand and help.

Once she'd addressed both letters she took them down to the hall. Lieutenant Colonel Hillier had said he would send her letters through the army packets.

He was there. He came from the drawing room as her foot left the bottom step of the stairs.

'Ellen.'

'These are the letters I spoke of,' she said quietly.

'Take them,' he said to a footman, who immediately moved forward to lift them out of her hand.

Lieutenant Colonel Hillier gave Ellen a stiff slight bow, his hands clasped behind his back. Then he straightened and met her gaze. 'Will you take tea with me?'

It would be impolite to refuse. 'If that is what you wish.'

'It is. Come then.' He lifted a hand, encouraging her to join him in the drawing room, while looking at the butler to fulfil the order for tea to be delivered.

When Ellen entered the room his hand momentarily touched her lower back as she passed him. A prickle ran across her skin, but she ignored it.

'Do sit.' He lifted a hand, directing her to one of the two soft chairs in the sunshine pouring through the window which looked out onto the garden.

Brushing her dress beneath her to stop the black calico creasing, she did as he said.

He took the seat opposite her. 'Your maid said your sickness has eased a little...'

'Yes.'

'And do you feel any better in yourself?'

No. She still missed Paul, like there was a burning hole

within her. 'I am able to think a little easier now. But I shall always miss my husband.'

He was silent, his eyes looking into hers, with unspoken questions. Then he sighed. 'Yes, I suppose you shall.' He leaned forward and held her hand. It was a habit he had formed, holding her hand on many occasions without asking her permission. She wanted to pull it away, but it was not within her to be rude. He lifted it. A shiver stirred across her skin as he pressed his warm lips against her glove. The grandfather clock in the corner of the room ticked through the seconds his lips remained on her glove, and her skin crawled with invisible insects.

Why did he not let go? Everything like this he seemed to do for a little too long. After a minute, or two, he released her hand.

She clasped her hands together in her lap, unable to meet his gaze, but he reached out and touched her chin. 'I know you are hurting, Ellen, I understand that, and I shall be here for you.'

His hand fell.

'Ah, here is our tea.' He turned to look at the maid as she carried it in. She was blushing as she set the tray down.

'Will you pour, Ellen?'

She did so.

She had lived in a sheltered safe world in her father's home, and then she had lived an ever-changing, unsettled life with Paul, but now... Now she did not know where she stood... What life should be, or could be...

25

PARIS, FOUR MONTHS LATER

Ellen had heard nothing from either her father or Paul's, yet she still looked at the post that arrived for the lieutenant colonel daily.

The months since the battle of Waterloo had passed slowly. She still lived with the lieutenant colonel, because she had no money and nowhere else to go.

He had hired a private carriage for her when the regiment marched to Paris and paid for her lodgings so she need not live among the men.

She supposed the lieutenant colonel paid for her keep out of the sum he had made by obligingly disposing of all of hers and Paul's possessions, before she had been sound enough of mind to even think about what to do with Paul's belongings. Perhaps if she had sold them, she could have paid for a passage home.

But some of his things she would have kept.

She missed the dress coat he had removed and left behind on the last evening most. The one which he'd worn to the Richmond ball. It would have held his scent.

Tears came into her eyes; they still did every time she thought of him, and she thought of Paul a dozen times a day. But how could she forget?

Paris was just as mad as Brussels had been before the war; flooded with British tourists. They had flocked to the city as though everyone wanted to claim it for themselves, as though they were the ones who had won the battle.

Ellen had no patience or time for any of them, and of course she had no husband to escort her to events, so she did not attend any of their lavish entertainments, not even the theatre.

She was uncomfortable about Lieutenant Colonel Hillier keeping her, but what other option did she have? Paul had been owed his wages too, so there must be money that was hers by right too. Was the lieutenant colonel also spending the salary Paul was owed to keep her here?

She looked left and right along the street, waited for a carriage to pass, then crossed. Megan followed.

Ellen had not seen Jennifer, her former maid, in Paris. Nor any of the women she had met in Brussels.

Unlike in Brussels, Lieutenant Colonel Hillier did not host dinners or entertainments, and at times, Ellen felt guilty because she thought it was in deference to her. But he had never spoken of dinners, or dances, or even card parties, and she had never asked why not.

In the evenings she dined with him, but beyond that she saw very little of him. More often than not, once they had eaten, he went out, and during the day he was out on business.

For many weeks he had been forever kissing her hand and offering compliments, but in the last few weeks, he had done so less. At times he even seemed to be impatient or angry, but he never said anything that implied his irritability was directed at her. His conversation had become more abrupt, though, and he seemed less tolerant of her desire to spend her time in her bedchamber and not downstairs.

'Megan.' Ellen turned and waited for her maid to catch her up as she reached the gates of the Tuileries Gardens.

They walked out every day, sometimes twice a day, because sitting in the house became too oppressive, and she would reach a point she wished to escape the silence and the walls about her.

She lived for her child. For Paul's child. She was only eating and breathing for his son or daughter. Between her thoughts of Paul, her mind filled with images of what his child might look like, and she longed for it to be a boy who would look like him.

She walked a full circle about the gardens. Though shrubberies looked bleak now the December frosts had withered the last of the greenery.

It was nearly a year since she had married Paul. It seemed a lifetime ago. Had she ever been that naïve girl? She'd been little more than a child then, so sheltered from the real world.

After an hour, Ellen walked back to Lieutenant Colonel Hillier's house. She could never call it home. It would never feel like home. Nowhere would ever feel like a home again without Paul.

As she neared the house, two of the officers from the regiment came out... Paul's comrades! She hurried to reach them, her heart leaping with an odd sense of being close to Paul again. They wore the same uniform he had worn.

'Captain Smith!' she called out, lifting her hand and waving a greeting. 'Captain Vickers!'

Captain Smith looked at her first. She was about fifteen or so yards away from them. He stared at her for a moment, his eyes widening, but then he turned to Captain Vickers and said something without acknowledging her. Captain Vickers looked over and his expression twisted with a look of disgust.

They looked away and walked on, their backs to her.

Ellen broke into a slight run, one hand clasping beneath the bulge of the child in her stomach, the other lifting the skirt of her dress a little. 'Wait!' She had no idea what she wished to say to them, but it suddenly seemed so important. They were a link to Paul when she had no other.

'Wait!' Ellen cried again, hurrying after them, leaving Megan behind her.

They did not stop, ignoring her cries and her presence.

When she caught them up, her fingers gripped the sleeve of Captain Smith's scarlet coat at his elbow. 'Will you not stop and speak with me? Please—'

He stopped walking and faced her, revulsion in his eyes. 'Madam, I have nothing to say to a woman such as you. I admit I was surprised by the news, as I am sure Captain Harding would have been. He would be disgusted. But there is no going back. Good day.' He turned away. As did Captain Vickers.

Ellen did not understand. She stood in the street, lost, as they walked on and then turned the corner. *Surprised by what news... Why would Paul be disgusted...* What did he mean? '*A woman such as you.*' A widow?

When she walked into the hall of Lieutenant Colonel Hillier's house she took off her bonnet and cloak, then her gloves, and passed them all to a footman, as Megan left the hall via the servants' door.

'Is Lieutenant Colonel Hillier home?'

'Yes, ma'am.'

'Where?'

'The lieutenant colonel is in the drawing room, ma'am.'

As she walked towards the door of the drawing room, the servant rushed past her to open it. 'Lieutenant Colonel, Mrs Harding.'

There were empty glasses by the decanters where the men had shared a drink, and a quill, ink and paper stood on a desk across the room, where the lieutenant colonel stood.

He came towards her, his hands out as if to take hers. 'Ellen, this is a charming surprise.'

'I have just seen Captain Smith, and Captain Vickers leave.'

The tone of her voice stopped him a few feet away from her. 'Yes, they were reporting to me about—'

'I do not care why they were here, what I am concerned about it is that they would not speak with me. Why would they not speak with me? They implied I have done something wrong...' Creases of confusion caught in Ellen's brow.

'Ellen...' His pitch became placating as if he talked to a child, and he stepped forward and clasped her hands.

She pulled them free.

'Why would they not speak? What have I done wrong? They said Paul would have been disgusted. Why?' Her last words erupted on a bitter whisper.

'There is no need for such distress, Ellen. I have said I shall take care of you and I shall. You must not worry about what others think...'

'Why would I need to worry about what others think? What do they think?'

'Ellen.' His hands lifted to hold her.

She stepped away; the expression in his eyes was similar to the one she used to see in Paul's eyes when he wanted to go to bed.

She could not stay in this room. 'I shall go upstairs.' She should not stay in this house.

'You do not want to join me for tea?' There was a cajoling, pacifying edge to his words; she did not like the tone.

'No. I am tired. It is the pregnancy. I shall rest.' With that, she left him, still not understanding why Captain Smith and Captain Vickers had refused to speak to her.

'I shall go out then,' he called after her. 'But remember, you are under my roof and you eat my food. You should respect that and respect me!'

She looked back, not knowing how to answer.

'I think much of you,' he said. 'You know that.'

What did he mean? She turned away and climbed the stairs, unwilling to pursue this disturbing conversation.

Before she even reached her rooms, she heard the front door close behind him.

* * *

When the dinner hour came, the lieutenant colonel had not returned to the house. All Ellen felt was relief; she did not want to see him this evening. She ate with Megan in her room, because Megan was the closest person she had to a friend.

They ate and talked, avoiding the subject of the scene in the street with Paul's fellow officers.

Immediately afterwards, Ellen asked Megan to help her undress so she could retire. Then she lay in bed, in the half-light of late evening, her hands holding the prominent bump in her stomach, cradling her child. If only Paul had lived... Her mind circled, think of ways to escape this house – to find a way to get home alone.

Lieutenant Colonel Hillier had promised her for weeks that

he would escort her when the regiment returned to England. She did not believe it was true anymore. But how would she find the money to travel? She dared not mention the possibility of leaving to Megan, in case she mentioned something to the other servants. But if she left, she should leave with Megan as her companion.

Sometimes sleep was difficult, but tonight it came quickly, despite her tumultuous thoughts.

She woke when it was still dark. There was a noise below, a candlestick, statue or vase, or something else heavy had been knocked from a mantle or table. 'Pick it up!' A low-pitched bark ran through the house.

Lieutenant Colonel Hillier was back and drunk by the sounds of it, yelling at his servants. It was not the first time she had heard him return in such a state, though she had never seen him in his cups. She never went outside her rooms once she had retired, and she certainly would not have walked about the house when he was in this temper.

His footsteps sounded on the wooden stairs as he walked heavily and unsteadily, bumping against the banister, making the iron struts ring.

His rooms were to the right of the house and hers to the left. She listened, expecting him to walk to the right, but his footsteps sounded on the landing, walking towards her room.

Cold fear clasped her stomach as she slid from the bed and rushed to turn the key in the lock of the door, the soles of her bare feet brushing over the cold, unyielding floorboards.

Before she could reach the door to lock it, the handle turned and it opened inwards.

'Lieutenant Colonel.' She spoke in a sharp voice, a voice that said, *get out* even if her lips did not. 'You have no business in my rooms.' Had he made a mistake? Was he too drunk to know where he was? But even as she thought those things she could see he knew what he was doing; his eyes were dark. This was no mistake.

She recalled all the times his stares had made her skin crawl.

'Go to your rooms.' Her voice was strong but she could not find the courage to yell at him; this was his house and she was here under his generosity.

'I think not, Ellen.' He did not sound so drunk now, not so drunk he was incapable – it sounded the sort of drunk that gave a man confidence and silenced his conscience. She had seen the difference in men when she camped with the army.

She stepped back, afraid of the hard intent in his eyes.

'I have a need tonight...' His pitch dropped to almost a whisper, but the bitterness in his tone matched the look in his eyes. 'I refuse to pay for a damned whore when I have a woman here. I desire you. I always have. You act as if you do not know, but you must know, and you have taken my protection and offered me nothing in return.'

No. The word did not come from her lips; shock had frozen her still. She would have backed away further but she could not gather her thoughts.

His hand lifted quickly and his fingers clasped the plait securing her hair. He pulled so hard it tore at her scalp.

'*Please do not...*' She could not say more. The words would not come and her voice was too quiet as fear strangled her.

His grip on her hair only tightened as he leaned forward and attempted to kiss her. She managed to turn her head, even though he held her hair.

'Why must you keep thinking of that man? Can you not appreciate all I have done for you?' He tried again to kiss her, but she turned again.

'You are so beautiful, Ellen. I have always thought you the most beautiful woman I have ever seen. I have been nice to you, kind to you, and bought you gifts and how am I repaid? By a melancholy woman pining for a dead man.'

No. A sob became tangled with a scream in her throat.

'Kneel.' It was a barked order, in the voice she had heard several times when he commanded the regiment.

'*Please, do not do this...*' Her voice was a pathetic whimpering plea.

'I said kneel! You have had everything you wanted, for months! You are under my protection! Do you hear? You owe me. How else will you pay? I want a woman. I want you!'

The servants must be able to hear his bitter shouting; she could not bear the embarrassment. '*Please let me go...*' she whispered, in another quiet plea.

'Enough of your refusals.' The hand that held her hair pulled her down, the pain in her scalp agony. Unless she screamed, she had no choice. But if she screamed, who would come? *He paid the servants.*

She had been brought up not to acknowledge servants. Not to share anything personal with them. She had been close to Pippa, but Pippa had raised her, she was like a second mother. She would have called out to Pippa for help, but no one else... How could she call for Megan? The lieutenant colonel would only hurt her too. If a footman came, what would he do? He was paid to do as this man asked. If a footman helped her, he would be dismissed.

'Kneel, damn you!' Her hair was jerked downwards, her knees gave way and she fell onto the floorboards.

With his free hand, as she overcame the pain of having fallen, the lieutenant colonel undid the two buttons which secured the flap of his breeches, he pulled her hair, forcing her

to rise to her knees, and in the next moment he filled her
mouth as Paul had used to fill the place between her legs.

My God. My God...

Despair reeled through her. She could not breathe...

The shame...

And would be foolish to try to wave at such privacy. He would not see want; but he... He would not sit... him too to keeping a... he... I felt for her to find pathway. Perhaps she should... he... here slowly joining...

She tried her... to move at... well and all.

26

She had prayed for it to end. Prayed to survive...

Now she lay on the floor. He had gone. But she could not make her limbs move and go to her bed.

A part of her did not believe what had happened. She was not certain of anything anymore. How could any man do something so vile? He was a senior army officer. She had trusted him.

He had secured his breeches and said, 'That is done then, Ellen. Thank you. You will not say no to me again.' Then walked away as though he had not just violated her in the cruellest way.

She longed to call for Megan, but she was afraid to admit what had just occurred. It was her fault. Yet the error had not been in the last few moments; in not locking her door, in not having said *no* more firmly and leaving the house. The error had been made months ago when she accepted his help.

Foolish... Foolish! It was foolish to have thought it was safe to accept anything from this man and think there would be no consequence.

Paul would be turning in his grave so many miles away. His body had been sent home to his family. He would be chiding her, too, for giving away the money he had left for her to find a pathway home. She should have left Brussels with Jennifer.

She held her stomach, protecting their child.

Megan's slight knock announced the arrival of Ellen's morning cup of chocolate. As Megan entered the room, Ellen could not look at her, she felt too ashamed. The servants slept in the attic above her room, Megan must have heard.

'I will return in half an hour to help you dress, ma'am,' Megan said, as she did every morning.

'I am feeling too ill to rise,' Ellen replied.

'You have not been sick...' Megan swept forward and pressed a palm to Ellen's brow. 'You do not feel hot, ma'am.' Her hand moved away.

No, she was not ill in the physical sense of the word, but she was sick of life and heart-sore. She missed Paul, and she did not want to rise and keep living today. How could she get up, when she knew what had happened yesterday?

She sipped her chocolate and felt bilious, holding a hand to her mouth. Megan rushed to fetch the chamber pot, and Ellen was sick.

'If you stay in bed, ma'am, should I bring you some toast?'

Ellen nodded and lay back. Her child, Paul's child, needed

her to eat. She turned her head, hiding her face, and the tears, as Megan left.

When Megan returned with the toast, Ellen feigned sleep so she need not speak.

At noon, Megan arrived again, with a luncheon tray. Ellen refused it. She had only eaten four bites of the toast. She would eat for the child tomorrow, but today she had no heart for anything.

Late in the afternoon, there was another slight knock on the door. 'Are you awake, ma'am?' Megan called in a quiet, apologetic voice.

Ellen did not answer.

'Forgive me, ma'am,' she called again, as though she knew Ellen was pretending to be asleep. 'Lieutenant Colonel Hillier has sent me...'

Ellen shut her eyes as her stomach turned, even at the mention of his name. But she knew then, Megan knew, she knew what had happened last night. She knew Ellen was hiding here and pretending to be asleep.

'I have told the lieutenant colonel you are unwell,' Megan continued, speaking on the other side of the door, possibly too embarrassed to enter and look Ellen in the eye. 'He still insists you come down for dinner this evening, ma'am...'

Shock pulled Ellen into answering. 'Then you must tell him, I will not.'

Megan did not quibble or even reply, it was as though that was what she wanted Ellen to say. Ellen heard Megan's footsteps walk away.

A few moments later, there was a much firmer, hard knock on the door.

Oh my Lord. She had not learned; she had not locked the door, but only to allow Megan to enter.

Ellen slid out of the bed and pulled a shawl off a chair near the bed, wrapping it about her shoulders.

'Ellen?' His voice carried the pitch of command. 'May I come in?'

Her stomach spun. If she ran across the room and locked the door, he would hear and possibly open it before she reached it – as he had done last night.

'I am not dressed,' she called back.

There was an odd sound, then a cough.

Ellen prayed he would not come in.

'But you are out of bed...' His voice was now coaxing. 'You cannot be so unwell. It will do you good to come down to dinner, I think, and I require your company.' The last was an order.

Ellen's arms folded over her chest, hugging the shawl about her. She wanted to run. But to where? Her fate might be worse if she was left on the street to beg.

'Do you agree to dine with me?'

She said nothing. Defiant – even though she had no escape.

'Ellen?'

She still did not reply.

'Ellen!'

She knew he would not let her say no.

'Yes.' Her voice was weak.

When Megan returned to help her dress a while later, Ellen did not speak. She could not. She stood like a mannequin and let her maid do what she needed to, dressing her up like doll for their master's games.

Occasionally she caught Megan glancing at their reflections in the mirror. Then her skin would redden as she avoided Ellen's gaze.

Megan knew. The servants serving her tonight would know too.

Her mind returned to the first days she had spent in the lieutenant colonel's house in Brussels – she recalled the fuss he had made purchasing things, walking her through the streets on his horse in that ridiculous procession. She could have walked. She saw the young maid in the house greeting her with constant blushes. Ellen was as certain as the sun would fall and rise, that the maid had known this was always the lieutenant colonel's intent.

He had sold Ellen's possessions so she would have no money, he must have stopped her receiving Paul's back payment of salary. He had not let her leave the house to the help the wounded... If she had gone, Mrs Beard would have helped her, or another of the women.

She closed her eyes. She had thought her naivety left behind in Pembroke Place with her life as the daughter of a duke. But no, she had known nothing of the dangers of the world.

'I am finished, ma'am.'

Ellen opened her eyes, looking at her image in the mirror. Her hair was curled, with ringlets slipping across her shoulders and pinned high, as though she were going to a ball.

Megan did not smile. Nor did Ellen.

As she walked downstairs, her heart pounding like a thumping hammer, Ellen's thoughts raced through the options she had now. She could open the door and run – but she had seen the injured soldiers, on crutches, begging in the streets; if no one helped them, who would help her? She could stay, simply let this happen, and in her mind pretend it was not, biding her time – then one day, surely, she would meet one of the women she had known in Brussels and ask for help. She could also write to her father...

She had written before...

Her feet stilled on the step of the stairs. She had placed the letters to her father and Paul's in the hand of the lieutenant colonel's servant. Were they ever sent?

Cold fear held her shoulders as she walked down the last few steps, her feet heavy and hesitant. The footman who stood beside the dining-room door opened it for her to pass through.

Lieutenant Colonel Hillier stood up as she entered, looking at her, though he had enough self-recrimination to be unable to look her in the eyes. Her back straightened, and her chin tilted upwards, she would not be cowed. If she had to remain here for now, she would not allow him to control her head or her heart – even though she knew he would invade her body again.

She looked at him, directly. Accusing him. Anger flooding her. She hated him, she wished to scream at him, and hit him, claw and scratch.

'Come, sit beside me, Ellen.' His tone sought to charm as he withdrew the chair.

Ellen could not move her feet; the floor had become thick mud.

He beckoned her with his fingers. 'Come, no need to be hesitant.'

The muscles in her jaw tightened with anger. There was every reason to be hesitant.

'I have a gift for you.' He lifted a small square box from the table.

He had still not looked into her eyes, when every other time, it was all he did. His skin was flushed red, she hoped with embarrassment. She knew she had not blushed, she refused to feel embarrassed when it was him at fault.

'I am sorry, Ellen. If I upset you, I did not intend to. But I have been very patient. Come and sit.' His voice changed in depth and strength at the last.

When he said the word sorry he had sounded remorseful, then his pitch had slipped into an order.

He had never intended kindness when he took her from the place she and Paul had called home in Brussels, he had only ever intended this, and slowly, carefully, slyly, he had closed a prison door on her. There would be no escape unless she found someone to help her.

She sat down. Her hand rested on her bump, the child reminding her she had a reason to stay alive – even if it meant enduring this.

'Wine?' He beckoned a footman forward.

Ellen lifted a hand. 'None for me, thank you,' she told the footman. Then she told the lieutenant colonel, 'It only makes my morning sickness worse.' She wanted him to remember she was with child. She wanted his guilt to grow and cut deep.

He reached across and lay the box he held before her. 'It is a little present to say thank you. Open it and let us be happy again.'

The box was made from a black wood, inlaid with a pattern of pale roses, probably made from rosewood. Ellen lifted the lid. There was a little slip of parchment there. He had written upon it, *To my love.*

A shiver tore through Ellen.

Those words had been precious to her when Paul spoke them.

His hand touched her forearm. Ellen jumped. 'Take a look.'

She lifted the parchment, wanting to crush it in her fingers and throw it in the flames of the fire.

Beneath, a little brooch, a blue enamel bird, lay on a bed of blue velvet.

Lieutenant Colonel Hillier stood. 'I thought of your eyes. Let me put it on for you.'

She stood too; she could not bear for him to lean over her.

He picked up the brooch and to her horror slipped one hand into her bodice. 'I would not wish to mark your beautiful skin, Ellen. I will prick my fingers, not your skin, if I am not cautious with the pin.'

With the back of his fingers on her breast he pierced the muslin cloth; bile rose in her throat but she swallowed it back.

Now he had put her in her place and embarrassed her before the footman. Now her skin burned as the footman looked on.

He smiled as her whole body trembled, while he pinned the brooch onto the fabric of her bodice, a little above her nipple.

It took only a moment to secure the brooch, then his hand slid away. 'There. It will brighten up your blacks.'

Ellen retook her seat, as he did. She knew now, the gift had been given to allow him a moment of control. To ensure she would know he could, and would, touch her when he wanted to.

'You need not buy me gifts,' she said in a quiet voice.

'But I wanted to. I wished to thank you.'

She looked at him. 'I do not want your gifts, and I do not want it to happen again. Will you give me your word that it will not?'

He met her gaze for the first time, now he had succeeded in embarrassing and belittling her. 'I cannot promise you that. But I will continue to take care of you, and I shall look after you well.'

'I do not care how well you treat me—'

'Ellen.' He barked her name so loudly she jumped. 'Let us be clear. You have no money, no family, and the titled men you appealed to have shown no interest. You have nowhere to live other than here, and if you live here, in recompense, you will repay me as I choose.' He did not even attempt to speak quietly, so the footman had heard every word.

After dinner, Ellen found a quill, ink and paper, and wrote to her father. Tomorrow, she would go out alone and take the letter to an inn that would transport post. No one would know, and she could send her letters with no money as the recipient was asked for payment. She would not even tell Megan what she was doing. No one could know she was trying to escape.

28

'Madam! You should sit up.' The midwife helping Ellen was a bulldog. She was physically muscular and from the way she spoke, the woman thought she could merely shout at the child to make it come out.

Her grip rough and firm she pulled Ellen to an almost sitting position.

Ellen had been in labour for a day and a half, and exhaustion overwhelmed her, urging her to lie down and give up.

'Madam!'

Ellen closed her eyes as she collapsed back. She was too tired to fight. Too much had happened to her, too many awful things. What was there to fight for?

'Madam!'

She wished to die. Let it all just be over now.

'Madam!' The last was shouted as her next contraction came.

Ellen's fingers clawed into the blood-stained sheet, gripping it tight as she cried out, longing for the one person who could never come – to come to her. 'Paul!' His name came on an agonised cry, not from the pain of labour, but from the pain of her broken heart. It was shattered. She was shattered. 'I cannot...'

'You have little choice, ma'am, the child is within you and it must get out,' the midwife told her bluntly.

'Ahhhhhrrg!' Ellen growled at the woman, baring her teeth.

In that instant she hated Paul for dying, and she hated fate for leaving her to survive alone and seek the help of a man who was cruel. Four more times he had used her mouth as Paul had used her body, urging her to be compliant and allow it. Each time he had been drunk, and each time, the day after, he could not look her in the eye due to his guilt. Though, he would send Megan to insist she came down to dine with him and find some way to belittle and control her.

Each time she had sat at his table feeling – *unclean* – hatred and anger and repulsion. The second time it had happened, she had ask him to take her home to England, or at least to pay for a passage for her. He had refused. He may feel guilty after doing what he did, but not enough to give her the means to leave him.

Life – was cruel. 'Ahhh!' She screamed her pain out into the room.

'Push,' the midwife urged her.

Ellen did not wish to push, or try, or live.

'Madam!' The glare she received when she made no effort at all condemned her. She would be bullied into bearing this child.

Her eyelids fell again, and behind them hiding in darkness she saw Paul's face. He leaned over the bed towards her. 'Ellen.' She heard him speak as his fingers touched her cheek, then brushed her damp, sweat-soaked hair away from her face. 'Ellen, remember how strong you are. You can survive this.'

His image disappeared and she screwed up her eyelids,

crushing them tightly closed as her heart poured out its misery. She was not angry with him; she missed him. She missed him so much. She opened her eyes and he was not there. Of course he was not. But his child was inside her, fighting to live.

'Ahhh!' She pushed.

'That's better, madam, and again.'

Ellen's fingers fisted, clinging onto the sheet as another contraction clasped at her stomach, tightening her muscles in an excruciating hold. She did push, she pushed hard, and she kept pushing, as though pushing might bring sanity back into her life.

'Oh, God!' The blasphemy slipped from her lips as the pressure was suddenly gone. A child's wail filled the air. She was panting, crying and laughing all at once as she looked at the little purple being curled in the midwife's hands.

'Hold your child while I take care of the cord and the afterbirth.' The infant was covered in white slime. Its arms and legs stretched out as the midwife passed the child to her. The child had come early. It was lean and it was a boy. A son. Paul's son.

Tears rolled from her eyes as she held the child to her breast.

29

Ellen watched John sleep. He was more like her than Paul. She had wanted for him to look like Paul, and yet now he was here, it did not matter at all – here he was to love and hold and draw comfort from. 'John.' She said the name she had chosen for her son quietly so not to wake him, with a note of reverence. She had chosen the name because the name John meant the grace of God. He was here with her by the grace of God. Even if he was not made in the image of Paul, he was a little piece of Paul on earth. Someone to live for.

She could not resist. Her fingers reached out and touched his little head, feeling the soft patch on the top.

He was sucking in his sleep, as if he were dreaming of suckling milk from her breast.

He was the most precious treasure she had ever had.

She straightened, rising away from the makeshift cradle she and Megan had created from an open dresser drawer. He had not long been fed. He would sleep a while longer.

She looked at the blank sheet of paper she had left on the small table across the room. She was going to write to her father and ask for his help again. There had still been no word after the letter she had sent a few months ago. She must escape Lieutenant Colonel Hillier, get John away from him, and their only hope of escape was via her father or Paul's. Leaving John to sleep, she sat down before the empty page, picked up the quill and dipped the tip into the ink.

> *Your Grace, Father,*
>
> *I have a child. Paul's child. A son. I am still in Paris, with Lieutenant Colonel Hillier, Paul's superior officer. He has been providing for me, but he cannot do so forever. I want to come home, with my son.*
>
> *I am asking you if you will either come and fetch us or send money for me to make my own way. Will you let me return to you now? I need somewhere safe for John to grow up. Please, father, let me come home.*
>
> *Please give my love to Mama and Penny, Rebecca and Sylvia also.*

At the thought of her sisters Ellen could write no more. They knew nothing of life – of the truth about the world. She said a silent prayer, that her father would receive her letter kindly, and she and John would get away from here and reach England soon. She also prayed that her sisters would experience none of the things she had in the last few months.

She signed the letter...

> *Eleanor.*

She never used her full name now. She had gradually, without even realising it, slipped into anonymity. It hardly mattered after what had happened over recent months, she did not want anyone to know who she was.

She had thought, when she sent her letters just after Paul's death, that Lieutenant Colonel Hillier knew, he had seen the addresses. He would have known the earl was Paul's father, perhaps he had thought the duke *'she appealed to'*, as he had put it, employed her family in the past. If he thought that, he would never imagine the duke was her father.

She wrote a letter to Paul's father too, telling him she had given birth to Paul's son. Then she sealed both letters with wax and addressed them. Her father's she held to her bosom for a moment, willing him to come as she asked.

She picked up her cloak, looking at John. She could not just leave, even though it would not be for long. She turned to the cord and pulled it so it would ring the bell downstairs and call Megan.

It was just past midday, the servants might be dining. But that would be a good time to leave when none of the other servants would be about the house.

It took a few moments for Megan to come. Ellen stood at the bedchamber door, waiting for her, dressed in her cloak, with her gloves and hat on. She was never sure of Lieutenant Colonel Hillier's comings and goings. He was not in the house now, but she had no idea when he would return, she wanted to hurry.

'Megan,' she said when the maid reached the upstairs landing. 'I am going out for a walk.'

'Shall I fetch my—'

'No. It is too soon to take John with us. Would you stay with him, while I walk? I will not go out for long.'

'Of course, ma'am.'

There always seemed to be a tone of pity rather than respect in Megan's voice these days – as though she felt sorry for Ellen.

Smiling her gratitude, Ellen walked past Megan and hurried down the stairs.

None of the footmen were in the downstairs hall, and there were four in the house.

It was the first time she had come downstairs since John had been born and it felt strange to find the place empty. She let herself out of the house and strode quickly along the pavement to reach the inn she knew would take letters and ensure they reached England via the paid coaches.

Then she returned to the security of her room and her son, thanked Megan, and bid her to leave. She pulled up a chair and watched John sleep, love overflowing inside her. It was wonderful to feel love again.

When the clock chimed five times, she was sitting on her bed, with John in her arms, singing to him after his feed.

A firm knock struck the bedchamber door. The sound jolted through her body.

It was the lieutenant colonel. The door knob twisted, but she had learned her lesson, she always turned the key in the lock now.

'You have spent enough time recovering from childbirth,' he called through the wood. 'I expect you to dine with me tonight, and I expect you to wear a pretty dress and not cover your beauty behind those dull black rags. I have allowed you to mourn for long enough.'

Her heart plummeted.

John whimpered in her arms, drawing her thoughts back to him. She held him closer, as love swelled and rocked inside her, like the surges of the sea when she and Paul had sailed to Ostend. She pressed a gentle kiss on his temple. 'I love you…'

She almost expected the tiny living soul in her arms to say it back.

30

Ellen's legs trembled as she walked downstairs. Megan had helped her dress and now was sitting in Ellen's bedchamber minding John.

She wore a pale pink dress, made of very fine muslin. The only part of this she did not mind was giving up her blacks. Now she had John, it was time to leave her mourning for Paul behind.

As she entered the dining room, she saw a box on the table, placed in front of the seat he liked her to use.

For a moment she could not make her legs walk on. Gifts meant payments. She did not want his gifts.

'I bought a new gift for you,' the lieutenant colonel said as she sat, as the footman withdrew the chair for her.

She sat down, staring at the box – it was a silent threat.

'Open it.'

She did not wish to, because she knew it meant he wanted a gift in return.

'Go ahead, Ellen.' His words became snappy, and his tone the one he would use on a parade ground.

He was in a beseeching mood – a dangerous mood.

She complied and opened it, only because when she refused he resorted to violence.

Inside the box rested a string of pearls.

He stood.

She did not.

She remained seated, facing the table; her legs would not have held her up. Her hands shook. She slipped them beneath the table.

As he leaned across her, his breath touched her neck, making the small hairs on her skin rise as they had done from the very first time Paul had introduced her to this man.

She wished she could run. But to where, and what about John? How would they survive without Lieutenant Colonel Hillier's shelter and food?

He slid the pearls about her neck, his fingers brushing her skin as he secured it.

She shivered. It felt as though he had secured a collar about her neck, as though she was his pet, to be secured with a chain. Perhaps a silk chain...

'There, they look perfect against your skin, and your hair, Ellen.' He returned to his seat.

Ellen said nothing.

'Are you not going to thank me?' The pitch of his voice changed from the tone he used when he believed himself to be expressing love, to the one he used when he gave up asking and forced her.

Ellen looked at him. *I hate you.*

He held her gaze, his expression becoming bitter. 'I said, say thank you.'

'I do not need them or want them,' Ellen answered quietly, hoping the footmen would not hear.

'You will be grateful for them.' His pitch lifted in defiance.

Damn you! All the other coarse words she had learned among Paul's men spun through her head. She wished to throw them all at Lieutenant Colonel Hillier... 'Thank you.' She whispered her answer, while she shouted the words *I hate you* in her head.

He looked away and bid the footman, 'Serve the meal.'

No matter her fear, when dinner was served, her stomach growled at the prospect of a proper meal; she had been eating only leftovers, cold meats and cheeses in her room.

The footman filled her plate, then poured her wine. She ate, listening to the lieutenant colonel speak without replying in anything more than words of a single syllable, desperately rushing to finish the meal and return to her room.

He drank constantly, taking a gulp of his wine between nearly every sentence. By the point her glass was empty his had been replenished thrice.

Ellen held her hand up, covering her glass when a footman sought to refill it.

'Let the man pour,' Lieutenant Colonel Hillier barked.

Ellen looked at him, discomfort unravelling in her nerves. 'I do not want more wine, thank you.'

'You are living in my home, if I say have more wine, you will have more wine.'

Embarrassment and anger prickled up Ellen's spine, as she removed her hand. She could not bear the servants hearing his rudeness.

She looked at the remnants of her meal. She was no longer hungry. She placed her knife and fork together, left them on the plate and lowered her hands to her lap as she looked at the unwanted full glass.

'Well, drink it as it has been poured for you,' he said.

The man was obnoxious. She looked up and saw that he had drained another glass and held it up to be refilled. Her stomach tumbled over, unease closing in on her as if the walls of the room were moving inward.

'Drink,' he ordered.

With the servant in the room to watch, she did, uncomfortable to even live within her skin. She would get out of this house.

Sipping only a tiny little taste of wine, she watched him smile, as if pleased. He talked again, between mouthfuls, as Ellen continued sipping her wine and watched him, saying nothing now.

The plates were taken away and dessert presented – a grand statement of meringue and orange jelly. The sweetness was oddly bitter in Ellen's mouth, as across the table she saw Lieutenant Colonel Hillier's glass refreshed again. He was edgy, and irritable, and she was afraid of doing or saying something which would lead to… *No*, she could not think of that nor endure it, not now John was upstairs.

But he had bought her a gift and she knew what that meant. The pearls lay heavily about her neck.

They ate the last course in silence, as the footmen stood back and watched, and while Ellen occasionally took tiny sips of her wine to prevent the lieutenant colonel's anger, he took great gulps and then waved a man forward to refill his glass.

Ellen longed for somewhere she felt safe. That had been her father's house for most of her life, and then it had been anywhere with Paul. Now there was nowhere.

When she set her spoon and fork down on the plate, he took another large swig of wine.

He was fortifying himself – building up courage.

Either that or he simply wished to be in his cups within the hour.

Ellen shut her eyes, searching for ideas – how to escape…

Once he had finished his dessert he let his cutlery drop sharply on the plate with a metallic clink against the porcelain, then looked at the footman. 'Clear this.'

Immediately, the footman moved and removed the used porcelain from the table.

Ellen counted down the minutes in her head to the moment it may not seem too early to leave, and when she went up to her rooms she would lock the door.

As the footman walked from the room, Ellen swallowed and stood. 'I shall leave you to your port.'

'No.' The answer was sharp. 'Shut the door,' he called after the footman.

Ellen froze, her heart kicking into a rhythm of panic.

'Sit.' It was an order.

She did so as the door clicked shut.

Lieutenant Colonel Hillier stood and walked across to his decanters, then poured some port into a glass.

The sound of Ellen's heartbeat pounded in her ears as well as pulsing through her blood.

He did not speak but turned and looked at her. It was a look of avarice – want.

'You know I love you, Ellen. I always have, and I have tried to make you love me, but I believe you will never let the ghost of Captain Harding rest. He seems to hover over us. I am bored with it. My patience has run dry. I have given you much, and you have given me very little in return.'

He came towards her, his fingers pressing on her shoulder to keep her seated when she would have stood. His fingers tucked a lock of her hair back behind her ear, then he held her chin and raised her head. 'Such a pretty face. I was envious of Captain Harding on the first day he introduced you. You are the grand prize, Ellen...'

She was just a woman, like any other. Or perhaps not like any other – after the things he had done to her.

'Do you not think you owe me more?' he asked in a quiet voice, that terrified her more than his orders.

He set his glass down on the pristine, starched white table-cloth beside her, then he bent.

As she realised he intended kissing her, she turned her head away.

His lips brushed her cheek.

'Not good enough, Ellen.' His hands held her head on either side, so she could not turn. It was what he did when he did that unspeakable thing. 'I have waited while you mourned, but you have had long enough. Now I want to be kissed.' His lips pressed against hers, hard and firm.

It was not with love... It was not love... It was nothing like Paul's kiss.

When he would have pushed his tongue into her mouth, she bit her lips and pulled back against his grip.

He freed her and straightened, staring down at her. For a moment he just stared.

She remembered all those times he had watched her when Paul had been alive. Had he been thinking of this then? Had he been planning this from the moment Paul had died?

'You know, Ellen, you have a choice. You can be my mistress and I shall continue to keep you. Or you may take your son and go and walk the streets, and perhaps become the mistress of a hundred different men to earn enough to feed and keep your son...'

She looked to the ceiling and prayed for help. *What can I do?*

'What is your choice?' he urged.

She did not speak. He could not really expect her to choose to be his mistress...

'If you stay with me now, Ellen. I expect you to be compliant. You must do all that I ask of you... Is that understood?'

She had a child upstairs. A child who needed a roof to sleep under, and she needed to eat to be able to feed him. It was icily cold beyond the door... She could not take her son out there.

'Shall we try this again, Ellen?' He did not even wait for her answer. He knew her answer could only be acceptance. His palms pressed against either side of her face. 'Open your mouth.' His words were spoken over her lips, hot and scented of wine. She closed her eyes and complied. His tongue slid into her mouth, making her feel sick with hatred and dread, and her body shivered with disgust.

He moved away. 'I said you must be compliant, Ellen. I also meant you must participate.'

No.

Tears burned in her eyes as his tongue pressed back into her mouth. She moved her own tongue, not in a caress, she felt too bilious, but just in answer... *How has my life come to this?*

One of his hands left her face and touched her breast.

* * *

Ellen lay curled on her bed in the dark. When the lieutenant colonel had left her in the downstairs drawing room, having taken what he wanted, she had run to the only place she could, to her room and her son. There she had used a bowl of water and flannel to wash her whole body clean. She still felt dirty inside.

The Commandments she had been forced to read over and over the day she had eloped with Paul, ran through her head... *Thou shalt not commit adultery...* She was an adulteress now. He had a wife in England. She would go to hell, but not willingly.

Yet her first sin had been her joy. Was this payment for that? *Honour thy father and mother.*

What could she do?

How could she have let this happen and done nothing?

How could she leave without money or possessions?

What am I to do?

Tears had run down her cheeks the whole time Lieutenant Colonel Hillier had touched her, and when he had done what Paul had done, she had sobbed aloud until he told her to be quiet. Then she had bitten her lip and wept silently.

'Ma'am... Forgive me, ma'am.' A very gentle tap knocked on the bedchamber door. Megan. Ellen sat up, wiping the tears from her cheeks. 'May I come in, ma'am?'

Ellen rose and walked to the door to turn the key and let her in. 'What is it?'

'May I come in and speak with you?' she whispered, her voice shaky.

'Of course.' Ellen stepped back, letting her into the room, then locked the door behind her.

'I thought... I want to say...'

'Please speak, Megan.'

She drew in a long deep breath, then spoke as she breathed it out. 'Ma'am, if you do not wish for another child. I can show you things you may do to help. There are no guarantees, but... I thought...'

Ellen stared at her, a fire of embarrassment flaring beneath her skin. But then perhaps what had happened had happened to Megan too if she knew such things.

'Do you want me to tell you?'

'Yes...' Ellen agreed; to become pregnant by that man would be unbearable.

'Then we must act, because if you are to do something to prevent it, you must do so now.'

31

Ellen picked up one of the small wooden horses and trotted it across the rug she knelt on beside John. Her tongue clicked against the bridge of her mouth, making a clip clop sound to make him giggle. John was sitting upright beside her watching this odd game that she had invented. He loved looking at the horses pass in the street, so she had begged the colonel for some money to be able to buy things for John and had asked a wood carver in the market to make these horses. Of course, there had been a price...

After the battle of Waterloo, she saw wounds stitched to hold the skin together so it might heal. John was the stitches in her heart. She only lived for moments with him. And these hours, when they played together and he laughed at her silliness, were her most precious; she could pretend the rest of her life did not exist.

The wood carver was mostly making items for the tourists who still hung around Paris like a swarm of locusts, invading every part of life and devouring any souvenir they could find. Every day she walked through the streets, hoping to see a face she knew to be able to ask for help, but she had not met anyone. She refused to give up hope of escape, though.

'Ball.' John's gaze reached past the horses to the leather ball they had played with earlier. John turned onto his hands and knees, and set off for it at a fast crawl. Her heart flipped as she watched him. She had never thought it possible to love anyone so utterly.

When he reached it, he pushed it towards her as best he could.

Ellen reached for it, her smile broad, and rolled the ball back to him, following it at a crawl. She nudged the ball against him, tipping him backwards, then caught him up in her arms and blew a loud kiss on his cheek so it would tickle and make him laugh. His laughter was the most beautiful sound, like water running over rocks in a stream, or a wave washing over pebbles on the seashore.

'Mama.' He pushed at her, saying stop. He had a stubborn streak, and a strength of will like his father's.

She did stop, smiling and brushing back his black hair, looking into eyes the colour of her own. 'I love you.' She picked up the ball and tossed it upwards. He looked up, watching it with a smile; her heart ached with happiness.

When it landed, he crawled off to collect it and bring it back for her to throw again.

Clunk. Clunk.

She stopped still.

That was the front door knocker.

'John,' she called in a low voice, urging him back to her.

Lieutenant Colonel Hillier was not at home. If it was someone calling for him, they would be turned away. But even so, her instinctive reaction was always to keep John close in this house, where she felt as though Megan was the only person she could trust.

Lieutenant Colonel Hillier's unpredictable nature kept her constantly fearful. Sometimes he was aggressive, or unbearably polite and gentle, as if he truly thought it was love he showed her. She had no trust for her son's safety no matter which guise he showed her.

Footsteps climbed the stairs.

She sat still, with John braced in her arms on her lap.

The footsteps came along the landing, towards her bedchamber.

Tap. Tap. The gentle knock struck the bedchamber door. 'Ma'am.' It was one of the footmen.

'Yes.'

'There is a gentleman below. He asked to speak with the woman living here.'

Ellen looked at the closed door. *'The woman living here...'* *What an odd thing to say?*

Had she become a completely nameless woman?

She moved John from her lap and stood, almost in a trance.

John raised his arms, hands reaching towards her, asking to go with her. 'Mama!'

I have a name.

'Come along.' She lifted him to her hip and stroked a black curl off his brow. She picked up one of his wooden horses to take with them, to entertain him as she spoke to the man who stood at the door. 'Here.' He took the horse from her hand, and immediately put its head in his mouth and chewed on his poor horse.

He had six teeth so far. She checked them every day to see if a new one had come.

She opened the bedchamber door. 'Do you know who it is?'

'No, ma'am.'

'Are they wearing livery or a soldier's uniform?'

'No, ma'am.'

She frowned. 'Is there a carriage outside?'

'Yes, ma'am.'

She carried John over to the bedchamber window and looked out.

There was a shiny black carriage outside the house. A coachman sat on the box, and a groom held the heads of two handsome grey horses, while a footman waited by the carriage door. They were all dressed in nondescript black. The carriage belonged to someone of standing, though, she could tell by the quality of the horses.

Why would they ask to see her?

'Horsees.' John pointed down into the street with his wooden toy.

She looked at him. 'Yes, darling, horses.'

'Ma'am, what shall I say?'

Ellen looked back at the footman waiting outside the open door. 'Nothing. I will come down. Where is the visitor?'

'In the drawing room.'

'Leave me to talk to him. You may go downstairs.'

He walked ahead of her on the stairs to the ground floor, then continued on to the basement level, to the kitchens and servants' spaces. They called her ma'am still, but the servants thought of her as a servant now, she knew that, and behaviour like walking ahead of her expressed it.

'Here we are to meet our mysterious guest, John,' she said brightly as she turned the drawing room's doorknob and pressed a kiss on his temple. Whoever this was, they could not bring any bad news.

As she opened the door, John's gaze was transfixed on the

wooden horse he trotted along her arm, as he tried and failed to make a clip-clop sound.

She took a breath, her heart pounding the beat of the marching drum as her fingers gripped John's leg over-tightly, causing him to squeal.

'Papa...'

He turned from the window and faced her.

As soon as she had seen the straight posture and black hair, she knew it was him.

His intent silver gaze studied her for a moment then fell to John. He stared at John as John stared at his toy.

Her emotions were a muddle of joy, fear and intense embarrassment. She could not remember who she was the last time she had faced him. Had it only been two years? 'You came...'

'Let me take the child.' He reached out.

Relief embraced her sore heart. She had asked him to come three times and he had not... Now here he was – come for them, to take them home to safety. Tears brimmed in her eyes. She blinked them away. He would not tolerate such feminine emotions.

'Oh, Papa, I am so glad.' She let him lift John from her arms.

'I do not expect your gratitude. I am taking him home...'

It was only then that Ellen realised there was someone else in the room – a woman. She came forward and took John from Ellen's father.

Ellen's brow creased in confusion. 'I should pack.'

'There is no need,' her father said. 'I have brought all he will need with me.'

He... Not you... Not me. 'I don't understand, Papa. Have you come for us?'

His eyes held no love, nor any other emotions. 'I have come to fetch my grandson.'

'Papa?'

'Stop calling me that. I am no longer that to you.' As he spoke, the woman carried John towards the drawing-room door. 'I will have nothing to do with a soiled woman. You are an insult to the Pembroke name.'

Not understanding, Ellen answered, 'I am your daughter.'

'Not now. You are a whore and nothing beyond it. You are dead to me. But the child is my heir...'

The truth struck her like a slap. He intended to take John but not her. She rushed after the woman. She was already in the street, about to lift John into the carriage. Ellen reached for her son and snatched him from the woman's arms. Thank God the woman did not fight her.

With tear-soaked cheeks, she pressed her head to John's, holding him close and tight, even though he fidgeted because he hated to be coddled. 'Mama.'

'Nothing is wrong, my darling, you are safe,' she whispered to his ear, rocking him in her arms and taking him back into the house.

The woman followed.

Her father stood in the hall.

'You cannot... I will not let you take him.' Ellen pressed John's forehead to her shoulder as he gripped the precious toy horse, and she raised her chin and stiffened her back. If this was a battle she would fight for her son.

'Would you rather raise him in this house of sin?'

The words pierced Ellen's heart with a knife thrust.

'This is not a place for a child,' he continued. 'I can, and will, give him a decent life, he will have an education and every-thing he will need to become a duke. I will protect him from this.' His hand swung out.

She clung harder to John.

'Have sense. This woman is a nursemaid, she can feed the child at her breast while I take him back to England, and there he shall have the house and grounds that will one day be his to grow up in.' His expression hardened. 'A duke cannot have a mother who has sold her body.' He spat the words at her. 'I will not leave him with a whore.'

'I did not... I am not... Papa. Take me? Do not leave me here. He may go with you if you take me too.'

'A duke cannot have a whore as his mother.' He withdrew a folded parchment from an inside pocket of his coat. 'This document says you have relinquished any right to the boy—'

'Why?'

'You must have nothing more to do with him, else he will be damaged by your sin.'

A crushing emptiness dragged through her, urging her to fall, she would not.

'Have sense. Think of the child.'

Her palm cradled John's head, the tears dripping from her chin wetting his hair. He fidgeted and fought to be free. How could she let him go? Yet she knew her father. He would not relent. If he had made up his mind he would not help her, he would not, no matter what she said. Yet he was willing to rescue John.

'Think of the child...' 'A Duke cannot have a mother who has sold her body... in a house of sin.' 'I can give him a decent life...' He could.

If she kept John, how would she hide what she had become from him as he grew? She was not even sure he was safe in this house. When he was older, he would at some point discover who she was, and what then? If he remained with her she would have to educate him herself, and she knew very little because her father had not paid for her to be educated.

She held him still. 'Mama loves you. Mama loves you so much...'

But if she really loved him then she would do the best thing for him, and her father was right – the best thing for John was to let him go.

New tears flooding her eyes, she nodded at her father, unwilling to say the word yes.

The woman came forward, her hands reaching out to take John.

Unable to speak for the pain in her throat, Ellen let her take him.

'Where may we sign this?' Her father raised the parchment.

She led him back into the drawing room and sat at a small table where there was an ink pot and quill. Her father stood behind her as she signed her name. Mrs Eleanor Harding. She did not know who that woman was now, she no longer wanted a name.

She blotted her signature and moved aside, leaving the quill in the inkwell for him.

He signed the paper too. Then called the nursemaid forward to make her mark as a witness.

Ellen reached out and took John back to hold him one last time. Her hand stroked over his hair. His gaze lifted to her eyes. 'You are to be good,' she whispered. 'And you are to always remember how much I love you. I am not letting you go because I do not, but because I do.' The breath of her quiet words stirred locks of his hair. 'I know you will grow up to be a clever and wise man, John, and you will be kind and honourable because you are Paul's son...' Her voice broke.

His fingers lifted and touched her lips, then the tears on her cheeks. He did not understand. He would not remember her.

She swallowed back more tears, though more still leaked from her eyes.

'Take the child,' her father barked.

Ellen's heart broke, shattering into tiny pieces, as she let the nursemaid lift him from her arms.

This will not be the last time I see you, she swore to herself. *I will come and take you back.*

'At least you are sensible,' her father stated coldly.

An urge to slap him lanced through her arm, but she did not. This anger, this grief, were merely more emotions to be buried deep and locked somewhere within. Lieutenant Colonel Hillier had taught her how to do that.

'That is resolved then,' he said, as matter-of-factly as though he had just bought a horse, not taken his daughter's son from her.

'Please take me with you? I am not... Papa, I am scared here...' She begged in a quiet voice.

His cold, emotionless expression ignored her. 'Take the boy to the carriage.'

He followed the nursemaid out of the room.

Ellen followed them outside and into the street. 'Let me hold him again.' Her voice expressed the desperation ripping her apart.

He waved a hand, telling the woman he would allow it.

Ellen held John as tightly as she could, breathed in his sweet scent, ran her fingers over his face and pressed kisses on his soft cheeks, trying to make sure she remembered what it felt like to hold him.

His large eyes stared at her. 'Mama?'

'I will miss you. I love you. You will have my heart with you, John.'

'Mama...' he said again as the nursemaid took him back.

The nursemaid held the footman's hand and ascended into the carriage with John balanced on her hip, and her father climbed in after the woman.

The footman closed the door as she heard John say, 'Horsees…' from within. Then he ran to the plate at the back of the carriage and hopped up onto it. The groom ran from the horses' heads to the perch on the other side.

'Mama?'

A vicious pain lacerated her heart as the carriage pulled away.

'Mama?'

She had thought when Paul had died she had felt as empty and heart sore as it was possible to feel, but now…

Her arms crossed over her chest and her hands clasped at either elbow, as she stood, deserted in the street, and watched until the carriage containing her beloved son disappeared out of view.

'I will get you back, John!' she called after the carriage. 'We will be together again!'

* * *

MORE FROM JANE LARK

Another book from Jane Lark, *The Great Western Railway Girls Do Their Bit*, is available to order now here:

https://mybook.to/GreatWesternBackAd

AUTHOR NOTE

I decided to write the prequel to *The Marlow Family Secrets* series because some readers who love the series asked me to. But it was an unusual book for me to write. The story had to be founded on facts because it is about a real regiment and a real historical event.

I named the regiment I chose as Paul's the 52nd (Oxfordshire) Regiment of Foot in earlier books. Which meant researching the truth of their whereabouts in the lead up to Waterloo and during the battle.

The first thing I found out was that the 52nd had returned from the Peninsular War to Britain in the summer of 1814. This gave me the window of opportunity for my fictional characters, Paul and Ellen, to meet at the beginning of the story.

The journey that Paul and Ellen took is real.

The 52nd were posted to America and sailed as far as Cork in January 1815, where they were stranded for weeks, waiting for the weather to improve.

When word came that Napoleon had escaped Elba, they were ordered to Ostend and then to Brussels. Many details of their journey are also true – for instance the wives did have to travel separately at one point, among the battlefield tourists.

I was extremely surprised when I learned the sheer volume of men who had fought in the battle of Waterloo; over two hundred thousand men took part. Most of the soldiers (not officers) were encamped outside Brussels for weeks. While within the city that was flooded with tourists and officers, they entertained themselves in a way that went on to change British culture forever.

The details of the Duchess of Richmond's ball, I discovered described in a letter written by one of her daughters; so, yes, it was in the coach house, and, yes, the paper was an ivy pattern.

I also fully researched the battles – yes, there were more than one – from the hours after the ball, to the end of the Battle of Waterloo. Yes, there was a moment when the occupants of Brussels were told the Allied forces had lost, and, yes, the wounded began to arrive in the way I describe in the story and within Brussels it was all hands to help save their lives.

Twelve thousand men were killed in the battles.

As for the 52nd...

Yes, they were ordered to move around to stop the last of the French Imperial Guard, who were making a final surge on the Allied army. There was a fierce firefight, which only lasted for four minutes, but during that brief period, right at the end of the battle, one hundred and fifty men from the 52nd (Oxfordshire) Regiment of Foot did die.

They shall grow not old, as we that are left grow old: Age shall not weary them, nor the years condemn. At the going down of the sun and in the morning, we will remember them.

ABOUT THE AUTHOR

Jane Lark is a writer of compelling, passionate and emotionally charged fiction filled with diverse characters. She is an international bestselling author of both historical fiction and psychological thrillers, and a finalist in British Fiction Industry awards.

Sign up to Jane Lark's mailing list for news, competitions and updates on future books.

Visit Jane's website: www.janelark.co.uk

Follow Jane on social media here:

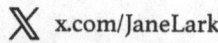 x.com/JaneLark

facebook.com/Janelarkauthor

instagram.com/jane.lark

youtube.com/@janelark3537

bookbub.com/authors/jane-lark

You're cordially invited to

The
Scandal
Sheet

The home of swoon-worthy
historical romance from the
Regency to the Victorian era!

Warning: may contain spice 🌶

Sign up to the newsletter
https://bit.ly/thescandalsheet

Boldwood

Boldwood Books is an award-winning fiction publishing company seeking out the best stories from around the world.

Find out more at www.boldwoodbooks.com

Join our reader community for brilliant books, competitions and offers!

Follow us
@BoldwoodBooks
@TheBoldBookClub

Sign up to our weekly deals newsletter

https://bit.ly/BoldwoodBNewsletter